Plagiarism

Plagiarism

Michael J Adams

Derelict Books

To Marty: One day, I hope to be as good a writer as you, my friend. Thank you for all your support.

ALSO BY MICHAEL J ADAMS

<u>The Osseous Series</u>
Prequel: Tooth & Nail
Book 1: A Tooth Fairy's Promise
Book 2: Exiles
Book 3: Insiders
Book 4: Vibrations
Book 5: Replacements
Book 6: Newhires
Book 7: Broken Promises

Chapter 1

Skylos – Los Angeles, CA – Monday Night

Dressed in a surfer's drysuit, green rubber kitchen gloves, and cheap safety goggles, Skylos hobbled down Vignes Street in the dark. The sweat-soaked hoodie beneath the tight outfit chafed something fierce. However, that discomfort was preferable to both the shard of broken glass stuck in his right foot and the pounding ache in his crippled left leg. Despite this, he refused to stop. He felt deep in his gut how close he was to completing the angel's final task: finding a prostitute and becoming a man.

His surroundings failed to live up to his mind's conjured images of Los Angeles. Instead of golden beaches or fabulous hillside houses fate led him before the looming twin towers of the city's massive correctional center. Neon signs in rainbows of red, green, and purple advertising the services of bail bondsmen and attorneys shone behind him. The tiny slits on the prison's facade held as little activity as the street. It had been at least twenty minutes since he'd seen as much as a car. Perhaps the internet forums had misled him.

Skylos scanned the block ahead and let out a haggard groan. The five-mile hike from the homeless shelter hadn't been kind on his bare feet. He longed for the foam sandals—stolen like the rest of his ensemble—in the sweatshirt pocket, but he couldn't put them on. The angel had been oddly specific about his attire.

I'll walk for another few minutes, and then find an underpass or somewhere to crash.

Headlights illuminated his shaggy brown hair from behind. He followed the red coupe with his eyes as it passed. The vehicle slowed, swerved into the oncoming lane, where it locked up its brakes and came to rest on the curb at the intersection. It stayed there for only a moment.

"Fuck off!" yelled the man in the car. Tires screeched and the car sped off. Skylos spied two women standing at the street corner opposite him. They waved their middle fingers and shouted obscenities of their own. After a moment, they crossed the street. Skylos hurried to catch up.

When the pair reached Skylos' side of the street he was still twenty feet away. The first woman looked roughly six foot and in her early thirties. The streetlamp's soft glow highlighted long black hair and a dark dress struggling to conceal her bosom. The second woman would've been closer to his own height, about five-seven, if it weren't for the heels. Dirty blonde hair fell to her jawline. An open, olive Peacoat obscured a similar dark dress.

Skylos had little time to determine whether they were escorts or simply returning to the Metro station from a house party across the river. Their hips swayed in an unbroken cadence as they walked. There were no signs of intoxication, it looked like he was in luck. Butterflies filled his stomach. He smoothed down his hair, sweat wicking off the rubber glove.

The taller woman elbowed her companion and nodded in his direction. The blonde placed her hands in her coat pocket and stepped forward despite her friend's nonchalant headshake.

"A bit late for a costume party, isn't it?" she said with a grin.

Skylos offered a half-smile but said nothing. He knew damn well how ridiculous he looked and couldn't afford to scare her off. The woman came closer, flaring the coat open to give him a better view of her plunging neckline.

"Candy," whispered the other woman, "we have an appointment."

"What brings you out so late?" Candy said, ignoring her companion.

"I'm lo-looking for..." he swallowed hard, trying to control his stuttering.

"A date?"

He nodded eagerly. As the woman came closer a bead of sweat dripped down the small of his back. His search was finally over.

"You can't need the money that badly," said Candy's friend, a little too loud for a whisper.

Skylos fumbled with the fanny pack zipper and withdrew a measly wad of small bills. A ten slipped from his grasp and he chased it as it tumbled a foot away. With a smile, he held up the money between his green-gloved fingers.

Candy looked over her shoulder and shrugged. "Sixty bucks is worth ten minutes of my time. I'll meet back up with you in front of Metro Plaza in twenty minutes. This won't take long." Her companion shook her head and walked off.

The escort grabbed the money and then his hand. "Come on. I know somewhere we can go." They walked a block ahead where she pulled him up the quiet palm-lined walkway of L.A.'s Union Station. Skylos paused for a moment in front of the building's massive glass façade while she dropped his hand and grabbed the door.

"Hurry," Candy said, motioning him forward. "The last train arrives shortly. They'll be locking up soon."

Skylos' heart pounded as they shuffled over large triangular floor tiles arranged in concentric circles forming a giant compass rose. A lone Amtrak employee mopping around the enclosed glass ticket booths gave a sly wink and smiled as they passed. Candy let out a soft giggle and ducked into the men's restroom. Skylos glanced over his shoulder and followed.

"In here," called Candy from inside the handicapped stall.

He took a deep breath. This was it. The proverbial two birds with one stone; he'd lose his virginity and fulfill the destiny the angel had spoken about. As the peach-colored, metal door's lock clicked into place a breeze swept through the still air. The space around him came alive with static electricity. Skylos shivered as the tiny hairs on the nape of his neck stood at attention and the taste of a nine-volt danced across his tongue.

Slit her throat, Skylos, whispered the angel's monotonous, static-filled voice.

Skylos froze, his eyes wide.

"What?" he said, looking right through the beautiful woman holding out a wrapped condom.

Candy and the angel spoke simultaneously.

"I didn't—"

KILL...

"Say anything."

HER!

Skylos whipped his head from side to side and threw himself back, cracking his head against the stall door. A deafening ring overtook him like a tuning fork the size of a Mack truck. Whatever words Candy mouthed fell on deaf ears as pressure built up inside Skylos' head. His eyes bulged and red filled the left half of one as blood vessels burst. He struggled to draw breath as the room faded to white.

Kill her! demanded the angel again. Its voice alone broke through the cacophony.

Visions projected onto the blank canvas replacing his failing vision. Knives pierced, slashed, and flayed porcelain flesh. Enough blood to drown a village. Faces of each man, woman, and child flashed by as well. And Skylos recognized every one of the faces of the people he'd killed. His body shuddered and his knees buckled. He tried to fight the images, to blink them away, but they remained. They weren't his memories; he'd never hurt anyone in his life. Nevertheless, each one was personal in a way, like it belonged to him all the same.

The memories ignited their own flavor of pain—like someone had sandwiched his head between the two halves of a waffle iron. He threw his mouth open, but his muscles were convulsing too much to emit any sound. There was only one way to make it stop. He had to obey. At that understanding, the ringing lessened enough to allow him a single gasping breath. Fighting through the lingering pounding in his head, he dug into the fanny pack and opened the largest blade of an old Swiss Army knife.

Before he could withdraw it, Candy drove her knee into his balls and ran.

You've failed me!

Fire exploding in his head prevented him from feeling the pain in his groin as he collapsed to the ground. He screamed, expelling what little air remained in his lungs as the ringing overtook him again. His voice failed to reach his own ears. That sharp resonating chime deafened him to everything around him. Skylos shut his eyes and longed for death.

The walls of the stall vibrated as the door burst open. A young man with a chiseled jaw flew into the stall, drawn by the screaming. Skylos opened his eyes, finding the man who'd been mopping when they came in. Tom—according to the lettering embroidered on his navy-blue Amtrak vest—stood in the doorway trying to make sense of the scene.

Last chance. Become a man!

Skylos nodded and managed to take in a gulp of air. He extended his left arm toward the heavens.

Tom reached down and helped Skylos to his feet.

"Thanks," said Skylos as he got to his feet and simultaneously drove the knife into Tom's neck. The ringing in his ears was immediately replaced by a whistling gurgle of blood from the man's nicked airway. Skylos took a step back. His lip quivered as he watched the deep red pour down the man's neck.

The Amtrak employee's hand fumbled in his vest pocket and a utility knife clattered to the floor between them. Skylos jumped and raised his blade again. His mind flashed back to one of the memories not his own. Using it as a guide, he flicked his wrist like an artist throwing paint on canvas.

Streaks of crimson erupted from Tom's carotid artery. Skylos watched the man's feeble attempts to stop the bleeding with both hands. Blood gushed between Tom's fingers before beading up and rolling off his attacker's drysuit.

The chronic, dull thud in Skylos' leg evaporated along with every other trace of pain. With a clear head, he finally saw the big picture. Stealing the drysuit from the unlocked vehicle at the beach and the other trivial thieveries the voice requested brought him to this point. It was a necessary formality to allow him to kill again.

Again? Skylos shook his head knowing he couldn't trust his memories. This was the first time he'd killed someone. Though, when looking down at Tom's body he felt only an odd calm. Repulsion, what he should have felt, was out of his grasp. He glared at the bloody knife in his hand. Maybe there'd never been an angel and...

You're not crazy, whispered a soft feminine voice, *but you do need to go.*

The voice was different this time. It was undoubtedly female. But the energy-laden vibrations teeming behind the words were the same. There was no doubt it belonged to the same *thing* he'd been conversing with the past week.

Crazy or otherwise, it was too much. Skylos wanted to stay put. If the prostitute hadn't called 911, the train would arrive soon. It wouldn't be long before someone wandered into the restroom and noticed the giant pool of blood. They'd surely call the police and he'd be locked up. And unable to hurt anyone else.

Go!

Embedded within that single syllable was a command he couldn't deny. Skylos hung his fanny pack over the toilet plumbing and shoved the still dripping pocketknife back inside. He peeled off the gloves, then the drysuit, and discarded them in the corner. Grabbing his pack again he reached for the door. The moment he touched the metal handle the static in the air dissipated, leaving him lightheaded. Although overjoyed that the 'angel' was gone, he found himself compelled to follow her orders.

Bloody footprints trailed behind Skylos from the handicapped stall. He drew the hood of his blue sweatshirt tight around his face and cracked the bathroom door. The foyer appeared as quiet as when he'd entered. The scrolling LED board above the ticket window across the foyer showed that the last train had just arrived at the station. He rushed to the yellow mop bucket, splashed his face with the dirty water, and then submerged his feet one at a time. With the blood washed away, he donned his sandals. The soft echoes of a handful of people reached his ears as he ducked out the way he'd come in.

An exhausted Ben Terrence stumbled north along Vignes, tears streaming down his cheeks. He'd killed someone. That didn't make him a champion—if that's what 'Skylos' even meant. His stomach knotted itself like an old pair of earbuds as he feared what else the voice may have in store for him. Exhaustion set in and he recalled passing an electrical substation on his way here. It was only a few blocks away and would at least be warm...

After he got some sleep, he'd walk to the police station first thing in the morning and turn himself in.

Chapter 2

Calliope

Calliope descended upon the boy she'd dubbed Skylos. The pitiful creature huddled beside a gray, paint-chipped electrical transformer for warmth.

She waited patiently until his heart stopped pounding and his head lolled off to the side. The work she had in front of her was easier if he wasn't conscious.

She hovered over him while he snored. As far as humans went, this one was an especially pathetic specimen. A sad crippled boy cast out from society and his family alike.

He had nothing, but that desperation worked in her favor, even though it disgusted her that she needed him at all. Skylos lacked the ruthlessness of her previous charges. If left unchecked his morals would get him caught and spoil her body count.

Still, she had faith it would work out. It had to because she'd already invested in him.

Luckily, eons of inspiring people served as a good primer for which seeds to plant. Humans were simple creatures. Ever since crawling from the primordial ooze and forming a societal infrastructure, power and money became everything.

The more advanced they became, the more they replaced their gods with greed. And greed paved the road to pride, lust, and the other famed deadly sins.

Skylos was an outlier. Even with as little as he had, he possessed few material wants. He desired family, to fit in, a purpose...

There was no better way to appeal to this than the longest-running social group in human history: organized religion.

The very idea of being chosen by an angel had him eating out of her hand. Granted, getting him to kill in her name had been a stretch. That would change.

Calliope drifted closer. Even though it was an abstract principle, time was a luxury she didn't have. The murder she'd inspired released a great deal of energy. More energy than she could absorb in this form. The excess traveled back on the silvery threads anchoring her to the physical realm. As clueless as her sisters were, it wouldn't have gotten past them.

They never appreciated her adventures and were certainly moving against her already.

Though weaker and slower, her younger siblings weren't stupid. More importantly, they outnumbered Calliope eight to one. But what had her ire most is that they always saw everything she did.

Calliope didn't share the same ability to track every dealing of her sisters. Staying amongst the mortals lent her strength but made her blind to their movements. Still, Calliope was certain they'd located their own puppets and were already feeding them details from the night in a feeble attempt to stop her.

She, and by extension, Skylos, were underdogs in this but facing overwhelming odds made every victory all the sweeter.

Calliope pushed thoughts of her kin aside and reached into the sleeping man's mind.

That time he got his head stuck in the railing of his childhood home? Gone.

His eighth birthday, when the neighbor made him a cake and taught him to ride a bike? Gone.

As Calliope poked around more, she got her bearings. It became second nature to pick and choose the optimal memories for replacement. She targeted those in which others showed him kindness. Anything that would have shaped his morals or helped make him... him.

In their place, she planted the experiences of those who came before him. Anger. Hatred. Death. Blood.

It would take him time for him to remember, but they were an inseparable part of him now.

Skylos whimpered and flailed his head back and forth but was unable to do little else.

Soon, her sisters would realize their true power and why the humans must suffer for no longer worshipping their kind.

Chapter 3

Skylos – Glendale, CA – Tuesday Morning

Ben Terrence rubbed the sleep from his eyes. The morning sun spotlighted the high voltage warning sign on the electrical transformer over his right shoulder. For the life of him, he couldn't recall how he'd wound up there or where exactly 'there' was.

He worked his jaw up and down, trying to summon saliva to his bone-dry mouth. The rest of his body felt far worse. This wasn't the discomfort a night's sleep on a concrete slab. He'd had worse accommodations over the years. This was something different entirely. Something closer to chewing on fiberglass insulation while a car dragged him through Death Valley.

"What the hell did you do last night, Ben?"

A mourning dove cooed and fluttered its wings from atop the barbed wire chain-link fence. As Ben took a step forward a new pain sprang forth from his right foot. He lifted his heel and carefully lowered himself back to the ground. Ben gingerly pulled his foot into his lap to investigate. Sunlight glinted off a speck of amber glass lodged firmly in his foot. While this was another thing he couldn't explain, it had a simple solution.

His fingers searched through the fanny pack for the old pocketknife he always carried. With any luck, the pair of tweezers hadn't fallen out since he'd last used it. As he withdrew the implement, maroon flakes sloughed off under his fingernail.

Blood?

Ben fully inspected the tool and found most of it covered with dried blood. A faint ring buzzed in his left ear as the largest blade snapped open.

The Swiss Army knife dropped to the pavement and skittered beneath the large unit beside him. His heart pounded. The blood on the knife belonged to Tom—the man Calliope had coerced him to kill. Though he inherently understood that was an oversimplification.

It was never about the prostitute. Why would an angel care if I were a virgin?

Calliope had led him miles from home under the guise of making him a man. Ben shook his head, feeling foolish that he'd fallen for the ruse. She'd misled him for the sake of both protecting him and making sure he didn't bail. If she'd told him outright that he needed to kill someone inside Union Station, he reckoned even the most devout Christians would have refused.

Ben's eyes tracked back and forth in his head. There was more than that. He suddenly remembered why he had to kill Tom.

Calliope had given him a glimpse of Tom's memories. The Amtrak employee had been using his job as a cover. He had been following lone riders off the train and killing them for weeks now. There was no choice but to kill him.

The angel knew that Ben could do what was necessary. Skylos was her champion.

Skylos straightened his back, pulled the shard of broken glass from his foot, and held it up to the light. It seemed the red-stained piece of glass was part of the big picture too. If he hadn't stopped to pull it, he may not have remembered the events of last night. He knew that this was part of Calliope's divine plan as well.

The dove flew off as he squeezed through a gap in the fence. He mindlessly followed north beside both the Metro tracks and the Los Angeles River. This route would take him in a wide circle around Dodger Stadium and, after another hour or two, bring him to I-2. Once there he'd determine where to head next. There were several options available: the Friends of Hope homeless shelter, the Silver Lake Branch Library, or Past Productions, the theater where he often squatted.

As he walked his thoughts gravitated back to Calliope. He longed to know what she had in store for him next, where she was now, and how he could get back in contact with her. Their interaction had thus far been fleeting, and she'd always been the one to reach out to him. He couldn't physically feel her now, but maybe she still watching?

"Hello?" Skylos called aloud. "Calliope?"

When no response came his stomach lurched. She may have left him for good like his mother did when he was thirteen. Even worse, he was certain it was his fault this time. Perhaps the thought of turning himself in after he'd killed Tom had left her disappointed in him. He had to find a way to impress her again.

The world was a wicked place and in such a crowded city Tom couldn't have been alone. If Calliope needed other sinners taken care of, he'd eagerly help. First, he'd need to get another knife. Candy had taken all his money, but though he had a small number of bills stashed in the theater he called home for such an emergency. Skylos compiled a list in his head as he continued his trek back.

...

The exterior of Past Productions boasted recessed arches and faux columns carved into the building itself. Skylos found the historic landmark to be fascinating.

The building housed a Performance Theater in the twenties which transitioned into a speakeasy during the prohibition era. Presently, the space operated as a four-screen movie theater. Skylos had been a long-time, though often non-paying, customer.

When Skylos approached, patrons filed out the single side door. He turned sideways and pushed against the flow of the crowd. Once inside he ducked under the velvet rope closing off half a dozen stairs leading down. He pulled open a black painted metal door bearing the faded white stenciling of a lightning bolt within a triangle beneath the words 'Electrical Closet'.

Breakers and conduit lined the wall of a cramped interior barely deep enough to accommodate the door. Skylos yanked on a red lever at the far left. The wall jumped forwards an inch with a guttural croak. He learned on the heavy wall, and it swung inward on its hidden hinges.

Skylos jostled the housing of an emergency light fixture and it cast a dull yellow light on a basement full of cobwebs, broken seats, and props from when the theater catered to live acts. Among the piles of rubbish sat an old bed that precariously balanced on a single intact leg. Although full of dust, like everything else, the mattress had surprisingly sturdy springs.

He moved through the piles of junk and left his heavy blue sweatshirt on the bed's headboard before stepping to the room's other corner. Behind a stack of dry-rotted pallets sat a utility sink. Skylos drank several handfuls of water before wiping down his chest with a rag hanging over the faucet. He grabbed a short-sleeved, grey T-shirt and slipped it on. A small cloud of dust rose as he dropped onto the old mattress.

What the basement lacked in accommodations was offset by the freedom it offered. He wasn't bound to the curfew or rules of the homeless shelter where he usually stayed. Also, after hours he was free to roam the kitchen, use the computer in the manager's office, or watch any movie he wanted. He'd been doing this for a year or two and no longer had any fear of being caught. Most of the employees were college kids and didn't really care. Besides, they saw him frequently enough to assume he was a cinephile and never questioned his presence. Since the basement stairwell was right next to the exit, he'd overheard the security system passcode when new employees were being trained. Nobody ever changed it.

Skylos' growling stomach reminded him that he hadn't eaten since last night. He swung his feet over the edge of the bed and dug his fingers inside a slot cut into the side of the mattress. He withdrew a few bills and walked toward the door. After untwisting the emergency light's bulb, he ducked back into the electrical closet. As he grabbed the door handle, a voice from the other side stopped him in his tracks. Kent Peterson, the theater owner, faded in and out as he paced the hallway.

"Yes honey, I'm leaving shortly. I needed to finish some billing before we leave for the cruise." His voice fell silent, waiting for his wife to finish speaking.

"No, I'm not bringing any work with me. That's why I'm still here."

Skylos held his breath until the conversation ended. He cracked the door a few inches and peered out. When he was certain it was safe, he ascended the stairs. After using the restroom, he purchased a hotdog and orange soda from the concession stand, and then carefully ducked back to the basement.

Skylos ate his lunch and sprawled out on the bed. While thinking of all the things he could accomplish with Kent out of town, he passed out.

...

Skylos awoke in the middle of the night to complete silence. He disabled the security system at the top of the stairs. The interface's clock read one in the morning. There was plenty of time before anyone would be in for work.

He slipped into the manager's office and ran his fingers along the spines of the novels resting on the bookshelf by the door. He sat down at the desk and pulled back a silver ball of the Newton's cradle and let go. The gentle clacking melded with the computer's humming fan as it booted.

When the Amazon page loaded Kent's account automatically logged in. Skylos smiled and without hesitation added the item's he determined he'd need to serve his angel: a large lock blade knife, a roll of duct tape, a backpack, and a tablet PC. He clicked the button to process with expedited shipping and crossed his fingers. It completed without any further password prompts. As he swiveled in the chair, he realized that while he'd have a new knife in a few days' time he would be empty-handed until then.

Skylos wandered to the kitchen and searched the metal prep table for a weapon. Within the last drawer, he located a trimming knife. He carefully slipped it into his fanny pack. The blade was long and thin, not terribly suitable for heavy applications. But it would have to do for now.

Chapter 4

Samantha Englund – Chicago, IL—Tuesday Night

Blood filled Samantha Englund's eyes every time she closed them. As an Indie occult writer, she'd envisioned her fair share of death. Though none painted the walls quite as vividly as the one stuck in her head.

It was a natural part of writing, habitually picturing gruesome scenes playing out like a movie in her head. With each draft's iteration, the picture solidified more and more until it was almost a separate reality.

This one was different. The inspiration, if not each individual word, had seemed planted in her mind as if taken directly from a dream.

The chair's casters struggled against the thick beige carpet of her Chicago apartment as she pushed back from her laptop. Samantha rubbed her watery eyes, smearing the dark makeup encircling them. She looked absently at the monitor and stepped through the young Metro employee's murder in her mind. She'd had the dream early this morning and wanted to make sure that it remained fresh.

Rhythmic notifications directed her attention back to the chatroom and she noticed it was nearly midnight. She winced upon seeing her own face in the livestream window. Blonde roots peeked out from her long black hair and large bags under her blue looked exaggerated by the room's overhead lighting. It was long past bedtime.

"Good night, guys. Thanks for working with me tonight." Samantha waved into the webcam. She paused to allow a dozen resounding 'Goodbye's' before shutting off her webcam.

By day Samantha worked as a copy editor for Windy City Publishers, an outfit specializing in children's books. She spent most evenings writing, hoping one day to be brave enough to pursue a traditional publishing contract. Despite it being her day job, she despised proofreading her own material. As an alternative, she utilized social media to handle that.

After posting her short stories garnered a small following it bolstered her self-esteem enough to step out of her comfort zone. As an experiment, Samantha created a website with a chatroom and webcam interface where she could write and communicate with her followers in real-time. Her following slowly grew and with it the site. Soon she had a burgeoning webpage including forums and a marketplace to sell digital copies of her work. While it didn't provide enough income to quit her day job, it generated a decent supplement.

With a yawn, she quickly scrolled through her work—eight pages and almost five thousand words. It was a new record for a single sitting. Despite the progress, she was aware of several plotting and character issues. While they were captured in the chat text, she took the time to document them formally in her repository of notes.

"One, consider killing the hooker along with Tom," she said aloud.

Several people begged for the pretty blonde to be hacked to pieces mid-coitus. They claimed that the story ultimately belonged to her readers, and it should be catered to them. However, it didn't feel right and was cliché as all hell, not that she needed an excuse to refuse the wishes of perverted weirdos. On second thought she deleted the note and moved on to the next item.

"Find a suitable name for the killer."

Her faceless and no-named antagonist frustrated both her and the readers. In the dream, she'd heard the demonic voice address him as 'Skylos'. While it had an interesting ring, it sounded more like a video game callsign than a ruthless killer.

One of her users, Heftyshark25, offered to donate twenty-five dollars to serve as the killer's namesake. While a tempting offer for such a minor detail, something stayed her hand. Besides, who in their right mind would want a serial killer named after them?

For now, she'd keep referring to him as the Bud-K killer, taken from the knife catalog her older brother drooled over in his teen years. Unfortunately, nobody understood the reference, making her feel old.

"Finish fleshing out the plot," she said through a yawn.

The concept was intriguing, and her fans loved it so far: a murderer walking the streets of L.A. in a diving outfit at the behest of a demon. Samantha hated to admit it, but she was as anxious to see where the story was going as her readers. Not that she didn't have a few surprises for them. They'd be expecting the unnamed killer to be an anti-hero. She knew better.

"Lastly, come up with a protagonist."

As much as it would fit in with her current series starring a 300-year-old vampire, she knew this one needed a human protagonist. Despite being just as cliché as the pretty blonde hooker, her leading contender was a detective coming out of retirement for one last case.

Samantha saved the open files, shut the laptop lid, and then stared at the wall behind it for a moment. There had been no time to create a formal outline for this story. The Bud-K killer had wormed his way into her head while she slept, pushing aside the story she'd previously been working on. She hoped for another dream, fearing she didn't have the skill to keep an idea like this alive on her own.

Fighting heavy eyelids, she got ready for bed and flopped down on her mattress. Reaching out, she groped for the phone charger on the nightstand. Despite her luck with tonight's progress, she didn't want to lose any late-night literary revelations.

Chapter 5

Skylos – Glendale, CA—Thursday Night

There had been no further contact from Calliope but Skylos kept operating under the expectations of her reaching out. That meant sneaking back into the office tonight. The items from his shopping spree had already been paid for and would be useful regardless of whether his angel had any further need of him. The springs of the old mattress squeaked as Skylos bounced his knees.

The booming bass of the theater above him finally cut out, replaced by the shuffling of a crowd out the door. Skylos got up and draped the blue sweatshirt with The Friends of Hope's cracked handshake logo and lettering over a stack of chairs. He'd be able to get the packages soon. If the staff rushed, as usual with the boss gone, they'd be cleaned up within an hour.

Avoiding piles of junk, he paced the room stopping periodically to peek through the crack he'd left in the door. After what seemed like forever, vacuums cut out and the exterior door rattled. Skylos rested his hand on the door handle and waited for the security system's telltale beep.

"Sweet, you brought two bottles," said an unfamiliar man's voice. "Mark's hooking up the consoles now. We're in theater one."

Skylos moved his eye to the slit. Two guys and a girl stood in the doorway. "Shit!" he said under his breath. It wasn't abnormal for the staff to party after hours, especially on the weekends or when the manager was absent.

His shoulders slumped as he let go of the door. If they'd planned a night of binge drinking and video games on the big screen, they weren't going anywhere soon. Skylos hadn't anticipated this, but at least they'd be on the opposite side of the building. Theater one was next to the kitchen and restrooms. If he moved quickly, he could still be in and out of the office before they knew he was there.

After giving them some time to get settled, he secured the fanny pack around his waist and crept up the stairs. A quick peek around the corner showed an empty hallway. He flinched at the faint sound of gunshots and explosions from the far end of the hall. They must have left the door propped open.

Skylos darted into the office and flipped on the light. Two cardboard boxes waited on the desk. Before he could grab the stack, the sound of humming came from down the hallway humming. He twisted the door handle so the door closed silently and then squeezed under the desk. As he pulled the chair in after him the door creaked open, and someone stepped inside.

Shit! They must have the light under the door. Skylos craned his neck but couldn't make out anything under the small opening beneath the desk's modesty plate. *Get what you came for and leave,* he commanded the intruder in his head.

"Hello?" a girl's voice called out, "Someone in here?"

Skylos' heart pounded as she shuffled into the room and the door clicked shut behind her. He was stuck. If the girl happened to be an employee, she'd recognize him. A throbbing ache started up in his knee. Skylos bit his lip. The pain had been with him for decades, he could endure until it she left.

Something thumped against the bottom of the desk causing him to jump a little. Moments later a similar thump hit the floor nearby. A third heavier object clanged onto the desk above him. Maybe a purse? The next sound was unmistakable; the jingle of a belt hitting the floor. She was undressing. But why wasn't she using the bathroom?

The office chair pulled away from his hiding place and the woman sat down. Skylos clasped his hand over his nose and mouth as her knees rested inches from his head. Tanned thighs and white lacy underwear flashed past his eyes as the chair spun counterclockwise. The strobing effect was hypnotizing, and he couldn't look away.

A dial tone sounded above the desk followed by a number being dialed. The line rang twice before a man answered. She stopped spinning, the chair facing away from the desk.

"Hey sweetie, I'm in the office waiting for you," she said in a seductive voice. "Wait ten minutes, excuse yourself, and come join me." She made a kissing noise and then dropped the phone back into her purse.

He recognized the half-naked woman's voice. Kara worked in the evenings and, judging by the books she always carried around, was a college student majoring in accounting. If her boyfriend could keep it in his pants, he had at most ten minutes to get out. Maybe if he shoved the chair into the wall and bolted, she wouldn't glimpse his face.

Skylos exhaled steadily and reached for the chair.

The temperature in the room seemed to drop a few degrees as a cool breeze swept through the room. Kara shivered and rubbed her legs together for warmth. Skylos jerked his hands back.

Calliope's voice filled every recess of his head. *Kill her.*

Skylos' eyebrows raised and he gave his head a quick shake. He remembered wanting this; longing for Calliope to return and give him another purpose. Tom was evil. And she'd shown him memories to prove it. But Kara was a student struggling to pay her way through school. She didn't deserve this.

Calliope disagreed.

Make it quick.

Skylos shut his eyes as a low tone started to build in his ear, but it didn't keep her voice out. *Look what she's done.*

Another memory, decidedly not his, began to play out on his eyelids. Hands stretching out, pressing a pillow down over an infant. Skylos snapped his eyes open, and the chiming stopped.

Slash her femoral artery.

Skylos blinked, his expression going slack. *I don't know where that is...*

Yes, you do. You just need to remember. Calliope said in a gentle, melodic coo. He closed his eyes again and a different memory showed a woman of similar height with dark, curly hair. His gaze focused on the midpoint of the anterior superior iliac spine and the symphysis pubis. The words were foreign, but he understood them, nonetheless. Suddenly the knife in his hands slashed back and forth so quickly he thought he'd get whiplash. As he opened his eyes, he realized that he *did* know exactly where to strike. Not only where to find the femoral artery, but all the vital zones of the human body.

Chapter 6

Samantha – Chicago, IL—Friday Morning

Samantha's heart jackhammered as she dreamt. The Bud-K Killer was poised to kill again. But from her viewpoint, it was all her. Thin, stiff carpet dug into her hands and knees as she waited under the desk on all fours. Reaching down, she unfurled the fanny pack zipper one tooth at a time. After taking a deep breath she leaned forward with the thin kitchen knife in hand.

Sexy lace panties flashed in front of her eyes. She counted the rotations in her head, waiting for the right time. Reaching out, she stopped the chair. The woman's legs were spread for her, inviting the blade in. Samantha knew exactly where to aim and slashed deeply. The unknown woman screamed as hot blood gushed all over Samantha's face. The taste of copper touched her tongue. She licked her lips and swallowed.

When her victim began to struggle, Samantha drove the chair against the wall and sprung out from beneath the desk. The Bud-K Killer's arms were wiry but strong. The woman in the chair struggled and tried to stand, but Samantha spun the chair and placed her into a headlock. Her forearm pressed into her throat so hard it hurt.

Samantha held her arm in place taking in the blood covering the desk, walls, and carpet. Her coughs and gasps quieted until they were overtaken by the distant sounds of gunfire and laughter outside the small room. When the girl stopped struggling Samantha let go. The body slumped down from the chair and onto the floor. She looked down at the baby killer wearing underwear a pretty shade of red.

The Bud-K Killer's eyes shifted to two boxes on the desk splattered with blood. Then she heard the demon's beguiling voice.

You've done well, Skylos. I'll be back soon.

A faint ringing faded in Samantha's ear as she shot up in bed and licked her lips. The coppery taste of blood woke her taste buds. She fumbled to turn on the nightstand lamp. Her hand slapped at her tongue, trying to rub the blood away. Holding her hand up to the lamp, she saw nothing.

When her heart rate slowed to normal, Samantha flopped back onto blue sateen sheets damp with sweat. Like the last dream, she remembered every grisly detail from the expensive Victoria's Secret underwear to the coffee stain on the cheap carpet next to the desk's leg.

She closed her eyes and walked back through everything The Bud-K Killer had felt. Aside from him and the girl, there was something else hanging in the room. It had spoken softly, the voice of an angel that was anything but. There were other things her senses had picked up upon too. A faint smell of popcorn butter on the woman's fingers and the deep explosions of bass from a movie theater.

The grisly images burned into her mind disgusted Samantha, but at the same time were exhilarating. After struggling with a backstory, she finally knew how to proceed. Her hungry fans, especially the perverts pleading for the prostitute's demise, would love this direction.

Samantha grabbed her cell phone from the bedside to record what she'd seen before going back to sleep. The phone's display read 7:30.

"Dammit!" she yelled, springing out of bed. "Melanie's going to be all over me if I'm late again."

She flew out of bed grabbing a dress off the chair in the corner of the room on her way. It wasn't clean, but it passed the sniff test. Once in the shower, she leaned her phone between shampoo bottles on the shelf. Samantha washed only long enough to dictate the details of the latest dream into the phone. After blotting her hair dry, she slipped on underwear, tossed the dress over her still damp body, and then ran for the bus stop.

...

When Samantha arrived at work Melanie's office was empty—thank the gods for small miracles. While waiting for her computer to boot, she pulled a compact from her purse. The mirror reflected how she felt; like she'd rolled straight from bed into the previous day's clothes. She pulled her wet hair across her face to hide from her co-workers. After opening her email and several applications, she grabbed the stick of deodorant from her desk's bottom drawer and went to the bathroom.

"Too bad I'm stuck here," she said into the mirror while brushing tangles from her hair, "instead of at home killing more girls."

"What the hell?" Called a voice from the stall behind her. "Samantha?" A toilet flushed and heels clicked against the dull, black and white bathroom tiles.

"Shit," Samantha said under her breath. It was her boss, Melanie. She'd been so preoccupied she missed the pair of feet beneath the door of the first stall. Holding her purse open, she swept the makeup from the counter into her bag with her brush and darted to the door. She was half a step away when her boss cleared her throat.

Samantha swallowed and turned around.

Melanie's frizzy hair gave her the appearance of Sideshow Bob in yoga pants, but her death glare was anything but funny.

"I'll see you in my office."

"Shit," Samantha repeated, trekking across the floor and taking a seat inside the large glass panels of Melanie's 'fishbowl'. The only enclosed space on the floor had floor-to-ceiling windows in lieu of walls. It allowed her to see everyone, and vice versa.

As she took a seat, Samantha pulled the phone from her purse and silenced the ringer. There was no point getting reamed out a second time. Melanie had a burning hatred for both interruptions as well as cell phones. The phone hit the bottom of the purse no sooner than her boss stepped in.

The woman closed the glass door and took her seat. Leaning against the desk, she rested her chin in her hand while giving Samantha a casual once-over. "Is everything okay, Samantha? Anything you want to talk about?"

Samantha closed her eyes in a long blink and reminded herself to stay professional. "No, I'm fine. I appreciate your concern though."

"You've seemed distracted these last couple of days. You were late this morning, which normally isn't a big deal, but..." she paused, still trying to process what she'd overheard. "Excuse my language, but what the hell was that back there?"

Unsure how to respond, Samantha kept her mouth shut.

"You realize there are often clients in the office and whatever that was isn't the portrayal of what this company stands for. Sometimes there are children in here!" Melanie closed her eyes and took a deep breath as she pushed her palms toward the floor. Samantha rolled her eyes. Probably a breathing exercise her yogi taught her, Samantha thought. Melanie opened her eyes again. "How long have you been working here again?"

"Since I graduated from college... So almost six years." Samantha bit her tongue and prepared for the rant. You need to set a good example for your peers, you have more potential than this, you need to focus, blah blah blah.

Melanie nodded. "And you've always been one of our star performers..." Samantha closed her eyes while she drew in a deep breath. "But like I was saying, you've lost focus. I've noticed you wandering, not only from your tasks but also from your desk."

Stupid fishbowl.

"Is it something personal you're dealing with?" Melanie leaned forward and whispered. "It's not drugs, is it?"

Samantha straightened up and waved her hand. Now she had to say something. "No," she said licking her lips. "I just haven't been sleeping well recently. Recurring nightmares." It was a half-truth but hopefully enough to appease the woman.

"Have you tried melatonin or meditation?"

If she said no, Melanie was bound to dive into a crazy tangent. Unfortunately, the pause alone was enough to spur her on.

"Well, you need to try something. If you're not eating a balanced diet and getting enough sleep, you're no good to me. I need you at the top of your game."

Samantha raised an eyebrow and Melanie sighed.

"I have an appointment with a potential client next week who is unhappy with their current publisher. They're looking to make a move to self-publishing but want to retain an editor. Truth be told, they asked for you personally." Melanie paused to take a sip of her Kombucha tea. "While not a big account, it could open other doors for us. I want to assure we put our best foot forward."

Samantha smiled. She hadn't expected Melanie to hand her an opportunity to redeem herself. "Of course. When are we meeting?"

"I'm meeting with them alone. I want you on the top of your game first." Samantha nodded and tried not to groan at the continual clichés. "I'll let you get back to work. Will you have the Anderson review done by the end of the day?"

"Yes. I'm working on it now," Samantha said rising from the chair.

"Great. Thank you."

Samantha returned to her cubicle and trudged her way through the Anderson's story again. Calling eh document a rough draft was a stretch. This was their second book, and it showed similar obfuscation as the first.

Their protagonist of their current 'masterpiece' was a Golden Lion Tamarin monkey in a spacesuit venturing through the Jungles of Brazil. It was way too preachy, reading like a Ménage à Trois between Curious George, Greenpeace, and PETA. And there was no good reason why he wore a spacesuit. Of course, she wasn't allowed to tell the husband-and-wife team that.

Candace Anderson ran an in-home daycare and was desperate to put her thirty-year-old English literature degree to use. Even if it had been a long time since she'd written, she didn't need an editor. Samantha hadn't seen tighter prose or punctuation in a first draft. It was the content that sucked. What they needed was to get a new Muse, ditch the preachy demeanor, and start from scratch. Providing an explanation for why the monkey was in a damn space suit wouldn't hurt either.

She drafted a new email and stared into space. This was the hardest part of the job. Despite maintaining the utmost tact, it was impossible to guess how someone would react after they read the critique of their hard work. Especially when that suggestion was to start over. She'd need to highlight the positive—her husband's beautiful illustrations. Unfortunately, if the story underwent changes, so too would his art.

Samantha leaned back in her chair. Maybe she was onto something with her initial assessment. The man in the yellow hat served as Curious George's moral compass. Tammy the Tamarin could do with the same sort of companion. Although... an antagonist would equally spice things up.

"A sloth that kills other jungle animals at the behest of a disembodied voice?" Samantha laughed, then clammed up when she realized she was thinking aloud again. She glanced around. Her coworkers were oblivious, except for the one that mattered. Melanie's eyes were locked on her. A shiver went up Samantha's spine. The woman had a knack for being at the wrong place at the wrong time.

Heh... A killer sloth. That gives me an idea.

She left the cursor to blink in the empty email and opened a document she used for notes on her cloud drive. Killing a zoo caretaker could be an interesting twist to her own story. Though she'd need to find a way to tie it into his twisted morals. She thought for a while. Punishment for animal abuse allegations ignored by the authorities seemed plausible. Before long, the simple idea became an entire page worth of text.

Someone cleared their throat behind her. With a deft string of keyboard shortcuts, Samantha saved the file and switched back to her email application. Samantha picked up her water bottle and took a drink without acknowledging the person behind her.

"How are things coming along?" asked Melanie.

Oh, come on! She was literally in her office a second ago! How long had she been standing there? Had she been reading over my shoulder as I typed? And then another worst-case scenario occurred to her. Maybe she'd been dictating again as she typed. Samantha bit her lip and spun the chair to face her boss. The motion caused her mind to flashback to the girl in her underwear from that morning's dream. Samantha shook her head, dismissing the memory.

"Good. I was typing up some notes on another file…"

"What file?"

"What file?" Samantha repeated. "Umm… The digital equivalent of scratch paper when I brainstorm. I'm trying to find a new angle for the Anderson story. My present recommendation is a total rewrite." Melanie raised an eyebrow. "Don't get me wrong. The character is adorable, and the artwork is amazing. It's overshadowed by a lackluster story. In fact, it's not a story at all. It's more of a lecture against diminishing the resources of the rainforest. We both know that doesn't make for a successful children's book."

"I see." Melanie placed her hand on her desk and stooped forward to look at her screen. Samantha pivoted her chair back toward the monitor to avoid the rotten egg smell of the Kombucha that always emanated from Melanie's mouth. "What do you have so far?"

The cursor blinked in the empty email document in the center of the screen, mocking her. Melanie let out a sigh and stretched back to her full height before turning and leaving in a huff. Samantha's only hope rested on the sloth.

"I know they're still new to this, so I want to make sure I approached in a tactful manner." Melanie turned back around. "I'd like to suggest a supporting character to serve as a contrast to the monkey. This will allow them to still convey morals in a back-and-forth manner." She paused to check for a reaction and to further develop the idea.

Melanie crossed her arms and framed her chin with her thumb and forefinger.

"A sloth. What better mascot to represent a character who's reluctant to change? Or do you think that's too on the nose?"

"Hmm... Do you have a name for this sloth?"

"Sammy." Melanie opened her mouth, but Samantha interrupted her by holding up her index finger. "The monkey's name is Tammy the Tamarin. I'm keeping with the alliteration."

Melanie gave a nod of approval. "I like it. Hopefully, Candace will too." She walked away with a smile on her face and returned to the throne within her glass room.

Samantha exhaled loudly and wiped a bead of sweat from her forehead. *The quicker I get through this the sooner I can get back to my own writing.* She began to frame the email with suggestions to spruce up Candace's story.

Chapter 7

Skylos – Glendale, CA—Thursday

Afternoon

Skylos rocked back and forth on the yellow parking block outside the gas station. With each car entering the lot his back straightened, only to slump with disappointment. Truth be told, he'd no idea exactly who he was looking for. Calliope gave him instructions to wait at this gas station and nothing more. He wasn't worried though. Something told him that he'd know who he was looking for.

Prior to this morning, it had been a week since he'd heard from Calliope. But she never left his thoughts. Periodically glimpses of other gruesome murders and atrocities filled his head. It worried him. Not so much due to the content, but because it hinted at the evil all around him. Sadistic monsters he couldn't identify without Calliope's guidance. When she reached out this morning, he was ecstatic. He longed to put the survival knife just purchased at the army surplus to good use.

A cool breeze accompanied by a sharp ringing jolted Skylos from his musings. He pressed his finger into his ear and worked his jaw until the discomfort faded. Before he could stand, a blaring horn drew his attention to the lot's south entrance. A station wagon swerved around a white pickup truck. Skylos pulled his legs back just in time as the pickup screeched to a halt in the parking spot on his left.

An unshaven bear of a man stepped out. His clothes, a faded red flannel shirt and blue jeans with patches on both knees, were stained with dirt and sweat. The man muttered something under his breath as he walked away.

Skylos didn't need Calliope to know who he was. His eyes followed the man into the convenience store.

Pedophile... Calliope whispered.

What flashed through Skylos' mind at that moment made him sick to his stomach. No matter his size, this man had to be stopped no matter the cost. Skylos tugged the truck's passenger door open. In the glove compartment, beneath old receipts and a can of chewing tobacco, was the registration for the vehicle. According to it, the owner was Thaddeus Jones of Altadena. Skylos slipped the paper in his pocket and closed the truck back up. Altadena was the next city over. It would be a hike, but if he hustled, he'd arrive shortly after nightfall.

Skylos followed into the store. He had an idea of what sort of person Tad was but wanted to get a good look at his face and see exactly what he was up against. The huge man had already headed to the checkout counter with a case of cheap beer under one arm and a bag of beef jerky in the other. The villain smirked as he knocked Skylos aside with his shoulder.

Beer bottles rattled as Tad slammed his purchases onto the counter. The bag of jerky slid off the counter and onto the feet of the middle-aged Chinese cashier. The clerk bent down slowly to pick up the item.

Skylos could smell the stench of sweat, oil, and sawdust as he stepped into line behind the man. The cashier, Zhang according to the name tag on his green smock, turned to him and smiled. Skylos wrinkled his nose and pointed at a display of tree-shaped air fresheners. Zhang stifled a laugh.

"Come on Wang, I ain't got all day!" Tad said.

"Sorry sir," he murmured while passing the scanner over the items. "Twenty oh four."

Tad threw a crumpled twenty onto the counter and pointed at the penny tray. "There's the four."

While Zhang dug pennies out of the blue tray Tad scooped up his purchases and moved toward the door. Skylos stepped up to the counter and pointed to the shelf behind the register.

"Two bo-bottles of lube, please."

Zhang turned around to retrieve the items. Tad stopped and cocked his head sideways. He repeated the word 'lube' and broke into laughter as he left the store.

"He'll get what's coming to him," Skylos said with a smile. Zhang raised an eyebrow and handed the items over after receiving the cash. Tad's truck peeled out as Skylos left the store. Taking a seat on the same parking block as earlier, he pulled the tablet from his backpack and punched in Tad's address. It was a three-hour hike to Altadena.

Chapter 8

Christopher Reyes – Chicago, IL—Thursday Evening

Christopher Reyes was an overweight sixty-three-year-old who kept his gray hair buzzed to hide male pattern baldness. He stood barefoot in the driveway of his red-brick bungalow leaning against the driver's side door of a dark green jeep. His daughter Jessica sat behind the wheel with her twin boys in the back. She was fit and pretty with long brown hair. Standing six feet tall had gained her the nickname 'Amazon' around the precinct. She looked every bit the part in her police uniform.

He'd been two weeks into retirement from the same police department as his daughter when Jessica's in-home daycare closed without notice. His wife, Martha, volunteered his services until she could find another. After all, the only thing on his plate these days was sleeping on the recliner in front of the television.

He agreed, thinking it would be an easy enough job. They were six, self-sufficient, and relatively well behaved. Famous last words. Their limitless energy coupled with his recent sleeping problems made the transition more difficult than anticipated. It seemed much harder than forty years ago. Though he only had one to deal with back then. Of course, he wasn't twenty-three anymore.

"Thanks again," Jessica said. "We'll see you tomorrow morning at the same time."

"No problem. Bye, guys," said Christopher.

"Something else you wanted to talk about, Dad?" Jessica said, cocking her head to the side after he didn't step back from the car.

"Maybe..." Christopher cleared his throat, leaned into the window, and spoke in a hushed tone. "Have there been any new unsolved murder cases. Particularly one involving a young, pretty girl?"

"You know I don't work homicide. If you were working something before you left, you should call your old partner." She paused. "Wait. Does this have anything to do with the nightmares you've been having?" She placed her hand atop his. "I know retirement is an adjustment, but it's normal. You should open up to the shrink."

He snorted and pulled his hand away. "Dammit. Your mother told you."

"Don't feel betrayed, Dad. She's been a paramedic for as many years as you've been on the force. She knows the statistics and it worries her."

Christopher locked eyes with his daughter. "I'm *not* suicidal."

"I wasn't suggesting you were. It's just... I don't mean any offense, but the department won't cease to function without you. It's time for you to relax and let someone else save the world." Jessica straightened her collar. "Perhaps a younger, more talented officer."

He chuckled. "Alright. Get out of here." He rapped the jeep's door and stepped back. "I love you."

"I love you too, Dad."

"We love you too Papa." The twins said in unison from the back seat.

Christopher waved as the car drove down the street. With a yawn, he marched up the concrete steps and back into the house where he collapsed into the recliner opposite the television. Before he could settle on a channel, he drifted to sleep. A warm breeze stirred the air in the front room and another dream overtook him. While he was aware that he was asleep, it was impossible to distinguish it from reality. And just like the previous two dreams, he maintained complete control.

A gas station parking lot materialized around him. There was a dirty white pickup truck parked against the building, and two other cars beside the pumps. What wasn't present, however, was a body. Despite that, he investigated as if it were a crime scene. A large flannel-clad man stood mid-stride; a statue carved by one of the masters. Christopher's head rolled to the left in his chair and his nose wrinkled. Even in the dream, the scent of sweat, oil, and sawdust was strong. Christopher circled the redneck, looking him up and down. From the stench and dirt on his hands, he looked blue-collar, likely a construction worker.

Was this the mysterious killer of the woman in the office?

Stepping back, he checked the license plate of the truck a few feet away. A jumble of strange symbols adorned both the front and back. Christopher moved away, looking for a street sign or something else to reveal his location. As he neared the street the scenery faded to a vast, gray nothingness. He took another step, pushing against the vision's constraints.

Suddenly, the man, the truck, and the gas pumps zipped upward into the sky. No, everything stayed put, it was him that was falling. Christopher's stomach twisted and bile danced on the back of his tongue. His dreaming form closed his eyes and his body in the recliner whimpered and flailed around until the motion stalled. He opened his eyes, expecting to be back in the recliner but the dream hadn't finished with him.

His surroundings had changed, the lot replaced with the interior of a convenience store. The construction worker stood frozen here too, inches from the door, with a case of beer under his arm. Christopher stepped around the man and looked outside. Though he'd been outside moments earlier, the exterior showed the unsettling gray expanse.

"I'm supposed to stay inside," he mumbled aloud. "I guess I'll have a look around."

A teenage boy stood at the soda fountain and the older Asian cashier held something over the counter. Behind him was a board displaying symbols like those on the license plate. They were still indecipherable, but they were paired in a format he recognized—lottery numbers. Instead of the rainbow and pot of gold symbol was a small logo of a stylized sun. He'd gambled enough money over the years to know this wasn't a gas station within Illinois. Hopefully, he could use that little sun logo to narrow things down.

As Christopher started down the aisle the gray haze crept back in. He explored until he worked out the epicenter—the area in front of the counter. Something had to be there.

He eyed the clerk with greater scrutiny. The cashier's name tag was illegible; it was written in the same alien script as everything else. There were two bottles of sex lube in his outstretched hand, but there was nobody on the other side of the counter.

Christopher spun in circles trying to determine exactly whom the cashier was looking at. He had a funny feeling that an important someone was absent from the scene.

An interior door slammed shut and the dream world disappeared in an instant. He sat up in the chair, bracing himself against the recliner's arm. It took him a moment to realize where he was.

"Ow..." he said as he pressed on the flap of skin outside his right ear canal. There was that ringing sensation again...

Something moving near the kitchen drew his attention. The man from the vision stepped into the room. *This isn't real.* Christopher blinked hard. The man was still there, like the afterimage burned onto your retina from staring into the sun.

"Sorry, did I startle you?" said a woman's voice.

He rubbed his eyes and looked back to the doorway. His wife, Martha, smiled back in her blue paramedic's uniform. A curvy woman ten years his junior with brunette hair pulled back in a tight bun, she was a far more welcome sight.

"Sorry, I must have dozed off," he said, prying himself away from the recliner. "I wish I could go back in time where those kids still napped."

Her lips went slack. "You were having another nightmare." Christopher shook his head unconvincingly. Martha kicked off her shoes and unbuttoned her shirt. "We've got dinner with Mary and Jeff tonight. I'm jumping in the shower. Will you be ready in twenty minutes?"

He nodded. "I'll be ready."

Martha closed the bathroom door and Christopher entered their bedroom. He took a seat on the bed and pulled a small composition notebook from the nightstand drawer. The department's psychiatrist had suggested he write down his thoughts throughout the day. And after the last dream involving the dead girl, he decided to follow the advice.

He hated the very idea of seeing a shrink, but Martha convinced him when the nightmares started. And she was the only thing that kept him going back. Dr. Bayer assured him that it was common to experience the transition back to civilian life. No shit, he didn't need a shrink to tell him that.

The bloody body in the public restroom had haunted him every time he closed his eyes. It wasn't until he transferred the memories to the book that he was able to rest. This was the third such vision, and he knew if he didn't write it down, he'd be thinking about it all night.

He opened to the sketch of a man's face on the first page. The drawing was crude, yet the smudged graphite summoned a crystal-clear image of the young man. Christopher clearly saw him slouched against the peach metal wall. A ton of bloody knife wounds covering his neck.

After flipping to the next blank page, he scrawled out the man's face from the gas station. He wasn't a sketch artist by any means, but the rudimentary pencil markings sparked something within him that allowed a perfect recall of the features. He documented the lottery symbol and everything else he'd seen. After committing the scarce details onto the paper, the ringing in his ear subsided.

"Huh..." he said, dropping the pencil.

This huge redneck was a puzzle piece of a completely different shape. Even without a corpse, Christopher *knew* he was somehow related to the two victims. With a frown, he tapped the pencil eraser against the page. He recalled each in sequence, looking for anything to tie them together. Unfortunately, there was nothing.

Maybe I'm going about this the wrong way. The memories were so crisp that he had no choice but to trust them. But where the hell were they from?

He'd already ruled out the few active investigations before retiring. That left old cold cases or maybe a lecture or case study from his rookie years.

Since it wasn't his case, there was no harm in conjecture. The two separate locales from this afternoon had one thing in common. The man in flannel. If Christopher had to wager, he'd put his odds on that man being the killer. He certainly looked strong enough to overpower the two bodies he'd come across.

The bathroom door in the hall clicked open as Christopher completed documenting his theory. He tossed the notebook in the drawer and jumped up. Martha stepped into the room in a long blue dress, still towel-drying her hair.

"You haven't changed yet?" she said with a sigh.

"I wanted to see what you were wearing first."

Martha rolled her eyes, reached into the closet, and shoved a red polo into his hands. She gave him a thumbs-up and returned to the bathroom. Christopher changed shirts, slipped on a pair of loafers, and met her in the kitchen.

"You look lovely." He bent down, gave her a kiss, and then ran his fingers over the short stubble remaining atop his head. "Just give me five minutes to fix my hair before we go."

Martha rolled her eyes and grabbed her purse off the counter. "Can you drive tonight? I start third shift rotation next week, so I'd like to have a few glasses of wine while I can." She picked up the keys for the van and tossed them to him.

Christopher caught the keys and nodded. "No problem. There's some old work-related stuff rattling around in my head. Doc said I should keep my head clear until I work through it."

Chapter 9

Skylos – Altadena, CA—Thursday Night

The full moon shone through the leaves of palms lining the block before Tad's residence. Skylos stuffed the tablet computer back into his backpack. Its battery was drained but it had served its purpose. He grew more anxious as the house numbers painted in white on the curb increased.

Tad's house was the second from the end of the block. Skylos calmly walked past. The street was quiet save for a car passing through the alley and someone dragging in their garbage cans. He circled back and followed the line of hedges to a brown wood fence with a 'Beware of dog' sign on the gate.

Even with the moonlight it was too dark to see through the fence slats, but he knew a man like Tad wouldn't own a Chihuahua. Bracing himself against the house's siding, Skylos kicked the gate. He flinched as something heavy slammed into the gate. The beast on the other side growled and clawed, as hungry for blood as Skylos himself.

Skylos picked a loose fragment of concrete from the fence's footing and flung it. A loud crack emanated from the back of the property. The dog barked wildly, giving chase. After waiting a minute, he kicked the fence again. Someone in the house yelled as the dog barked uncontrollably again. He repeated the process several more times until the sliding door scraped open.

"There's nothing out there!" yelled a gravelly voice. "Get your dumbass in your crate before the dipshit next-door calls the cops."

Skylos waited patiently for the automated floodlight to shut off before easing open the gate. The well-greased hinges swung inward without a sound. He stepped through, closed the gate, and then set his backpack near the corner of the house.

A swimming pool surrounded by a low metal fence dominated an unkempt yard of dry grass. Stairs led up to the garage and alley. An offshoot of the perimeter fence concealed the pool's heating and filtration units. Jugs of pool chemicals and cleaning implements lay scattered against the wall.

He hugged the house and took a few steps around the corner near the flickering glow of a television illuminated the drawn Venetian blinds. Despite the glare-reducing film on the sliding glass door Skylos had an unobstructed view inside. He dropped to his knees and crawled closer.

"What the fuck!" yelled Tad.

Skylos ducked back and fell on his ass. He scooted backward and grabbed blindly for his pack.

"Put the ball in the damn net!"

Skylos breathed a sigh of relief and then crawled back. The television illuminated Tad sitting on a worn sectional in a dingy undershirt and boxers. His feet rested in the middle of a glass coffee table flanked by a pizza box and at least a half dozen empty beer cans. There was no sign of the dog at his heels. Hopefully, Tad locked it up in another room. Skylos moved back and steeled his nerves. Tad was a big man, which only meant he'd fall harder.

He returned to his bag and removed the bottles of personal lubricant, a roll of duct tape, and the large survival knife with a compass built into the handle. He laid the items at the patio's edge. Keeping an eye on the window, he retrieved the pool skimmer and attached the knife to the end with duct tape. He swished the polearm through the air. It was slightly awkward but would keep him out of Tad's longer reach.

Leaning the weapon against the house, he tore the metallic seals from the bottles of lube and then emptied them around the sliding door into the house. He dribbled the remaining strands of liquid onto the knife and spear shaft. With his preparations finished, his angel announced her arrival. The weapon became a lightning rod as the muscles in his right hand twitched from pulses of Calliope's energy. It was impossible to drop the weapon at this point.

Show him how we treat sinners.

Resting the makeshift spear in the crook of his arm, he grabbed a handful of volcanic rock from around the pool mechanicals. Taking a deep breath, he whipped them at the glass and hurried beside the door. The television muted, allowing Skylos to focus on his pounding heartbeat and the buzz of Calliope.

Tad flung open the sliding door and bypassed the patio step entirely. His left foot landed in the middle of the lube puddle and slid out from under him. There was a sickening thud as his head struck doors threshold. The revolver in his hand skittered across the patio, striking Skylos in the foot.

Tad groaned. His hand touched the back of his head and came back bloody.

"You deserve this more than Tom and Kara combined," said Skylos, taking a step forward.

"Huh?" Tad jerked his head to the side, his eyes narrowed at the figure hovering over him. Their eyes locked and recognition flared in his eyes. Tad reached for his gun, but Skylos kicked it aside and jabbed at the man's knuckles.

Skylos smiled. Thanks to Calliope, he knew every vulnerable point on his miserable body. However, he didn't want to take him out quick. This man deserved to suffer. Skylos thrust the spear into his flesh, alternating strikes between the gut and groin.

Tad yelled and grunted as he fought for control of the spear. His hands slid down the slippery shaft and went rigid as the blade severed flexor tendons in his fingers. Skylos' pulse raced as he continued stabbing.

A light came on in the yard to his left. It was followed by gravel being displaced by a pair of flip flops. Skylos drove the blade deep into Tad's neck with all his might, severing his windpipe.

"Are you okay Thaddeus?" Skylos became a statue. The voice came again. "Tad?"

Tad let out a gurgle that sounded like a clogged drain struggling to empty. Skylos stared deep into the man's fluttering eyes and cleared his throat.

"Fuck off!" he said, in as gruff a voice as possible.

There was a snort on the other side of the fence. A grumble and more shuffling gravel followed. A door slammed and darkness enveloped the neighbor's yard again.

Skylos spit on Tad and then heaved the body into the pool. The thin blue tarp offered no resistance to the bulky construction worker. Skylos stood triumphant at the pool's edge and celebrated, pumping the spear above his head with both hands. He understood how David must have felt after felling Goliath.

A warm hand rested on his shoulder. Skylos spun around, swinging the tip of the spear in a wide arc. No one was there, but the pressure remained.

I'm proud of you, whispered Calliope.

Her warmth radiated through his body like a warm summer day. The spear clattered to the patio as he attempted to embrace her back, yet he grasped nothing but air.

I'll see you again soon.

Her words didn't register until the warmth slipped away. "Wait!" he cried out, stretching his fingers into the night. She was gone.

Skylos stood on the patio trying to savor the last vestiges of her touch. Like the first time, she'd left him alone miles from home without further instruction, but he found it difficult to be angry. He knew she'd done it to teach him something. Skylos turned and looked up at the large house. There was no reason why he couldn't stay here for a few nights until he knew where he was headed next. And he could help himself to whatever valuables were inside the house.

After collecting his gear and the revolver, Skylos stepped into the house. Other than a light in the hallway, the flat-screen TV atop its cheap wooden stand was the only source of light in the room. Even so, he had a better view of the place now. The desk sitting in the corner by the front windows supported mounds of paper and more dirty dishes and empty beer cans. As if there was any doubt, Tad was a bachelor. And it seemed there was little to no risk of running into a cleaning lady.

Skylos dropped his bag on the couch and devoured one of the two remaining slices of room temperature sausage pizza. A partially disassembled clock with a gold finish sitting on the fireplace mantel caught his eye. Stepping closer, he realized it wasn't broken. The face was ajar, concealing a hidden compartment large enough to hold the gun Tad had rushed outside with. Skylos shrugged and placed the firearm back inside before closing the hinged door. He grabbed the last piece of pizza and toured the first floor.

Barking picked up as soon as Skylos stepped into the kitchen. He grabbed a large chef's knife off the counter and followed the noise to the back of the room. Opposite a walk-in pantry was a small nook with a washing machine and dryer. A Doberman inside a large, metal crate barked with renewed ferocity.

"Shhh... The bad man's gone," Skylos said, reassuring the animal. He reached toward the cage with steady hands. The dog lurched forward, nipping his fingertip. Skylos swore and kicked the cage. Setting the knife on the washing machine, he wrapped a linen towel around his hand. He pulled it away from the wound and peeked. The finger was bleeding but not bad enough to require stitches.

"Fine, stay in there." Skylos slammed the utility room door and checked the rest of the house.

The second floor was much like the first—a dump. The patched blue jeans Tad had on during their earlier encounter sat on a disheveled bed in the master bedroom. Skylos checked them and pocketed the wallet and keys still inside. The dresser contained a couple of hundred dollars and a bottle with two round Oxycodone pills. Skylos took these as well before moving onto the second bedroom. It was empty except for a twin bed—still made up—and an empty suitcase.

There wasn't much else to see upstairs so he ignored the sound of the dog downstairs and went into the bath. Skylos drew a bath and soaked in the tub, making sure to scrub all of Tad's blood off his body. The entire time the dog never stopped its incessant barking.

He lowered his head under the water and still heard the beast clearly. In a way it was worse than the annoying ringing he used to get in his ear. Eventually, he jumped out of the bath and dug through Tad's closet until he found something that fit—a faded high school gym tee-shirt and pair of mesh drawstring shorts.

Grabbing the sheets and blanket off the spare bed, he marched downstairs and draped them over the cage. Not even that muffled the noise. He sighed, put his hand to his temple, and closed his eyes.

Once his eyes were closed, his mind raced. More visions came to him: people setting out rat poison to kill their neighbor's beasts, slipping razor blades into apple slices, throwing rocks... He snapped his eyes open again. He didn't want to resort to that. It wasn't the dog's fault. There had to be something more humane.

In the bottom drawer of a refrigerator stocked mostly with beer was a package of long expired hot dogs. He pushed the remaining Oxycodone pills into a slimy link. Tossing the coverings aside, he shoved it into the cage. The dog ignored the sausage and renewed its attempts at biting Skylos through the bars.

"I'm trying to help you," Skylos said, closing his eyes.

Based on the homeowner's demeanor, he imagined the police were used to issuing warnings about the loud dog. He was going to have to get rid of it. He snatched the knife off the washer and thrust it between the kennel bars. The dog pressed its large body against the opposite side, avoiding his reach.

Skylos grabbed a metal hanger, straightened it out, and used it to push the bedsheet through the bars. He tied it off to the other end and slipped it over his shoulder. Deep scratches carved into the wood floor as he dragged the cage through the den. The dog growled and chewed at the sheet as Skylos yanked the cage outside and to the pool's edge.

A single firm kick sent the entire kennel plummeting to the bottom. The barking ceased and hundreds of tiny bubbles rose to the water's surface. The dog thrashed within the cage. One final bubble popped the surface as the last breath escaped from the

German Shepard's lungs. Skylos breathed a smile of relief. With both beasts put down, he could finally rest.

He went back into the house and sat in the uncomfortable wooden chair at the corner desk. Once the old computer booted and the internet browser opened, it loaded directly to an adult website. Skylos cringed and went to Amazon's site.

Tad's account logged in automatically, just like Ken's had. Though Tad wasn't on vacation, and therefore Skylos could order anything he liked. Not knowing what Calliope's grand scheme detailed, the first thing that came to mind was gift cards for large chain establishments. This would ensure they'd be usable no matter where Calliope sent him next.

The next thing he needed was a no-brainer—a buttton of knives. There was a huge variety available, but what he needed was a bulk supply of disposable blades. After a brief search elsewhere, he came across a government-sponsored site that sold items confiscated by the TSA. Knives were available for purchase in lots of five pounds. As he proceeded, he found that all internet sales required an in-person pickup from a warehouse in Sacramento. Unfortunately, a five-hour drive was not part of his plans. Further searching yielded similar offers on eBay.

After waded through dozens of posts he found a local seller. Unfortunately, the pictures were all blurry. He shrugged. It wasn't his money.

The chair creaked as he leaned back and added other miscellaneous items to his Amazon cart: a flashlight, small first aid kit, and a lighter. As he added the items to the cart and prepared to check out a sponsored advertisement caught his attention—a zombie survival kit. Included was a hatchet, a folding shovel, and other ludicrous items. While those things would only slow him down there was one thing that stood out to him. A set of lockpicks.

He searched through the site some more and found a transparent padlock with a set of picks and added them to his order. Calliope's appearance was unpredictable, and it should leave him plenty of opportunities to practice. He submitted the orders and requested a guaranteed shipment by Saturday.

Skylos turned off the desktop and looked around the room. The clutter around him was reminiscent of the theater's basement but somehow felt dirtier. He yawned. In the morning, he'd clean and conduct a more thorough search for valuables.

He headed upstairs to the master bedroom and threw Tad's dirty clothes onto the floor. He crawled into the bed and pulled the comforter up to his neck. The stained blanket paled in comparison to the warmth of Calliope's touch, but it wasn't long before he fell fast asleep.

Chapter 10

Christopher – Chicago, IL – Thursday Night

"Honey? Honey, wake up!"

Christopher kept his eyes shut and tried to hold onto the vision through his wife's vigorous shaking. It was no use. She'd already pulled him away from it.

"I'm up," he mumbled.

"You were flailing and talking in your sleep. You're still having nightmares?"

He nodded, working his jaw up and down to alleviate the ringing in his right ear. "Yeah. Sorry if I woke you."

"It's been a week. I thought they were over. Do you want to talk about them?"

He wiped the sweat from his brow with his forearm. "No. I'm going to step out and document it as Dr. Baker suggested. Go back to sleep."

"Are you sharing them with her at least?" she said with a yawn.

"Of course." He lied. Dr. Baker had been working with the department for a dozen years. In that time, she'd no doubt been party to discussions of gruesome scenes. But Christopher was no more likely to discuss a man whose genitals had been skewered than a near-naked coed with her thighs slashed to ribbons. Those sorts of things were best unsaid to an attractive psychiatrist almost half his age. And even though she didn't push him, he knew she was smart enough to know he was holding back. He kissed his wife on the forehead. He was sure Martha knew he was holding back too.

Clutching his notebook, he walked out and closed the bedroom door behind him. He went to the kitchen and filled a glass with cool tap water. As he downed the glass, the dot on the oven's digital clock switched from PM to AM.

Christopher took a seat at the kitchen table, licked his finger, and flipped to the last page. He jotted down the time without looking, instead staring at the murdered construction worker's face. This was the first time since the strange dreams started that he'd dreamt of the same person twice. Christopher angled the pencil so the metal securing the eraser nub didn't tear the page. He was wrong the other day. The redneck *was* a victim.

This time he had an actual, the murder weapon. A large knife attached to a pool skimmer was nothing if not unique. If it were a case that came across his desk, he would have remembered it. Jones would have found a way to crack some stupid joke or another about it.

The weapon wasn't the only clue either; the location of the body itself was significant. It was a house exterior. And one rife with clues. The pool was behind a large mission style house with a barren and rocky yard. What few trees he could make out in the dark bore an odd, scaly texture. They reminded him of palm trees, so he was probably looking for a southwestern state, or possibly Florida.

He rested the pencil tip on the small sun logo from earlier. He hadn't investigated it in depth but knew New Mexico's state flag bore a sun. Even though the styles didn't match, it was another supporting detail.

"Okay," he said aloud, "Definitely not an old case." Every year he'd spent on the force had been in the city of Chicago. He dropped the pencil and rubbed his eyes.

If this is the plot to an episode of CSI or Criminal Minds. I'm going to be furious.

Christopher picked the pencil back up and revised his theories. The burly construction worker didn't fit the other two deaths, but his gut said it was related, nevertheless. "Did the dog have something to do with it?"

Martha had woken him before he could investigate the cage at the bottom of the pool though he could tell it was a large dog, maybe a German Shepherd. Their bite strength didn't rank as high as a pit bull's, but they weren't an uncommon dog fighting breed. If the owner owed money in fights, it could have been an aspect in his death. It was a decent theory but missed a link between the Train Station employee and the young woman. In fact, the only commonality they shared was the efficiency of the strikes. Ignoring the fact that the last body was toyed with for a bit, each suffered severed arteries.

After everything had been written down, he returned to bed, careful to avoid disturbing his wife. He rolled onto his side and slipped the notebook back into the nightstand. Martha scooted closer and rubbed his back.

"Feel better?"

"Yeah." He lied again. With tonight's killing, there were now three unsolved murders floating around in his head—potentially the work of a serial killer.

"Will you ever let me read through that notebook?"

He rolled over, facing her. "I wouldn't want to subject you to that. It's nothing interesting. Merely the scribblings of an old man who's seen too much shit on the force."

He kissed his wife on the forehead and rolled onto his back.

Martha drifted off to sleep but the gears kept turning in Christopher's head. Suddenly it hit him. Perhaps he was trying to make a connection where there wasn't any. His brain was keeping itself busy during retirement. Maybe it was a creative spark for the next chapter of his life. Plenty of former police officers went on to become successful writers. Gene Roddenberry was a police officer during the time he wrote the script for Star Trek.

Christopher fluffed his pillow and closed his eyes. He had both the procedural knowledge and life experience to weave something intriguing. With a little work, he'd be writing the next great American novel.

Chapter 11

Samantha stared at the metal T-pin stuck in her low cubicle wall. It was proving to be more interesting than Candace Anderson's third revision. More frustrating than that though was the fact that her own story had hit a snag. It had been a full week since she'd had one of the unsettling dreams and just as long since she'd written anything worth keeping. This wasn't typical writer's block. She plugged away at the keyboard every night but none of it was good enough.

Over the last week, her story ebbed and flowed like the tides. On Monday evening she added five pages, only to delete them Tuesday morning. Tuesday night was the same—three new pages that received the executioner's axe the following day. Wednesday and Thursday were more of the same. She missed the dreams and hated feeling like she was incapable of producing the same quality of work without them.

When her usual creative exercises failed, she turned to the internet for remedies. She tried every suggestion no matter how ridiculous—such as taking her keyboard to bed and whispering to it before she slept. Last night's attempt was the worst mistake. Her co-worker, Charlie, convinced her to "Come out for a few drinks to get your creative juices flowing." What Charlie failed to consider was that she hadn't drunk at a professional level since college. Now she was learning the hard way that alcohol was like violence. It didn't solve any problems.

From the corner of her eye, a bright purple pants suit swished toward her. She groaned. As if the fluorescent lights overhead weren't murder enough on her head, she was going to have to deal with Melanie too. Samantha downed the fizzing cup of Alka-Seltzer.

"Everything good over here?" Melanie asked in an all too cheery tone.

Samantha looked at the pen on the desk and gave serious thought to jabbing it into Melanie's throat. "All good," she said sarcastically and gave a thumbs-up.

"Set to finish our deadlines for the week?"

"Two remaining," Samantha replied as she squinted up at her boss. "They won't be a problem to knock out before the end of the day."

Melanie checked her watch and glanced at the doorway onto the office floor. "I'll be occupied for the next hour but let me know if you get overwhelmed and need something."

When Melanie strayed out of earshot Charlie stepped over. He switched his coffee cup to his left hand and leaned against the cubicle wall. He was a short, clean-shaven man dressed in a sports coat, blue jeans, and thick square-shaped glasses. If he was as hungover as she was, he hid it masterfully.

"Well, that was painful," said Charlie. He gave an exaggerated recoil when he saw her face. "You look like crap, Sam."

"Thanks?"

"You need a big, greasy slice of pizza. Always does the trick for me. I can order. My treat."

"Ugh. It's barely 9 A.M. I'll stick with dry heaving instead of throwing up grease."

"I'm telling you, it's a miracle cure." He winked and flashed a smile that made her wonder if he was hitting on her. She held her stomach and shifted in the chair. Melanie walked the client to her office and Charlie waved as she went past. "So, are you coming out with us again tonight? We were going to try..." Charlie's voice trailed off as he craned his neck toward a commotion at the office entrance.

Whatever it was attracted the attention of several other colleagues. The office fell quiet and people all around her stood up one after another. Samantha leaned back in her chair to look around Charlie. Two uniformed officers, one male and one female, were talking to Dawn at reception. A third guarded the door, scanning the floor. Dawn pointed in her direction.

"What's going on, officers?" asked Charlie as they approached.

"Samantha Englund?" one of them said. Charlie backed away.

Her stomach dropped like the downtick of a rollercoaster and her initial thoughts went to Dad. He suffered a mild heart attack a few months ago. Did something happen to him? Wouldn't Mom have called?

"I'm Samantha," she said, rising from her chair.

Both officer's hands instinctively reached for their holsters. She froze. Something was wrong.

"I'm Officer Davis," the man continued. "This is Officer Reyes. We have some questions we'd like to ask you at the station. We'll be placing you in handcuffs for everyone's safety." Samantha looked up at the tall, well-built female officer as she withdrew a pair of cuffs from a leather case and stepped forward.

"I don't understand. Is this necessary? Am I under arrest or something?" Samantha protested but knew better than to struggle as Officer Reyes restrained her. The male officer grabbed her cell phone and purse off the desk.

"You're not under arrest at this time."

Whispers floated over the cubicle walls as the officers escorted her away. Melanie's mouth formed a large 'O' as she watched from inside the fishbowl.

"At this time... What does that mean? You're obligated by law to inform me of whatever crime you think I've committed."

"No, we aren't," said Officer Davis.

"Conspiracy to commit murder," Officer Reyes blurted out. Charlie dropped his coffee and several co-workers gasped. A faint smile graced the corners of Officer Reyes' mouth. It seemed she had already made up her mind.

"This is a mistake!" Samantha said, shaking her whole body.

Officer Reyes gripped Samantha's shoulder firmly and guided her out of the building. Samantha kept her head high. Come Monday morning, they'd all be laughing about the misunderstanding. As they exited the elevators in the lobby Samantha noticed a news van already parked across the street. One of the male officers hurried over, intercepting the camera crew.

A clean-shaven man with a buzz-cut in a meticulous gray suit waited outside the building watching the gawkers gathered on the street. When Officer Reyes placed Samantha into the back of her squad car, he jumped into the passenger seat. The female officer asked him if he was ready. The unidentified man nodded and studied Samantha via the rearview mirror.

"Can someone please explain what's going on?" When neither of them obliged Samantha sank back into the stiff plastic seat, closed her eyes, and tried to ignore her churning stomach.

At the station, Officer Reyes dragged her into an interrogation room and removed the cuffs. Samantha rubbed her wrists and sat in silence on the cold metal chair. She wondered what they had done with her personal belongings, particularly her phone.

The interrogation room door opened only a few minutes later. *That's a good sign,* she thought. The silent passenger from the police escort stepped inside and took a seat across from her. He looked her over with cold, calculating eyes and then placed a manila folder onto the metal table. Samantha couldn't help but feel like she was stuck in the middle of a police procedural drama.

When it was clear the man wasn't going to start the conversation, Samantha spoke up. "Why am I here? I haven't done anything wrong."

The man cleared his throat. "Ms. Englund, I'm Agent Montgomery with the Federal Bureau of Investigation. I'd like to ask you some questions about your relationship with the L.A. Ripper." He studied her eyes and lips for a reaction.

Samantha's eyebrows rose as she cocked her head. "My relationship with whom?"

The agent hesitated for a moment before unwinding the string-sealed folder. He withdrew a single piece of paper and slid it across the table. Samantha picked it up and skimmed over the text—a search warrant for her person and apartment. She looked up at him, the puzzled look still taking over her face.

"We seized your laptop and will have what we need before long. However, it would save us all a great deal of time if you'd cooperate and answer my questions."

"I'd love nothing more than to cooperate. But I don't know what you're charging me with." Samantha let the search warrant float down to the table. "Maybe I should be asking for a lawyer."

"Let me get your phone." The FBI agent stood, bringing the folder with him to the door. His hand lingered on the doorknob for a moment before he turned around and loomed over her. He pulled two photos from the envelope and lined them in front of her. "These may help jog your memory while I'm out." He swung the door open and took a step outside the room.

Samantha looked down and gasped. She picked up the first photo—a young man whose throat had been slit. "Tom?" *How was this possible?*

She dropped the picture and turned away, but it didn't help. Her mind was already conjuring the foundation for her story. Samantha watched herself stabbing Tom in the throat again. She shook her head hard until the image cleared. She didn't have to see the other photo to know who it was. "Stephanie..."

A vise twisted in her stomach and bile danced on her tongue.

Agent Montgomery stopped the door from closing with his foot. "So, you're familiar with the victims?"

"I'm going to be ill."

The room spun violently as she got to her feet. She fell forward into the edge of the metal table, and everything went black.

Chapter 12

Elliot Thompson – New York City, NY—

Friday Morning

Elliot Thompson's long black duster flapped behind him as he walked into the offices of Penguin Random House in New York City. He waved off the receptionist at the front desk, Larry or Barry or something, and went straight to the elevator. He no longer had an office space in the building; it had been a decade since he'd ascended from lowly editor to an author that often graced the bestseller list. His goal was to snag an unused office for a few days and hammer out as many pages as possible.

Aside from a few voices starting their day with coffee and socializing in the breakroom, the fourteenth floor was quiet. Elliot lowered his head and hurried past them. He didn't want to talk with anyone. Dragging his tired feet down the halls, he found a room near a corner office without a name on the door. He flipped on the light and understood why the door was closed. The amount of clutter made the small office look like a mailroom. Elliot shrugged. The leather chair looked comfy enough.

Two heavy cardboard boxes rested on the chair. He tossed the first into the corner of the room and the second on top of it. It landed with a thud and split, spilling papers on the floor. He looked at the desk through heavy eyelids and scratched at the stubble on his throat.

It's too early to deal with this crap.

Grabbing his laptop case at both ends, he plowed everything over the edge. A mug shattered and countless papers dropped like the leaves of a great oak succumbing to autumn. He shut the lights off again and returned to the chair where he draped his coat over himself and fell asleep with his feet propped up on the desk.

...

"What the hell?"

The voice roused Elliot from his slumber. A baby-faced intern in a cheap suit stood in the doorway with his arms akimbo.

Elliot rubbed his eyes and raised his head. "Something..." he said through an exaggerated yawn, "I can help you with, chief?"

"You can start by getting your feet off my desk and cleaning up the mess you made."

"This is how I found it. And I don't see your name anywhere on the door." Elliot rested his head back against the chair. "Shut the light off on your way out."

The intern glanced back at the mess floor and, in a moment of bravery, attempted to swipe Elliot's feet off the desk. Elliot shifted his weight forward in the chair and the intern's hand slapped feebly against his boots.

Taking his time, Elliot removed his feet from the desk. He looped his left foot under the chair leg and lifted it as he stood. The intern jumped as the chair crashed to the floor.

"The legal distinction between assault and battery confuses a lot of people," Elliot said as he stepped over the chair and toward the intern. "Assault is an attempt or threat to bring about harm to someone. Only when acting upon that threat does it cross over to battery."

Marcie, the office manager and senior editor, flew into the room. She was of slight build and stature, standing around five and a half feet. Despite this, she commanded a lot of respect, and fear, in the building. She took one look at Elliot and sighed. The intern took a step back, almost tripping over a stack of boxes, and looked to Marcie. A smug smile cracked the corner of his lips.

"Oh. I see..." Elliot said pointing. "You're going to let her fight this battle for you."

"Elliot, what the hell are you doing?" Marcie said.

He smiled and kept his eyes fixated on the intern while addressing Marcie. "Good morning, Janet." The slight upturn in Marcie's nose reminded him of a character from an old sitcom. Elliot's smile grew broader as he caught her eyebrows sharpen out of his periphery.

Marcie raised her hands to her head. With another loud sigh, she grabbed the intern's arm and pulled him into the hallway. "Go get some coffee, I'll sort this out."

"What an asshole," the intern grumbled as he walked away.

"An asshole who's still within earshot!" yelled Elliot, determined to get in the last word.

After she returned but before she could chastise him, Elliot embraced her. "Good to see you." Marcie pulled away. She stood on her tiptoes to look him in the eye. With great restraint, she pressed her pointer finger into his chest instead of slugging him.

"He's right. You are an asshole. Did you *have* to trash his office?"

"It looked like old storage. Who the hell uses paper anymore?" Elliot looked down at the floor and shrugged. "Just have another intern to clean it up. That's why they're here."

"No. They're not janitorial staff. You're going to clean this up before you leave." She cocked her head and glared until he nodded. "Why are you here anyway? You hate people. Go home and write."

"Remember the old house to the east of me? Someone bought it and tore it down. It's been nonstop construction since. It's so loud I can't even think. The noise ordinances prevent them from working before seven in the morning. That apparently doesn't pertain to them having trucks idling outside my window for over an hour. I figured I'd be better off here."

"So, you're here for the foreseeable future?" Elliot shrugged. Marcie closed her eyes and took a deep breath. "Since you're here we should talk about your..." She furrowed her brow. "Revisions... But first I'm going to need a coffee and to check on Rob."

"Who?"

"The intern you assaulted."

"Technically it wasn't..." Marcie gave him a death glare and he shut his mouth.

Marcie returned twenty minutes later just as Elliot threw the last jagged shard of the ceramic mug into the waste bin. She looked around the room. Faint boot prints marked piles of papers pushed together in a mound against the wall. At least it was something. She shook her head slightly and took a deep breath before sitting down.

Elliot righted the chair, pulled out his laptop, and turned his attention to her. "Well? Give it to me straight," he said, typing his password into the computer.

"Where to begin..." Marcie swiped her fingers across the tablet in her hand. She soon gave up and tossed it onto the desk. "Two weeks ago, you had a dozen solid chapters. Where did they go? Suddenly you've started over entirely and relocated your detective from the French Quarter to Los Angeles. Is this what a mid-life crisis looks like?"

Elliot laughed. "Whoa. Tell me how you really feel, babe." He checked her face for a reaction. Nope, still a scowl. "I guess I wanted to breathe some new life into the series."

Marcie sighed and took a deep breath, the strategy she typically employed with Elliot. "Change is fine but start with subtlety. Let's see your revised outline."

Elliot bit his lip. "Umm... Outline?"

"We both know what happens when you try to pants stuff. Give me a synopsis, or something. What is this new direction and where did it come from?"

"I don't know. It struck me early one morning. Shower thoughts."

Marcie reached across the desk, placing her hand on his. "I'm talking to you as a friend now. I think the lack of sleep from the construction next-door is getting to you. Get a hotel room in the city and take a few days off. Come back when you're rested. I'll have an office set aside for you. Trust me, you will alienate your readers by a sudden genre shift. If anything, do another one centered around voodoo. That book was well-received. Ditch the demon and the southwest backdrop."

"I haven't decided if the voice is an actual demon yet. I at least want to allude to it though. I can always fall back on it being a visual and auditory hallucination. That's common enough among serial killers."

"Look, I'm trying to help but if you want to start a debate, I'm going to have a hard time finding where to start." Marcie cleared her throat and then continued. "You open with a nameless orphan who steals a scuba suit, tries to kill a hooker, fails, and settles for a lowly janitor. All of this at the behest of a demonic voice demanding he copycat killings detailed in an Indie author's blog posts. Tell me you wouldn't toss this in the trash without a second thought if it came from a first-time author."

Elliot lowered the laptop lid. "So, you're saying you don't like it."

Marcie sighed for the hundredth time. "Your writing's tight, it's the content that's lacking. Unless you're targeting a younger audience that eats up the supernatural/demon/vampire subculture you will alienate your readers. You'll see. I sent an excerpt to my fifteen-year-old niece. This is right up her alley."

He raised an eyebrow. "Did she enjoy it?"

"I haven't heard back from her." Marcie picked up the tablet and swiped a few more times. "I emailed you my comments. But only because it's my job and I'm being paid to. My professional—and personal—opinion is for you to revert to your previous draft... But since I know you'll ignore me, at least look at my suggestions."

"Alright," Elliot said waving his hand to dismiss her. "Go and let me write already."

Chapter 13

Christopher – Chicago, IL – Friday Afternoon

Luke and Jake ran circles in Christopher's front room. The six-year-old identical twins ignored the muted television. Chasing each other with crude weapons constructed from Lego bricks proved far more interesting than the local news.

Christopher navigated the minefield of plastic bricks guarding the recliner with a fresh mug of coffee in hand. Exhausted from another week with the twins, he set the mug on a TV tray and fell back into the recliner. Immediately, a burning pain shot down his back and into his legs. He groaned out a little curse at the bulging discs in his lower back. It was a necessary reminder of his orthopedic's recommendation to stay active.

He let out a wide yawn while stretching his arms above his head. The twins seemed content, but they'd be just as happy running at the park. There was also a tiny chance it would get them tired enough to take a nap. *After this cup of coffee. And the crossword. And maybe one more cup of coffee.*

Before he could pick up a pencil and make any headway on the crossword puzzle, Luke bumped into the TV tray. Hot coffee drenched the morning paper and poured onto Christopher's lap. He shot to his feet, knocking over the entire tray.

"Shit!"

Both kids stopped in their tracks and stared. "Aww, you said a bad word!" they shouted in unison.

"Are you okay, Luke?" The boy nodded. The coffee had managed to miss the boy entirely. "Alright. Go and grab grandpa a towel and then we'll go to the park." He tousled the boy's faded, skunk-striped, blonde hair and chuckled. After the first day of watching them, he dyed a large black stripe into his hair to tell the boys apart. Jessica was still pissed about it, which only made it funnier.

"Here, papa," said Luke holding out a kitchen towel with a blue stripe along the edge.

"Thanks, buddy."

Christopher knelt and soaked up the puddle on the wood floor. As he rose to his feet with the soggy newspaper, something in his subconscious alerted him to the scrolling closed captions on the television.

Chicago police detain local author for connections to Los Angeles slaying victims.

He fumbled for the remote and raised the volume, but the promo spot was already over. He stared at the TV. Had he really read that right?

"Can we go to the park now?" asked Jake.

"Yeah, I want to go to the park!" said Luke.

"Give me a few minutes. I need to change." Their faces fell and Luke stomped his foot. "How about cartoons until we leave?" The twins cheered as he flipped the channel until he found a channel depicting robots fighting anthropomorphized farm animals.

Christopher changed into a different pair of khaki shorts and brought the notebook back to the front room with him. He dug through the kids' backpack and sank back into the recliner with their iPad. A parental restriction blocked access to the internet. He entered the obvious dates: the twin's birthday and his daughter's.

"Hey, what's the password for this thing?"

The boys didn't budge an inch, eyes glossed over and fixated on the screen. He may as well be talking to the wall. Christopher grabbed the remote and changed the channel.

"Grandpa!" they both whined.

"What's the password?"

"Oh. Two. Oh. Four," said Jake. Christopher snorted. *The divorce finalization. It figures.* He typed in the code and returned them to their show.

He flipped open the notepad, though it was a useless formality. Every small detail of the three crime scenes were fresh in his memory. He traced the words scattered across the page like a macabre word association exercise. As his fingertips passed each, their corresponding images sprang to life in his head. The bloody surfer's suit on the bathroom tile, a still packaged condom dropped behind the toilet, the embroidered name badge on the jumpsuit...

His hands trembled as he searched for the news story on the tablet. He was both terrified and excited to see the results. The body of a Janitor was found within the restroom at L.A.'s Union Station last Monday. He compared the date of the article against his notes. The death had occurred the night before he'd dreamt of it. Christopher scanned the story, matching the details to his synopsis. The broad details matched, but there was nothing about the condom or the drysuit. Not surprising. Were he still a homicide detective, he wouldn't have disclosed the full details to the press either.

How was this possible? he thought, staring at the wall with his mouth agape.

He moved onto the next murder, already knowing what he'd find. Three days later another body was found. A woman slain in a small L.A. movie theater. No mention of her being half-naked, or the Amazon boxes that looked like they were hastily torn open. Still, he was two for two. He chewed his lip and searched on, needing confirmation of the last body. Strangely nothing surfaced regarding a construction worker in the pool.

He tapped his fingers against the bulky tablet case. The third murder took place behind a private residence, not a public place like the others. It's possible no one had found the body thus far.

Christopher moved on, looking for details about the local author. None of the networks had anything on their sites about the story. He broadened his search and found a video posted to YouTube only a few hours ago. *L.A. Ripper's Accomplice Arrested in Chicago.* It already had a thousand views and counting.

He tapped on the video and suffered through twenty choppy seconds of police activity around an indistinguishable downtown building. Two officers emerged from the said building and deposited a dark-haired woman into a police car. Christopher re-started the video and leaned in close. While he couldn't make out any features of the alleged accomplice, the numbers on the front quarter panel of the squad car were familiar. It belonged to his precinct. He squinted and tapped replay a third time. There was no mistaking the tall female officer escorting the suspect. It was his daughter.

"You've got to be shitting me."

Whoever posted the video identified the woman as Samantha Blackblood. An obvious fake name, but one he could work with. A search on the name led Christopher to her website. It contained a series of blog posts as well as several chapters of a story she'd been writing. Instead of reading it immediately he skipped to the forums section. Several posts linked to the same L.A. news stories he'd just read. Others linked back to the YouTube video.

He went back and skimmed through the untitled story posted on the main page. The first chapter served to recreate Tom's murder in a startling degree. What was even more startling was that it included additional details that accounted for some of the things he'd seen in his dream—mainly the addition of a prostitute which accounted for the presence of the rubber. The retelling matched every piece of evidence that Christopher had seen left behind. An outside observer would mistake his notes for an outline of Samantha's story. He read through the remainder of her work and found a single exception. Like the news, Samantha's story was devoid of a third victim.

Christopher scrolled back and cross-referenced each of his dreams with the dates of the blog posts on the site. They matched to the day. He shut off the tablet and put it back in Jake's bag while he thought. If she was detained this morning, she may not have had time to write about it.

Not only was he dreaming about unsolved murders, but they were murders that had just taken place. Somehow, he had to find a way to talk to Samantha. If she were still in police custody, it would be relatively easy. Not so much if she'd been cut loose. Either way, Jessica had the information he needed.

"Come on boys. We need to visit mom before we go to the park."

As Christopher packed snacks he envisioned the possible outcomes of meeting with this woman. *One – 'Samantha' knows what's going on and can fill me in. Two – she's as clueless as I am, but together we can figure something out. Three—She thinks I'm a madman and calls the police.* While ushering the kids into the minivan he thought of another possibility. *Maybe she is involved and straight-up attacks me.*

Chapter 14

It had taken all morning, but Skylos finally cleaned up the house. Though exhausting, it was a worthwhile exercise. Not only was the space more comfortable, but he also found useful things during the effort. From Tad's closet, Skylos found a handful of old or shrunken clothing his size. He added these items, along with a few bandannas and a hat, to the suitcase he'd found the previous night.

A safe was also anchored in the closet floor. Unfortunately, it was locked tight and there were no keys to be found. After an hour of entering incorrect combinations, he gave up. If it contained cash or additional revolver ammunition, it was inaccessible. The rest of the house contained little of value.

He lugged the last bag of garbage down the stairs and through the kitchen. Depositing it outside the back door with the other five, he wiped the sweat from his brow. As he looked up the two dozen stairs to the alley his eyes settled on the garage. It was the one place he hadn't yet checked, and he was sure it was as disorganized as the rest of the house.

Skylos abandoned the garbage and opened the side door into the garage. Power tools, construction equipment, and crates of junk littered the floor and hung off the walls leaving little room for the huge truck. But it was clear that this was where Tad kept all his valuables. It was a veritable gold mine of machines and gadgets. Without familiarity with each item, it would be an impossible feat to assign a fair value to each. Even if he received a fraction of their value, it would still be a hefty sum.

It would take forever to sort through everything. He reminded himself that he couldn't sell all of it. While Tad didn't pay for a cleaning lady or lawn care company, he wouldn't remain undetected forever. Despite being a child molester, someone would eventually notice his absence, even if only his employer. Skylos dropped the truck's tailgate and climbed into the back to get a better view. He needed to focus on the most expensive things, the largest items. He rolled up his sleeves, jumped down, and dug in.

An air compressor scraped against the concrete slab as he dragged it out. With great effort, he managed to hoist it into the truck bed. He returned to the massive pile of tools and wheeled a gas generator over. Once he got it behind the truck, he realized it was too large to lift alone. He put it back. *On second thought, let's not go for things that big.*

He tossed in a large circular saw, a paint sprayer, and a drill, documenting each item on the back of the instruction booklet for a miter box. He continued to pile items onto the truck until it was full. When he looked back, the pile was barely dented.

Dripping with sweat from the poorly ventilated garage, Skylos returned to the house. He sat back down at the computer and created a post in the 'For sale' section of Craigslist.

'My uncle recently passed away and I need to clear out his possessions before selling the house. He worked in construction for the last 20 years and has many tools. I am motivated to sell and will accept all fair offers. Included in the lot is a Craftsman circular saw, Ryobi drill, Ryobi belt sander, Wagner paint sprayer, Milwaukee band saw, Milwaukee nail gun, DeWalt air compressor, and several boxes of assorted tools. The asking price is $500. Cash only. Must clear out ASAP.'

He submitted the post and retired to the bathroom for a long, steamy shower.

When he made his way back down, there were several inquiries about the tools. The first was willing to meet outside the Altadena Community Center at eight PM. Skylos looked up the address and frowned. The building shared a parking lot with the Sheriff's department.

It seemed unwise to drive a truck belonging to a man he'd killed less than twenty-four hours earlier to a police department. Though, five hundred dollars was more than he'd ever seen at one time in his life. And maybe the parking lot of a police department was the most ideal place to meet. The anonymous buyer would be less likely to rip him off. Besides, everything was already loaded in the truck. All that remained was to reap the rewards. Skylos accepted the offer and agreed to meet.

Chapter 15

Samantha – Chicago, IL – Friday Afternoon

Samantha stared down at the bald man in his underwear who was tangled in the pools tarp. The tip of her spear glinted in the moonlight. Blood dripped into her hair as she rose the weapon above her head, celebrating his death.

The vision faded as quickly as it came, chased away by a jackhammer pounding her head. Samantha's eyes flickered open to the drab, gray ceiling tiles of the interrogation room.

"Where am I?" she groaned.

A hand gently pressed down on her collar, preventing her from sitting up. Agent Montgomery was almost on top of her. Her eyes followed the contours of a muscular physique no longer covered by a suit jacket. She could make out a portion of a tattoo on his right bicep beneath his rolled-up sleeves. A globe and anchor—he must have been a Marine.

"Sit still. You lost consciousness when you struck your head."

Samantha's cheeks turned red as he caught her checking him out. "How long was I out?"

"Not even a minute. Can you remember your name?"

"Yes, I'm fine," she said, attempting to sit up a second time. Again, he restrained her.

"I'm not letting you up until I'm certain you're alright. Can you tell me your name, the day, and how old you are?"

Realizing he wouldn't let her up until receiving satisfactory answers, she complied. "Samantha Englund, twenty-seven years of age..." *And single.* "Today is Friday the second. Other than a headache, I feel fine. I'm declining further medical attention. Now can you please let me up?"

Agent Montgomery gave her another visual inspection before extending his arm and helping her up. He picked up his suit jacket that had been propping up her feet and then righted the tipped chair. Samantha took a seat again.

"You're sure you're okay? I'll go get you a bottle of water and an ice pack."

"I'm not going anywhere..."

The agent disappeared for only a minute and returned with a cold bottle of water and a frozen bag of blue gel. He slid them across the table and sat in silence, giving her time to regain her composure.

Samantha probed the lump on her forehead and took a long drink of water. "Thanks," she said and replaced the bottle's cap. The agent smiled and nodded. Pressing the ice pack to her forehead she looked across the table at him, ignoring the photos on the table. "Tom and Stephanie... When?"

"Tom and *Kara*," he corrected. "Both died around the same time, and in the same manner, as your narrative." Samantha moved her lips to say something but had no good explanation to give. "I've read your... documentary several times. There's a lot of things I can't figure out. For starters, why you changed the second victim's name, but not the details of the murders. Either you have a relationship with the murderer or source within the L.A.P.D. I'd like to know which."

The twisting in the pit of her stomach returned. "Someone must be copycatting the murders from my story."

Agent Montgomery shook his head. "As unlikely a scenario as that would be, the coroner put the time of death for each victim *before* you wrote about them."

"Check my phone records," Samantha offered. "I haven't been in communication with anyone from L.A."

He raised his eyebrows. "You're saying your site doesn't have any registered users in California?"

"I have readers all over the United States. Not to mention ones overseas. Because I have readers in Syria doesn't mean I have relationships with terrorists." Samantha regretted the words as soon as they left her mouth. "Shit. I didn't mean it like *that*. You know what I'm trying to say." Agent Montgomery's face didn't move.

Samantha put down the ice pack and picked up the picture of the janitor. As she looked at it, she didn't believe her explanation any more than the agent did. It was the same face she saw in her dream—down to the chickenpox scar over his left eyebrow. Even if one of her fans killed him, there's no way she could have known his face.

"My dreams..." Samantha said, not realizing she was speaking aloud.

"What?"

"I saw both of their deaths in my dreams..." she stammered.

Agent Montgomery crossed his arms over his chest. "Your official statement is that you received unreleased case information by way of psychic premonitions?"

"I don't know," she said, throwing up her hands in frustration. "I don't understand what's happening. If you have a more logical explanation, I'd be glad to accept it. All I know is that I'm not involved." Samantha dropped the photo and pushed the items across the table. She looked the agent in the eye. "Are you charging me with something?"

He responded without hesitation. "No. After sitting here and talking with you, I don't believe you're involved. At least not directly. I've spent plenty of time around guilty individuals. You're not one of them. I *do* believe you know more than you're letting onto though. This may be a complex situation, but there's a simple explanation... Somewhere."

"So, I'm free to go?"

"Yes," he said sliding over an embossed business card. "But I want to know if you think of anything else."

She hesitated to pick it up, thinking of the body she'd just seen floating in a pool somewhere. There was no point in mentioning it. The vision was too short to learn anything useful. "Can I ask you something before I go?" she said, nervously turning the card over in her hand.

"Sure."

"Can you tell me what led the FBI to my site?"

"An anonymous tip. But your site is, without a doubt, suspicious."

Samantha shrugged. She couldn't argue with that. "I'm trying to piece together what's going on the same as you," she stammered.

The FBI Agent led Samantha out of the interrogation room. Officer Reyes, the woman who'd placed the cuffs on her earlier, waited with a large, sealed plastic bag. When she handed Samantha the bag, it was clear it didn't contain everything.

"Excuse me. Where's my laptop?"

"Still in evidence," Officer Reyes said. "There's a slip in the bag."

"I'm sorry. There must be a mistake. The agent said they're not filing charges."

"Just because you're not being charged now doesn't mean that you won't be in the future. It's evidence that still needs to be processed." She turned around and walked away.

"When will I get it back?"

Officer Reyes continued down the hall without responding.

Agent Montgomery, still standing behind her, answered in the officer's stead. "They'll release it once the investigation is completed. I'm sorry I can't be more specific."

Samantha walked out with the bag and wondered what kind of mess was waiting in her apartment. She called Yvonne, her neighbor. Yvonne was a bartender, and while they had conflicting schedules and didn't hang out much, Samantha considered her one of her few close friends.

"Sam, thank God you're okay! The cops were here. I was afraid that your stalker was back."

"No, it was a misunderstanding, but I'm stuck at the station." Samantha gave a long pause. "I hate to ask, but could you come and pick me up?"

"If you need me, I'm there. I'll grab my shoes and see you in twenty."

Finding no benches on either side of the street, Samantha resigned to leaning against the short metal fence in the building's shade. While waiting for Yvonne, she fiddled with her phone. Three missed calls and an overwhelming number of emails vied for her attention. She'd forgotten that she silenced the ringer at the bar last night.

She listened to the first voicemail. *Hey Sam, it's Simon, did you piss off someone? Your site was getting hammered with a DOS attack – sorry—denial of service. It means the server can't keep up with the number of access requests. I increased your bandwidth temporarily to accommodate for now. I'll try to track down the bastards coordinating this.*

Samantha shook her head as Simon babbled on. She wasn't illiterate when it came to tech, but her web administrator always spoke to her as if she were. The only reason she tolerated it was because they attended high school in Missouri together and somehow both ended up in Chicago. He was a wizard with code and gave her a generous 'friends and family discount'.

The second voicemail was also from Simon, thirty minutes later. He wanted to make sure that she'd received the first message and ensure her that he was on top of things. Samantha marked it for deletion before listening to the entire message.

The final message had no callback number and the distorted voice sent a chill down her spine. *Samantha, we know who you are, and the terror you're spreading via your site. If you don't take it down within the next three hours, we will nuke it and dox you.*

She shook her head and deleted the message. "Damn you and your paranoid delusions, Simon." He'd likely gotten wind of her detainment. Samantha stood and paced back and forth while dialing his number. Knowing the conspiracy theories he believed in, the threat was genuine. Simon wouldn't hesitate to delete the entire site if it would save his own ass. The line rang several times before someone answered.

"Crystal Web Services, how can I help you?" said Simon after clearing his throat.

He never answers the phone like that. Would he know if someone was monitoring my calls? No. Don't get caught in Simon's web of paranoia.

"Cut the crap, it's Sam. Don't you dare wipe out my site."

"Sorry; I wasn't able to make that out. Are you calling from a mobile phone? There's interference on the line."

"I'm fine, by the way... You know what. Forget it." Samantha hung up, slumped back against the fence, and rested her head against her knees.

There was little time to wallow in sorrow before a black jeep without doors pulled up to the curb. Yvonne sat behind the wheel singing along with the radio in her typical tight black T-shirt cut above the midriff and frayed jean shorts. The sun glinted off the stud in her nose and her long red curls danced on her shoulders as she bounced about in her seat. When Samantha jumped into the passenger seat Yvonne lowered the radio volume.

"Here," she said, handing over a brown paper bag spotted with dark grease stains. "I'm sure you haven't eaten in a while."

"You didn't!" Samantha snatched the bag and opened it. Inside was a burger and fries from her favorite fast-food joint. "I love you, Von." Yvonne winked, pretended to shoot her with her thumb and forefinger, and then seamlessly picked up the chorus.

She handled the burger with one hand and swiped through her emails with the other. Most of them were automatic notifications from the site regarding donations and manuscript purchases. She skipped over them and opened a message from a site moderator. He reported an influx of user bans for spamming external links.

Another moderator called out the video footage and wanted to know whether she was okay. He surmised that a user must have made a connection to the murders and contacted police. Like Agent Montgomery had said, her site was damning. What was most disturbing though, was that the person who turned her in knew where she worked.

A glob of ketchup fell from the half-eaten burger onto her blouse. Yvonne held out a handful of napkins. Samantha let the phone drop back into her purse and dabbed it away. After finishing the meal, she licked her fingers and actually smiled. The greasy burger was a small step toward normalcy.

Samantha was appreciative that Von hadn't put pressured her to talk. Although she wouldn't have any insight, it would be good to talk to someone. And knowing her wild side, she wouldn't cast any judgment. Samantha reached over and shut off the stereo. Yvonne followed suit and let her singing trail off.

"Thanks again for the burger."

"Mmhmm," Yvonne replied, keeping her eyes on the road.

"Could you tell how badly my place got trashed?"

"I'm not sure... The officers pounded on the door several times before management opened it for them. They practically pushed me back into my apartment when I stuck my head into the hallway. I couldn't make out much through the peephole. I can tell you that several officers went in with guns drawn and then left shortly after with your laptop."

"I know, it was in the search warrant."

"What did you do? Software piracy? Catfish the wrong person?"

Samantha let out a soft chuckle. "You're not going to believe me, but here goes..." She took a deep breath. "After being inspired by some incredibly vivid dreams

I started writing a new story. Turns out they're more nightmares..." She paused. Unsure if she believed what she was about to say.

"Sorry, I'm not following. Is this a writer thing?"

"There were two murders in California this past week. And they happened exactly as I wrote them."

"Seriously? Someone's copycatting your story?"

"No. That's where it gets even weirder. The murders happened *before* I wrote about them. That's why the authorities were interested. One of my viewers must have contacted the police after recognizing the similarities."

"Your viewers?" Yvonne asked.

"We haven't talked about how I live stream while I write?"

"That's what you're doing over there at all hours of the night? I thought you were doing stuff over the webcam."

Samantha raised an eyebrow. "Yeah, I am..."

"No. I meant like topless, cam girl stuff." Yvonne grinned.

"What? No!"

"Don't knock it. You can make serious money that way." Samantha wondered if that's how Yvonne afforded to stay in the building on her bartending income. Yvonne reached over and placed her hand on Samantha's leg. "If you need anything, an alibi or whatever, don't hesitate to ask."

"Thanks, but they understand I don't have anything to do with it."

They drove a few miles in silence until Yvonne spoke again. "So, the conundrum is how you knew things you couldn't possibly know. Isn't this the stuff you write about? The supernatural?"

Samantha nodded. "I've always claimed to believe in the things I write about. That it's possible vampires and magic are part of our world, but deep inside I know it's fantasy. I'm seriously starting to rethink that."

Yvonne pulled into her assigned parking spot in the garage, and they walked into the elevator together. The door to her sixth-floor apartment appeared undisturbed.

"I expected police tape or something."

"Hollywood," Yvonne said with a shoulder shrug. "In the real-world police departments don't have budgets for fancy tape."

Samantha smiled and unlocked her door. She closed her eyes, preparing for the worst. From the doorway, it looked like everything was as she'd left it that morning.

"Want me to come in with you?" Yvonne asked, peeking into the apartment.

"I'll be okay. They were only after my laptop, which was sitting in plain view on my desk."

"As long as no one was digging around your underwear drawer," Yvonne said, nudging her in the ribs with her elbow. "I dated a cop for a few months who turned out to be a major freak. It wasn't until I dumped him that I realized I was missing several pairs of panties." Yvonne smiled and then unlocked her own door. "I'm right across the hall if you need anything."

Samantha let her door swing shut and locked it behind her. A second copy of the warrant sat on the kitchen table. She walked throughout the apartment and took inventory. The only absent items were her laptop and an old tablet on the bookshelf. She didn't care about the tablet, but the laptop was her livelihood. She'd freely trade her entire underwear drawer to have it back.

Samantha returned to the front room and sprawled out on the couch. It was barely past three o'clock, but she was exhausted. Her first instinct was to use her phone to continue the story. The man in the pool somehow tied into things. If she wrote about him, she might gain more insight into the murders. Unfortunately having to rely on her phones on-screen keyboard would suck.

She sat up, remembering the Bluetooth keyboard that came with the tablet when she purchased it ages ago. There was no reason it wouldn't work with her phone. She dug through a drawer in her kitchen filled with miscellaneous crap: a palm-sized projector, several flash drives, and old power cords, but no keyboard. As she crammed the items back into the drawer a promotional key chain from her office clattered to the floor.

"Shit!" Before she did anything, she needed to smooth things over with Melanie. If she took a cab right now, she'd probably catch Melanie before she left but she needed to be sure. She picked up her phone.

"This is Melanie speaking, what can Windy City Publishing do for you today?"

"Hi Melanie, it's Samantha."

There was a long pause. "I wasn't sure I'd hear from you again."

"I'm sorry about the scene this morning, there was a big case of mistaken identity. I still have a couple of hours of work left to wrap up. Unfortunately, my personal laptop isn't working, but I can be in the office in about thirty minutes, and I'm willing to stay late and work through the rest of my deadlines."

"It won't be necessary. They've already been taken care of."

"I can't convey how sorry I am. I'll make it up to everyone on Monday."

"Samantha... I don't think you're a good fit for this company's ideals any longer."

Samantha moved her lips, but couldn't find anything appropriate to say other than, "What?"

"You were dragged out of the office in handcuffs. In front of a prospective client, no less. While it may have been a misunderstanding, it was a clear sign. Something's changed in you recently. Which is okay. People grow out of their jobs all the time."

"But..."

Melanie interrupted her before she could get another word in. "Please stop in on Monday for your personal effects. You'll be compensated for your remaining PTO and given a generous severance package. I'd also be happy to write you a glowing recommendation. You've always done good work. Think of this as a window opening for you."

Melanie rambled on, offering other encouraging words. Samantha hung up the phone, tears streaming down her face. On top of making her a person of interest in a murder case, the dreams had cost her the job she loved.

She talked aloud to calm herself down. "It'll be okay. Melanie promised me a recommendation and a severance package. Between that and my savings, I'll be fine for a few months. Though I did just hang up on her..." She looked around her apartment. It would make sense to move into something smaller and less expensive until she could secure another job. Her lease was up for renewal in October anyway.

She cursed again. While she'd always been diligent in backing up her writing to the cloud, she'd never done so with other important documents. Thinking about having to interview and needing an up-to-date resume was never on her priority list. If she could even find a hard copy, it was probably half a decade old. She darted from room to room, checking the barely touched recesses of the apartment. It wasn't on the bookshelf in the front room or the top shelf in her closet. She had one last location to check. Samantha pulled a large plastic storage bin from beneath her bed and removed the dusty lid.

There she found a wireless keyboard sandwiched between expensive college journalism textbooks she couldn't bear to get rid. "Heh." She tossed it onto the bed and continued digging. Beneath an old photo album at the bottom of the container was a faux leather padfolio. Samantha grabbed it, kicked the bin back under the bed, and then returned to the front room.

She paused in front of the couch in the front room and flipped open the padfolio. Tucked into the left pocket were her resume and leftover business cards from interviews that happened eons ago. The attached pad of paper still bore the notes from her interview with Melanie. It highlighted a brief job description, what questions were asked, and a column listing perceived pros and cons. After being in a room with Melanie for only an hour she'd written "overbearing and micromanaging boss".

She set the documents aside and let out a long breath. Even with the aid of an external keyboard creating a new resume would be a challenge.

Samantha made a cup of chamomile tea and sat down on the L-shaped couch. She took a sip and went back to piecing together the puzzle. According to Agent Montgomery, both murders happened in California. That's where she'd start. After pairing the keyboard to her phone, didn't take her long to come across an article about the murdered Metro employee. Accompanying the text was a black and white photo of the bloody footprints in the entry hall of Union Station.

However, that photo didn't adequately portray the actual crime scene. When Samantha closed her eyes, she was back there again. The news article glossed over all the gory details. But Samantha knew the contour of the rusty knife with a loose casing from a long-absent screw, the smell of the rubber drysuit, and the bloody prints covering the stall like a macabre game of Twister. She shivered.

None of those details were the embellishments of a skilled writer...they actually happened.

Her stomach lurched as she thought about the second murder. The police statement claimed that one was a robbery gone wrong and unrelated to the first. Samantha knew the murder wasn't planned, but it wasn't an intended robbery. Smaller media outlets suspected the same and were already referring to the killer as The L.A. Ripper.

Samantha searched further but found nothing about a body found in a pool. Maybe it was only a nightmare. It was brief and didn't have the same quality... The same vibrancy. She touched her forehead. It was still tender.

She typed 'Prophetic Dreams' into the search bar then erased it. It didn't fit. She was dreaming of things that had already happened. It was reminiscent of some sort of psychic phenomenon, but not prophecy.

Early in her writing 'career', readers gave her flak about the lack of realism in her stories. So, she dove deeper into the occult. She knew all about Wicca and the lore behind vampires, werewolves, and demons. Unfortunately, psychic abilities weren't something she was well versed in.

After some digging, she found a few some consistent schools of thought. It was agreed that psychic gifts tended to reveal themselves in one of three manners: through excessive training to develop latent abilities, via spontaneous development at puberty, or passed down genetically. And she was a long way from puberty. While she couldn't recall her family ever discussing the subject it would be easy enough to find out. Samantha rang her mother, who picked up right away.

"Hi honey, did you just get in from work?"

"Yeah..." Samantha licked her lips. She couldn't exactly explain what was going on. Not now, and probably not ever.

"Is everything okay?"

"Yeah. I just wanted to ask when it would be a good time to come visit. I've got some time off work coming up." She hadn't been back to Kansas City since last Christmas. Chicago sucked her in ever since she moved there for college.

"Anytime is good. Let us know when you're thinking, and we'll free our schedules. Something else bothering you?"

"I have a sort of odd question... Do we have any history of psychic ability in the family?"

Her mother paused. "Only if you count your father's schizophrenic uncle who believed he could hear spirits. Though I guess there was that weird thing around your birth..."

Samantha straightened her back. *You've got to be kidding me...* "What *thing*, Mom?"

"I'm sure you've heard the story. Your father used to love telling it. The moment you were delivered the hospital briefly lost power. Roger swore he heard a voice and witnessed you smiling when it happened. He used to tell people you were the Antichrist."

A temporary brownout? She relaxed. She was letting her imagination get the better of her.

A heavy knock came at the door—probably Von checking up on her. "Sorry to cut this short, but someone's at the door. I'll let you know when I book my flight. Give Dad my love."

Chapter 16

Christopher – Chicago, IL – Friday Afternoon

It wasn't until after Christopher unloaded the twins that he realized he'd parked the minivan in a spot no longer reserved for him. He shrugged his shoulders. While it may cause a lecture, they wouldn't tow him. He put his arms around the kids and corralled them into the building.

A skinny officer looked up from the front desk and smiled at him. "Did you forget that being retired means you don't have to show up at work, old man?"

Christopher offered a feeble laugh. "Funny, Jones. I need to have a word with my daughter. It's important."

"I think so." Jones leaned over the counter and yelled to another officer. "Hey Parker, is Jessica still in the building?"

Christopher shook his head. *I could have done that.*

A man with a buzz cut answered without looking up. "The Amazon? Yeah..."

"Parker!" Jones yelled.

Parker looked up to Christopher's glaring eyes. He cleared his throat. "Umm... Sergeant Reyes is at her desk finishing some paperwork." The man picked up a stack of papers and scurried down the hall.

Christopher smiled and gave Jones a playful punch. "I'll let you in on a little secret. Both of us know that everyone calls her that. She may pretend that it irks her, but it gives her a certain sense of pride. And if you ever tell anyone that, you're a dead man."

Jones mimed zipping up his lips and throwing away the key. "Want me to keep these two occupied for a few?" he said, eyeing the twins.

The retired Sergeant nodded. "If you wouldn't mind."

"You boys know how to dial nine-one-one if grandpa falls over and can't get up, right?" Jones asked.

Christopher shook his head and worked his way down the hall to his daughter's office.

Jessica looked up as she tossed a brown folder on top of a stack of others in a three-tiered plastic tray. She did a double take upon seeing her father in the doorway. "Dad, what are you doing here? Where are the kids?"

Christopher pointed behind him with his thumb. "Up front with Jones. They may not be in the best hands, but we're in a police station. What could happen to them?"

Jessica cocked her head and raised her palms. "I've still got a few hours on the clock. You're not dumping them here, are you?"

"No, we were on our way to the park. I thought they might like to see where their mother works."

"They've seen where I work plenty of times..." Jessica narrowed her eyes. "Either you miss this place, or you want something."

Christopher laughed. "I'm sure that's it..."

"Spit it out, Dad, what's up?"

"Is Samantha still in the interrogation room or did they cut her loose?"

"Englund? No. The feds cut her loose about an hour..." Jessica growled. "Dammit, you're fishing. I hate when you do that." Her eyebrows squished together. "Wait, how do you know about that?"

"It's not important. Save me the trouble and fill me in so I don't have to manipulate it out of you like when you were a teen."

Jessica rose from her chair. "This is what made me want to be a cop growing up. I figured if I could determine how you extracted information from me so easily that I could find a counter. Still, you were always fair with what you learned, so I'll give you the details." She narrowed her eyes. "But first I want to know why you're interested."

"Curiosity."

Jessica shook her head. "Not good enough. Elaborate."

"I saw something about it on the news." He shrugged and looked at the floor. "I've read some of her stories..." Jessica's eyebrows rose. "A few of them deal with psychics. I thought I could ask her a few questions and see if she was for real."

She smiled, which caught him off guard. "Wherever you're going with this is a bad idea."

He nodded. "I know."

Jessica shuffled papers around on her desk in a sudden frenzy. "Hang on. I should put this down in writing and have you sign and date it."

Christopher grimaced. "Alright, wise-ass. What can you tell me?"

"I'm serious. I don't want you getting involved. Especially since your daughter helped bring her in." When Christopher didn't move a muscle, Jessica shook her head and let out a loud sigh. "Shut the door."

He did as she asked.

"Since I know you won't let this drop... We received an anonymous tip yesterday afternoon. The caller fingered Ms. Englund as an accomplice to some killings in L.A. Her website had enough compelling evidence for us to execute a warrant this morning.

"Since the crimes took place in California, we forwarded the case to the FBI. An agent from the Chicago field office rode along earlier today. We picked her up at her office, the agent handled the interview, and then he let her go."

"There wasn't enough to charge her with anything?"

"If it were my call, I would have at least held her for a few days. The details in here writing were pretty condemning." She shuddered. "Fifty bucks says she's involved."

"Did you record the..."

"Nope. Agent tall, dark, and handsome took the tape," she said. Christopher rubbed his chin. "I can see the gears turning in your head. And I don't believe for a second you're some goth writer's fanboy. I'm not sure what your interest is, but I'm telling you again. Keep your nose out of it. I'd like to make Lieutenant, and this is exactly the type of thing to get in the way of that."

"So, you're not going to hand over her home address?"

"Dad!" she said through clenched teeth.

"Okay. Okay. I'm heading to the park with the kids. We'll see you in a few hours." He turned to leave her office.

"I'm serious, Dad! Leave this alone."

"Fine, you win," he said, backing out with his hands in the air.

I'll get it myself.

Chapter 17

Elliot – New York City, NY—Friday

Afternoon

It was two o'clock when Elliot returned to the office with a sandwich and chips from the deli down the block. The boxes previously littering the room were gone. Elliot chuckled at the image of the intern scurrying around like a scared rat, waiting until he left to remove his belongings without further confrontation. As he raised the pastrami on rye to his mouth Marcie rushed into the room. Her lip quivered.

"Did your cat die in the twenty minutes I was gone?" Elliot took a large bite of the sandwich.

"I... Just look at your email."

Taking another monstrous bite, Elliot pulled the laptop closer. He slid one finger on the trackpad and opened a forwarded message from Marcie.

"Natasha Martin? Is that your niece?" he asked, spitting bits of bread as he talked.

"Yes. Read it," Marcie said, moving to his side and swaying anxiously.

Elliot swallowed, set the sandwich down on the butcher paper, and wiped the crumbs from his hands. "She loved it, didn't she?" He scrolled down to the original message and read aloud.

"Aunt M, I can't believe one of your authors are collaborating on Samantha Blackblood's newest work.

That's exciting news. Keep me up to date, I want a signed copy!" Elliot pushed the chair away from the desk. "What the hell is this?"

"Samantha Blackblood," Marcie said pointing at the laptop. "Look her up."

Elliot ran his tongue over his teeth with a sucking noise. He humored her and clicked on the first search result. An Indie author's blog site opened in the browser. "She's just a crappy amateur writer with a blog. Quit it with the scavenger hunt and tell me what's going on."

Marcie walked around the desk, bent over, and navigated the site. Elliot turned his head and leaned back to stare at her ass. When she reached the posted story, she grabbed his cheeks and turned him back toward the screen. As he read, she took a step back. Elliot's eyes darted left to right as he took in the first few paragraphs. His neck craned closer and his jaw dropped a bit with each pass.

Samantha's story opened with a drysuit-clad transient failing to kill a hooker and settling on the mop-boy. The same thing that happened in his story. The only difference was that he'd preceded the murder with an artfully created backstory.

Elliot spun his chair around until he was face to face with his editor. "Is this some kind of joke?" Marcie shook her head. "So, some untalented twat is trying to make a name for herself by stealing my work?"

"That was my first thought too. On the surface, it looks like plagiarism, but after investigation, I don't think that's the case,"

Elliot cocked his head. "What are you saying?"

"She's posting a serial. A single story, written it in separate sections, on separate nights."

"I know what a serial is..."

"But that's the thing. Her timestamps are legitimate."

"Huh?"

A chair puttered across the thin carpet as she dragged it over and sat down. "What you're looking at is the product of several days of writing."

"So?"

"Her shtick is writing in front of a live audience. There are corresponding chat logs and forum posts backing it up. Her followers provide commentary as she writes: plot, characters, prose, spelling, et cetera. It's all digital so it could be fabricated... But that's an awful lot of work to do just to cover up stealing from an established author."

"Are you accusing me of copying her material or are you putting faith in the infinite monkey, infinite typewriter theory?"

"I'm saying that this whole thing is odd. There's plagiarism all over the internet, but I've never seen anything this complex." She wagged her finger at him. "I know you, Ell. Don't go creating an account and starting shit on her forums. All it's going to do is paint you in a negative light. Let the lawyers handle it."

He frowned and sat still for a minute before unplugging the network cord from the laptop. "Get someone from IT down here. There could be a Trojan or a keylogger on my machine and that's how she's gotten my work. Have them check your laptop too." He rested his chin in his hand for a moment. "Screw it. Make them check every computer on the office network. After that, have legal send a cease and desist to this broad. Make sure it goes to the web host and ISP if necessary." He tapped his fingers on the desk lost in thought. "Can we pass her name around to other publishers? Make sure she doesn't go to print ahead of me?"

"I think you're getting carried away. While she has books for sale on her site, they're all in PDF format.

They don't even have ISBNs. Ignoring the logistical difficulties behind trying to reach out to every possible publisher, it wouldn't prevent her from self-publishing. Next, you'll be telling me that you want me to figure out her identity and address and then fly out to kick her ass."

"That sounds perfect babe. Thanks." Marcie let out one of her patented sighs.

"Let me reiterate my previous suggestion. Take some time to cool off. Get a hotel room so you can rest. In the meantime, I'll talk to IT and legal and then get you a temporary nameplate for the door. There's no need to terrorize any more interns."

Elliot gave her a thumbs up and stuffed the sandwich back into his mouth.

Chapter 18

Christopher and Samantha– Chicago, IL –

Friday Evening

Christopher Reyes walked into the lobby of the apartment complex from the department's files. He didn't expect a copy editor and amateur writer could afford to live in such a luxurious building. Leather low backed couches, ornate glass and metal tables, and chandeliers decorated the space. The furniture alone looked more expensive than all the pieces in his house combined. To top it off the building boasted both a concierge and doorman.

"I may have chosen the wrong career," he mumbled as he approached the counter.

A man in his early thirties wearing a crisp white shirt and red vest looked up. "How can I help you this evening, sir? Are you visiting a resident?"

After staring for a second Christopher let the look of awe fall off his face. "Can you direct me to Samantha Englund's unit?"

"I'd be happy to ring her apartment for you."

Christopher instinctively reached for his badge. His hand stopped near his breast coat pocket like he was reciting the Pledge of Allegiance. "Detective Reyes, badge number one five nine eight eight. Her apartment number, please."

"Uhh..." the man said without moving. His eyes darted back and forth, trying to determine the protocol for this type of thing.

Christopher glanced over his shoulder and then back into the young man's eyes. "I'm undercover, so I'm not going to flash my badge. Nobody's in any trouble. The apartment number wasn't listed on her CI file."

After a brief pause, the concierge typed onto the console built into his kiosk. "Sixth floor. Apartment two."

Reaching over the counter, Christopher patted the man's shoulder. "Thanks. Just act casual." The man stood frozen, his eyes darting over each lobby occupant as Christopher walked away with a smile.

Once inside the elevator, he glanced down at the notepad in his hand. Hopefully, it was enough to convince her of his story. He shook his head. Of course, it would be. If she were going through the same thing as him, being detained and questioned by the FBI would be one hell of a wakeup call. The elevator dinged, signaling his arrival on the sixth floor. He headed a short distance down the hallway, knocked on her door, and waited.

"Who's there?" a woman asked through the door.

"Samantha, my name's Detective Christopher Reyes. Could I please come in and ask you a few questions?"

...

"Reyes?" Samantha mumbled while looking through the peephole. *That was the name of the lovely female officer from earlier in the day.* The balding, overweight man outside her door was definitely not her. However, it was a common name... "Can I see your badge?" The man's lips whispered a curse. "I don't know who you are, but you should leave before I call the cops."

"Hang on," he said, holding his hands up to show he was harmless. "Does your door have a chain on it?"

The muscles in Samantha's legs tightened. *He's going to force his way in.* She ran for the couch to get her cell phone.

"I came to discuss the dreams we've been sharing. I have something that'll explain." Christopher waved the notebook in front of the peephole.

Samantha's blood ran cold when the door across the hall opened. A metal baseball paved the way for Yvonne. She was dressed for work—a fringed, red-leather halter top and a pair of blue jeans tucked into knee-high boots. The stranger stood his ground despite the business end of the weapon hanging inches from his chest.

"Is everything okay, Sam?" Yvonne called loudly.

Samantha opened her door. "I'm okay," she said with a smile. "You look badass, by the way." Yvonne did a little curtsy before straightening back up and slapping the bat against her open palm.

Christopher looked back and forth between the women and slowly extended the black and white notebook.

Samantha took the book and flipped from the back until she found a page with writing on it. A bald man's face took up the middle of the page. If the stranger really was a police officer, he wasn't a sketch artist. Words and short phrases haphazardly adorned the space around the drawing. Instead of coherent sentences, they were more of a list of hasty observations. 'Pool'. 'Spear'. 'Drowned dog'. The word 'Doberman' scratched out and replaced with 'German Shepard?'. 'Same man from earlier – premeditated?'

Pool? Spear? It could have been a coincidence, but he mentioned the dreams... She flipped back another page. A crudely drawn sketch dominated the center of this page as well. Words were aligned in the same hectic structure, but these were easily decipherable. And the face was unmistakable. The round cheekbones, and button nose of Stephanie... or Kara, according to Agent Montgomery.

The notes could have been recreated from pieces of her story, but not the woman's face... She turned again, partially ripping the page from the binding in her haste. Tom stared up at her. Samantha's knees buckled and she reached out to the wall for support. Somehow the man in front of her had received the deathly details as she had.

"I think we should go inside and talk," Samantha said.

Yvonne raised one eyebrow and looked Christopher up and down. "Sure you're okay, Sammy?"

"All good. Thanks."

Yvonne shrugged. "If you need me, just scream," she said, and then returned to her apartment.

Samantha turned back to Christopher and held out her hand. "My name's Samantha Englund, but I have a feeling you already knew that." He nodded and shook her hand. "Come on in," she said, turning to the side. She guided him to a small circular table against the kitchen wall where they both took a seat.

"I came because I thought you might have some insight into these dreams. I didn't mean to scare you— or your warrior princess neighbor. I also didn't mean to misrepresent myself as a police officer. I retired just last month. And by some strange coincidence it was my daughter Jessica who brought you in this morning."

"Yeah. She was charming." Samantha bit her lip. "Sorry, that was kind of rude." She hung her head and glanced back down at the book.

"It's okay," Christopher said with a chuckle. "She's not much of a people person."

Samantha let the notebook cover close but didn't yet return it. "You're having dreams of the murders too?" She felt silly asking the question, but the evidence supported the theory.

"Not the murders, per se, but the aftermath." Samantha furrowed her brow and rubbed her forehead. Christopher narrowed his eyes. "What did I say?"

"From your notes I presumed we were having the exact same dreams, but you didn't mention the prostitute. In my dreams, I'm forced to watch through the killer's eyes."

"Really?" Christopher reached across the table and placed a hand on his notebook. "May I?" Samantha raised her hand and let him take it back. He pulled a mechanical pencil from his coat pocket and put it to the page. "If you're seeing things from his point of view, do you know what you...err...he looked like?"

"No, I never passed in front of a mirror, but I know for a fact they're a he." Her ears turned red, and she dipped her chin. "While crouched under the desk in the theater's office, I could feel the discomfort of his... junk."

Christopher smirked and then let the pen drop. "It's infrequent that I recall my dreams. But these aren't like any other dream I've ever had. They're more vivid. More like memories, but..." He scratched the stubble on the side of his neck, "Limited. If I had to compare it to something, it's akin to walking around a crime scene preserved in a single moment of time. Something always felt missing around the dream's focal point. But now I think it was a *someone*."

"Are you referring to the demon or the killer?"

"Wait," Christopher said, shuffling his feet beneath the table. "You wrote about him being guided by a demon. You don't actually think there's a demon, do you?"

"If this itself isn't a dream and the two of us are sharing dreams about a killer, then yes. I'm inclined to believe that otherworldly forces are at work here."

Christopher stared. "He's killed a handful of people—the first while dressed like a cut-rate SeaWorld employee. I think that qualifies for a poster child of mental illness."

"Both times I could hear a faint voice egging him on. I didn't see anyone else and neither victim noticed it. If it weren't for the *feeling* of something else, I would have chalked it to hallucinations on his part."

"I don't believe in demons," he said, shaking his head.

"But the fact that both of us are dreaming about murders happening on the other side of the country is easier to swallow?"

"While the mind is a powerful thing, memory's fragile, especially at my age. Maybe we're regurgitating things we've seen or heard from the news? And since our minds don't process things the same way, our individual subconsciouses are crafting different dreams from that information."

Samantha shook her head. "I was ignorant of the actual murders until an FBI Agent threw the crime scene photos in my face. I don't read the paper or watch the news, online or otherwise. I pretty much work and write." She frowned. "I have some other theories, but they require some amount of faith."

"Faith?" Christopher asked, raising one eyebrow.

"Belief in something supernatural: oneiromancy, astral projection, group dreaming, or remote viewing. Maybe something else... I don't know."

He shook his head. "I'm not going to pretend I understood any of that. But it sounds like you're blaming this on black magic Voodoo."

Samantha sighed and talked with her hands. "Black magic and Voodoo are two completely different... Sorry, forget it. There is no rational explanation behind what we're experiencing."

"I don't think we have all the facts," he said.

"All the facts? I know it's a tough sell, but what do you think we're missing?" Samantha paused for a response, but Christopher remained silent. "Both of us are dreaming, in explicit detail, about murders taking place thousands of miles away. There's no such thing as a coincidence.

"There is something else that I wanted to ask you about though," she said. "The last page—this bald man." Christopher flipped to the page and spun the book so that the sketch faced her. "Yeah. I only got a glimpse of him. I didn't see the actual murder."

"Really? I saw him yesterday afternoon and this morning."

"You dreamt of him twice?"

He touched the pencil to the back of the page. "You didn't?"

"No. Well, barely. I had a grainy and short-lived vision of a body floating in a pool this morning. Though it was during the time I'd passed out after hitting my head on the metal table in the interrogation room. The last full vision I had was the theater murder—Kara."

Christopher flipped back and documented her name. "Is blacking out a common thing for you?"

Samantha shook her head. "A combination of the crime scene photos, a hangover, and whatever's happening to us, I guess."

"The best thing for a hangover is a big greasy burger with a fried egg on it."

She found it funny that Yvonne had brought her exactly that.

"Have a few too many drinks last night?" he said, jotting down more notes on the page.

Samantha groaned. "Yeah. With my former coworkers." She leaned over and inspected his additional comments. "You think me being intoxicated prevented me from getting the last vision?"

"Maybe? Booze impairs not only motor function, but also brain chemistry and memory. I'm no expert, but it's feasible it prevented you from dreaming. Maybe all we need to do to stop the visions is to start drinking like a fish. Or start taking mind-altering drugs."

"Let's keep that as our last-ditch option. Not sure where we go from here though..."

"I don't know," Christopher said with a shrug. "Discuss the murders like the Manson Family book club?"

Samantha smiled. "I guess. I have a feeling that if we can figure out a way to help, the visions will stop naturally."

"Help?"

"Figure out the identity of the killer. Find a way to stop him."

Christopher shook his head. "That's a job for the police. Everything about him screams amateur. With the number of bloody fingerprints and other evidence he leaves behind, it's only a matter of time before he's caught."

"I'm not sure. My fingerprints aren't in the system. I could leave them everywhere too and it wouldn't lead anyone to me. What isn't amateurish is *how* he's killing. And what if he *is* being guided by a demon? How would the police handle that?"

"Alright. Point taken. Suppose we presume for a moment that you're correct. That we're having these dreams because we're... destined to unmask the killer. How do you suggest we go about doing that? For starters, he's in California. Second, we're receiving visions after the murder has already been committed. Any information we get is already in the hands of the police. But most importantly, I've seen enough films and TV shows to know it never ends well for a cop who comes out of retirement for one last case."

"But police don't have the same information as we do. For instance—the prostitute saw his face. There's also no media coverage about the last murder. We could call and..."

"Tell them what? That there's a third victim lying in a pool somewhere in California? I know your heart's in a good place, but it wouldn't be wise—especially since you're already on their radar. Think about how this looks to external observers. I'm having these dreams the same as you, and I'm still having a hard time believing neither of us is involved."

Samantha nodded. He had a point. "I'm curious. Do police agencies ever actually work with psychics?"

"No," Christopher said laughing. "As much as you hear about it the media, I've never heard of such a thing. Agencies only act on credible information. They only make exceptions when a call comes in regarding the welfare of a child. Most, if not all, will operate on a better safe than sorry principle when kids are involved." Christopher looked at his watch and then stood from the table. "I should probably head home before my wife sends out a search party."

Samantha stood and walked him to the door. During that time, she never took her eyes off the notebook. "Do you mind if I make a copy of your notes?" she asked, pointing at it.

He handed it over. "Knock yourself out." Samantha took it to her desk and printed each page. "It would be a good idea to start keeping your notes offline. The FBI and police are likely still monitoring your site." Samantha frowned and returned the book.

"Do you know what 'Skylos' is?" she asked.

"No... Should I? It feels familiar somehow."

"I think I heard the disembodied whispers utter it. I think it might be the killer's name..." she shrugged. "Anyway, it was nice to meet you, Christopher. And thank you. I may be going crazy, but at least I know I'm not going through this alone."

"I should be thanking you. You seem to be a little more knowledgeable than me." Before stepping into the hall, he fished an old business card from his wallet. "The cell number is still current. Call anytime if you need to talk."

"Careful, I'll take you up on that." Samantha punched his number into her cell phone. Christopher's antiquated phone beeped in his pocket. "You've got my number now too. It seems like we're stuck in this together. Maybe I should start writing about a group of people who have the same shared nightmare night after night and are powerless to stop it." She let out an uncomfortable laugh and frowned at the empty desk in the corner of the next room. "Except I can't. The police still have my laptop. Which I also need if I'm going to find a new job."

"Call a lawyer. They can most likely expedite the release," he said as he walked out the door and said goodnight.

Chapter 19

Skylos – Altadena, CA – Friday Night

Skylos sat at the table in Tad's kitchen and enjoyed the last few bites of his steak. It was the first time he'd eaten one and he now understood the appeal. It was exquisite. As he chewed the last piece, he counted the money again. Even after the expenditures at the grocery store, he still had five hundred and thirty-two dollars. He creased the bills down the middle, put them back in his pocket, and cleaned up after himself.

He returned to the den and flipped television channels, giving each a moment to pique his interest. Cop drama, feminine hygiene product commercial, baseball replay... With a yawn, he continued pressing the worn remote button. More commercials.

A man in a suit appeared on the screen. "Do the recent stabbing deaths have a tie to the Windy City? Tune in at ten o'clock for more." Skylos pressed the button again before his brain even processed the news anchor's words.

"Wh-what?" he stammered. Raising the remote he hammered his thumb on the back button. But the promo was already finished. Another newscaster rattled off a recap of the day's sports scores.

Skylos sprang from the couch and paced in front of the fireplace. They were talking about *him*. Why did they mention Chicago? According to the mantel clock he had at least fifteen minutes before he could find out. When he'd met Calliope, she mentioned someone was hunting her. Was this related to her? After what seemed like forever the ten o'clock news began. Skylos parked himself a foot from the set until the segment began.

"One of our top stories tonight is the two recent stabbings in the L.A. area. Does this case have ties to Chicago? David Howell at our news affiliate in Chicago has more on the story. David?"

"Thanks, Tom. I'm standing outside the Chicago precinct where a woman was taken into custody earlier today. Chicago P.D. received an anonymous tip about a website that had intimate details about the recent string of murders. Local Police have not confirmed the validity of these posts and has not been forthcoming with information. All that they've shared is that at this time, no arrest has occurred. We'll continue to follow the story and provide updates as we learn more. Back to you, Tom."

"That's it?" Skylos said aloud, continuing to stare at the screen. As he reached out to press the power button on the television, a spark jumped to his finger. The shock traveled up his right arm, tickling him as he went. The sensation looped around his collarbone and trailed up his neck. It ended with a soft nibbling at his ear.

This is the work of my sisters trying to stop us. You need to take care of this.

"How do I find this woman?" Skylos said. There was no response. Calliope was already gone. He was going to have to figure it out on his own. He went back to Tad's computer.

The online version of the news story offered no additional information. However, the discussion section was abuzz. Users spewed all kinds of crazy theories. The detained woman was a psychic or a puppet master who was directing the killer from afar. Skylos scrolled through page after page of comments, hoping to find something else to go off. As the page refreshed all the comments disappeared, replaced by a note that commenting had been disabled by the site administrator.

Skylos wondered what others had to say but was more concerned about the large picture. If someone were legitimately aware of his dealings, they could unravel everything they'd been working toward. Protecting himself and Calliope was foremost in his mind. He had to get to Chicago and eliminate the threat.

He drummed his fingers on the desk as he looked through other news sites. They had taken to calling him the L.A. Ripper, a name that was neither original nor flattering. Though, the infamous Jack was doing his own part to clean up his city...

Pulling the keyboard closer, he scoured the internet for other references to the "L.A. Ripper". The search engine yielded thousands of results. After wading through dozens without success, he came across video claiming to show the arrest of the Ripper's accomplice—what the reporter from Chicago was talking about. The video showed a long-haired brunette being escorted into a police car. However, the woman's face couldn't be seen clearly. He was prepared to wade through the hundreds of comments to find something further. And he found it without any effort at all.

Whoever posted the video claimed her name was Samantha Blackblood. And that name subsequently led him to a writing blog. His heart beat faster as he browsed its contents. Samantha's last post recounted in detail his attack on Kara. His eyes grew wide and were glued to the monitor as he devoured everything she'd posted for the last week. A chill went down his spine.

Aside from Tad's death, Samantha somehow knew everything.

The short author bio offered no clues regarding her real identity, but it confirmed she lived in Chicago, Illinois. Skylos investigated the forum posts. The majority discussed character and plot points for her stories. The most recent, however, centered around him. Users pointed out the similarities between her Bud-K Killer and the L.A. Ripper. It seemed others had come across her site in the same way he had.

Skylos registered an account. Henpecking at the keyboard, he created a post under the guise of a publisher looking to put her unique insight into the killings into print. It was a long shot, but someone on the site had to have more information.

Opening another browser tab, he brought up a map to plot his trek to Chicago. Nearly two thousand miles separated him from Samantha. In a perfect world he would have taken the four-hour flight the map suggested. Unfortunately, he couldn't get on a plane without proper identification. Or while carrying a large bag of knives.

At best, he had a thirty-hour drive by car. After studying the map Skylos noticed how I-15 turned into I-80 in Salt Lake. The latter highway ran all the way to Chicago. It seemed a good path as any. He chose four large cities roughly equidistantly spaced to maximize the likelihood of hitchhiking or finding a rideshare: Las Vegas, Salt Lake City, Denver, and Kansas City.

He thoroughly researched each, identifying shelters or churches where he could rest comfortably. In no time he'd devised a formal itinerary. With a smile, he printed a copy. Skylos flipped through the warm pages, reciting the cities and stops in his head. He'd readjust the plan along the way if necessary, but little doubt existed in his mind. With the angel of death at his side, he couldn't fail.

Skylos tapped the pages against the desk to get them in alignment, folded them in half, and put them into his backpack. His stomach did backflips. He'd never left the state before, but tomorrow he'd be traveling halfway across the continent. And it was only fitting that his first stop would be in Las Vegas, the city of sin.

Chapter 20

Elliot – Greenwich, CT—Early Saturday Morning

Elliot lay on his bed wearing only a pair of green boxer briefs. Despite the cool silk sheets and the soft pitter-patter of rain he tossed and turned, unable to sleep. The rain had kept the construction crew at bay all day. Without that noise or Marcie constantly in his ear, made good writing progress all afternoon. It was a glorious escape from the Samantha debacle.

However, now that the house was dark and quiet, his mind wasn't. Samantha dominated his thoughts. Being powerless to stop her ate at him. But Marcie was right, not that he'd ever tell her that, the legal department would take care of everything.

For a third time since he'd come to bed, he glanced at the laptop sitting on the nightstand. Samantha's site called out to him. Were there clues within it that could reveal her identity or give insight into her motives? Maybe he wasn't the only author she was stealing from. For a third time he stayed his hand. He refused to give her site any more traffic.

The tech nerds found nothing, so how she was physically stealing his work was still a mystery. There was no malicious code on his laptop or any signs of a company-wide data breach. They suggested he check his home network. When he told them that he only had one laptop, they told him to check for physical surveillance devices. While a ridiculous theory, it was still an uncomfortable thought.

He tossed and turned for another hour before sleep came. As his eyelids finally yielded, his phone rang. Elliot shot upright, his heart pounding. It wasn't until the third ring that he recognized where he was.

"It's one in the morning. What the hell do you want?" he grumbled.

"I'm outside Ell, can you come let me in?" came Marcie's voice.

"What? Why?"

"I'll explain inside."

"Fine."

Elliot grabbed a shirt off the floor but didn't bother with pants. His hand ran along the ornate wooden banister as he went downstairs to the front door. Without an invitation, Marcie marched inside and looked down at his pale legs.

"Can you put on some pants?"

"My house, my rules." He closed the door behind her and started up the stairs. He looked back after a few steps. "Are you coming?"

"What?" Marcie shook her head with gusto. "This is *not* a booty call. We need to talk about Samantha."

Elliot groaned and tilted his head back. "New rule. If you say her name again, you're going back out in the rain."

"This is important. Something's going on," said Marcie as she sat at the far end of the blue, microfiber couch. Elliot mumbled unintelligibly as he descended. He fluffed a pillow and laid down, resting his feet in her lap. Marcie shoved his legs aside before addressing him again.

"Saman..." Elliot glared at her. "She-who-must-not-be-named was taken in by the police for questioning yesterday morning..."

"Let me guess. Samantha," he said, making air quotes, "Is an obese, thirty-plus year-old man living in his mom's basement. Police caught him with a stolen credit card he got from hacking into several systems, including ours. He also figured he could make some quick cash by self-publishing other author's work. How close am I?"

"Not even close. The police didn't release much, but there's plenty of rumors that say she's a murder suspect."

Elliot sat up. "Murder?"

"I've done some digging. There were two murders in Los Angeles last week. They match your story."

Elliot blinked his tired eyes and shook his head to clear it. "An obsessed fan is re-enacting the murders from my stolen, work in progress? Grim, but flattering I suppose."

"I don't think that's it. The timing doesn't make sense. While the news coverage is vague, one thing was clear. The first killing occurred the night *before* you wrote about it. It was also before the chapter was stolen. Where did the idea for these rewrites of yours come from?"

"I don't know. It just came to me one morning. You think I fell asleep with the television on?"

"I thought about that. But why would New York outlets cover a seemingly random murder on the opposite coast? Besides, your death scenes are much more detailed than the news articles." A shiver ran down her spine as she pictured them. "And I'd wager that's exactly why the police took her in for questioning. The writing contains details only the police and the killer could know."

"What exactly are you saying? That we wrote two identical stories because of a psychic link?" Marcie shrugged at the question. "Have you read all of her stuff?"

"Yeah," Marcie said with a nod. "And it's not what you'd expect. Aside from her skipping your prologue, the story isn't an exact copy. Her story lacks a protagonist and has a different backstory. In general, she's been placing more emphasis on the demon. That's her go-to genre: supernatural thrillers. The other interesting thing is she suddenly stopped another work in progress to write this. Just like you."

"I still think it's nothing more than blatant plagiarism with a lazy attempt to hide the fact."

Marcie threw her hands in the air. "You're missing the point, Elliot. Two people are dead. They were murdered in the exact same manner you've depicted, which matches what she's written down to every detail."

Elliot laughed. "I think you want them to be real. A poor janitor who nobody would miss. A pretty, young blonde with a great rack who's killed while waiting to ride her boyfriend. They're victim archetypes. You see them in every book and movie so much it has its own name—anti-mimesis, art imitating life. I shouldn't have to explain this to you."

"Don't preach art history 101 to me. People are dead."

"I agree it's an eerie coincidence, but that's all it is. A coincidence." Elliot covered a yawn. "Is there not enough gossip in the office to keep you entertained? I can start pushing around more interns."

Marcie narrowed her eyes and glared at him. "Oh, there's been plenty to talk about with you in the office. And for what it's worth, I convinced Rob, the intern you harassed, not to file a complaint with human resources."

"Cool. I'm going to bed now. Are you staying?"

She shook her head. "I can see I'm not getting through to you. If you're not going to take this seriously, I'll go home."

"Suit yourself. Have a good night and drive safely. I'll see you in the office on Monday."

Elliot returned to bed. He swatted at an invisible bug buzzing around his ear. As he started nodding off, he entertained having the killer find Samantha's website and resolving to hunt her down. If he couldn't get payback in the real world, doing it in the literary one was going to have to do.

"Take that, Sam," Elliot said aloud before passing out.

Chapter 21

Skylos stretched in Tad's bed, craning his neck to see the alarm clock. It was already past ten. He jumped out of bed and raced down the cold stone stairs. The porch was empty save for a local freebie newspaper. He threw the paper in the house and returned to the second floor where he showered and packed everything into the suitcase. He left it by the front door then brought a bowl of cereal back to the computer desk. He checked the tracking information for his delivery. According to the computer it was out for delivery. With any luck, he could start his trek to Chicago within the hour.

While raising the spoon to his mouth, a thought struck him. A delivery uniform would make excellent camouflage. If he could lure the deliveryman into the house and make him strip, he could easily catch Samantha off guard.

After breakfast, he pulled a bandanna from the suitcase and folded it into a triangle. Slipping it over his shoulder, he let his left arm rest within the fabric. Next, he grabbed a page from the newspaper and took it to the bathroom. Watching the mirror, he rubbed it on his face. The newsprint left a convincing dark ring around his eye. Skylos grinned into the mirror. Who could refuse a beaten cripple?

Sitting back down at the computer, he returned to Samantha's site and reread the story in its entirety. He had to admit that despite being pegged as the villain, it was nice to be immortalized. Skylos pressed the refresh button several times. There was still nothing about Tad.

This was both disappointing and worrisome. It had been a day and a half since he'd killed Tad. Where did she go? If she were still locked up it would be harder to get to her. He logged into the forums and checked for any updates there. The post he'd made was now locked, but it had half a dozen replies that were still accessible. The most recent was from an admin criticizing him for breaking the sites terms of service. None of the posts were helpful. Everyone had seen through him. He clicked back into his account page to check out the other notifications. The private message was nothing more than a reiteration of the terms of service.

As he closed the site, a large truck hummed outside. He pulled the shade aside revealing a telltale brown UPS truck at the curb. He shuffled into the kitchen and grabbed a small paring knife the block. He had the door halfway open before he remembered the other part of his plan. With a quick pivot, he slipped on the sling and tucked the knife alongside his arm. When Skylos turned around the deliveryman was on the stoop. The man had fair-colored hair and was about the same height as Skylos, though more muscular. An electronic signature pad sat atop three packages resting in his arms.

Skylos smiled. "Sorry, co-could you bring them inside for me?" he said.

"Ouch. What happened to you?" the man said while looking him over.

"Gang initiation," Skylos stammered with a smile.

"No problem." The driver said with a laugh.

Skylos nodded with his head toward the family room, making sure to keep his arm still so the bandanna didn't come unfurled. "Over by the TV, if you could."

Skylos followed close behind. When the man bent over to place the packages down Skylos grabbed the knife and let the sling drop. A slideshow of anatomical images flashed through his head. Bringing the knife down above the shoulder blade would sever the axillary artery and he'd bleed out in no time. He crept up and lifted the knife above his head.

The deliveryman dropped the boxes and caught Skylos' reflection on the TV. He pivoted on one knee and lashed out with the electronic signature pad. The heavy device cracked against Skylos' knuckles and sent the knife tumbling near the brick fireplace. Skylos yelled out in pain and comforted his aching hand.

"What the hell, psycho!" the man yelled, adjusting his grip on the pad.

Skylos stood between him and the door. The deliveryman advanced and took another swing. The thick plastic brushed over Skylos' hair as he ducked at the last moment. He backpedaled as the driver flailed the pad and advanced toward the front door.

An idea dawned on Skylos as he caught the reflection of the sun on the clock's face. If he stepped aside, letting him pass, he could get the revolver from its hiding place. Skylos lifted his arms to the heavens. "I'm sorry. I'm off my meds... Go."

The deliveryman shuffled forward, not taking his eyes off Skylos for a second. As he passed by the fireplace, he kicked the knife further across the room. Skylos backed up as he passed, then lunged for the clock. He swung it open, grabbed the gun, and took aim.

The truck driver stopped in his tracks and raised his hands. The device clattered to the floor with a heavy thud. "Please... I have a family."

"Your u-uniform! Take it off," demanded Skylos. The revolver shook in his aching hand.

"Okay." After fumbling with the top button, he slipped off the brown shirt. The shorts followed, leaving him in an undershirt and a pair of red plaid boxers.

"Throw them on the couch," said Skylos, stepping closer. "The hat too." He'd never fired a gun before, but at this range, he couldn't miss.

The man stepped out of his clothes and stood trembling in the entryway. "Can I go now?" he asked, licking his dry lips.

A crackle of arcing electricity filled the air. The gun steadied as his muscles locked up from the surge of energy. He pulled the trigger halfway without him realizing it.

Should we let him go? whispered Calliope, running her fingers ran through his shaggy hair. Skylos closed his eyes and reveled in her touch. *Well?*

Skylos' eyes snapped open. "Go."

A heavy sigh of relief escaped from the driver's lips and he bolted for the door. The revolver bucked in Skylos' hand. The echo from the shot reverberated off the walls followed by the thump of the gun hitting the floor.

The driver let out a cry and a small spray of blood exited the middle of his back. Unlike the movies, he didn't collapse immediately. Instead, he continued to stumble forward, clutching his chest. He moved toward the open door taking shallow, raspy breaths.

While life-threatening, the wound wasn't fatal. Skylos still had work to do. He snatched the knife from the corner of the room and slammed the heavy front door on his leg as he took his first step out of the threshold. The deliveryman cried out in a painful wheeze.

Skylos stabbed him in the back several times, but his ribs prevented the knife from doing any serious damage. He rotated the knife ninety degrees and thrust again. The blade slipped through the rib cage puncturing the other lung. After that, he finally collapsed.

The man clawed at the floor as Skylos dragged him away from the doorway. Blood settled between the floorboards and into the scratches from where he'd dragged the dog cage the other night. Avoiding the wavy trail of blood, Skylos stepped onto the porch and looked up and down the street. Besides the low growl of the truck in front of the house, all was quiet.

Skylos locked the door and went to wash his hands. While the driver still crawled at a snail's pace, he was no longer a threat. When he came back, Skylos retrieved the wallet from the uniform pants. It was devoid of pictures of family and contained less than twenty dollars.

"So much for a wife and kids... Walter Kevins?" Skylos said, kneeling. Guttural sounds escaped Walter's blue lips as he inched forward.

"Sounds like the made-up name of someone trying to hide from something. You wouldn't have found yourself in this situation if you weren't guilty of something."

Walter lifted his head, took one last rasping breath, and slumped over.

Everyone's guilty of something, whispered Calliope.

Skylos smiled, pocketed the bills, and tossed the wallet inside his backpack with the others. He looked back to the door; he couldn't leave the truck where it was. Doing so increased the chances of both bodies being found. Police would figure out the identity of the homeowner quickly, and likely put out an APB for

Tad's truck. That limited his chances of getting to Vegas.

After moving the UPS truck over a few streets Skylos hurried back to the house. He hurdled the couch, avoiding the growing puddle of Walter's blood. Throwing aside the packing material of the largest box, he found a large plastic bag containing roughly two dozen assorted knives. He removed each, gave it a once over, and then set it aside. Most were simple, medium-sized, lock blades, but two stood out above the rest.

Those he inspected more carefully: a double-edged boot knife with a leather sheath and a curved knife with a ring built into the end of the grip. He picked up this last knife and unfolded it. The blade glowed with brilliant emerald green swirls. It was a knife fit for an angel. And he knew then that it was the knife that was destined to kill Samantha.

Cradling the blade in both hands, he closed his eyes. The weapon—a Karambit knife—suddenly became familiar to him. He connected with the weapon and slipped his pointer finger through the hole in the handle. A smile crossed his lips as he spun and flipped it around in his hand like a professional drummer would a drumstick. Skylos gingerly placed the knife inside the center pouch of his fanny pack so it would always be close and then distributed the rest of his provisions between his suitcase and backpack.

He glanced at the revolver lying on the floor. While it hadn't eliminated Walter in a single shot, he figured it may be useful in the future. Skylos packed it up as well and took his things out the back door.

Skylos held his breath as he passed by Tad's bloated body floating in the pool and hurried up to the garage. He shoved both bags into the passenger seat and took off into the alley.

His printed directions took him out of Altadena by way of the Foothill Highway. After sitting in traffic for an hour he reached the next strip of highway. Interstate 15, called the Ontario Freeway for reasons unbeknownst to him. This would take him north all the way to Las Vegas.

The scenery gradually made the shift from residential to desert to mountains. The surroundings were bleak and held nothing to entertain his eyes other than scrub brush, other cars, and the occasional dirt road leading to a tiny oasis of human development. He shifted over and over in the seat, trying to find a position to ease the pain growing in his bad leg. If he didn't get out soon, it was going to lock up.

"Calliope?"

Things had happened so quickly that he almost didn't notice the faint hint of static lingered in the air. She was still close. Watching, but just outside his grasp. The only surefire way to get her attention, and deaden the pain in his knee, was to kill again. In the aftermath of Tad and Walter she was almost tangible. It was an indescribable high. And he needed more.

Many options for isolating someone along a desert highway came to mind, but they all had some tactical complexities. If he wandered down a dirt road to find someone, he'd likely become lost. Rear-ending someone would force them out of their car, but road rage and a good Samaritans would make it a difficult situation to control. And the blue call boxes lining the roadside every few miles further complicated things.

He continued driving, trusting that he'd find some sort of sign. After several miles, he spotted a small sign indicating a fuel station ahead. He checked the gauge. The truck had enough fuel. He stayed his course. Another mile down the road was another sign. Rasor Road—Three miles.

Razor? The phonetics of the word were too uncanny to be coincidental.

Butterflies flitted in his stomach as he floored the accelerator. He loosened the seat belt and leaned over the dash. Another sign—Rasor Road, one mile. Skylos took the exit ramp and followed the yellow Shell sign to a gas station. Pulling over at the stop sign he shut off the truck and got out.

The station housed eight pumps, including the four diesel ones. And unfortunately, the place was a popular truck stop. Several eighteen-wheelers sat in the gravel lot beside the properly paved one. In the short time he'd been stretching his legs, a dozen cars had come and gone, filling their tanks, or buying provisions within the small, corrugated metal building. Skylos shook his head. There was too much traffic here. He got back in the car, rolled through the stop sign, and got back onto the highway.

"Razor. How was that not an omen?" Another green sign appeared on the horizon. As he got closer, he was able to make out the words. The town of Baker was eleven miles ahead and Las Vegas one hundred further. Halfway there. Skylos kept his eyes peeled for other opportunities.

A dozen more miles ticked up on the odometer before Skylos straightened up in his seat. Off the road ahead was an old, beige sedan with its hazard lights blinking. A man in a dusty suit sat crouched beside the back passenger tire. Skylos reached across the seat and grabbed the first knife his fingers touched; a folding utility knife bearing a single-edged razor. He snorted at the irony.

Skylos slowed, kicking up a cloud of dust as he pulled within a few feet of the car. The man backed away holding the tire iron firmly. Patches of sweat highlighted his blue dress shirt. Skylos scrutinized the man whose suit was far nicer than the vehicle. He was on the right track. The cheap car looked like a smokescreen someone embezzling money would hide behind. Skylos palmed the knife, exited the truck, and approached.

"Need any help?"

"Do I need any help? You almost hit me!"

Skylos looked back at the gap between the cars. "Sorry," he stammered. He took a few more steps forward, his limp pronounced form the long car trip. "Just wanted to make sure you were okay."

The man sighed and looked down at the ground. "I'm almost done here." He returned tightening the lug nuts. "But thanks anyway."

Skylos' bruised knuckles throbbed as he looked at the heavy tool. He needed that out of the man's hands before he made a move. Looking up at the setting sun, he had an idea.

"I've got an extra bottle of cold water from the last oasis. Would you care for it?"

"That would be great. Thanks," the gentleman said, tightening the last nut.

Skylos returned to the truck and dug into his bag. He winced as his sore knuckles brushed against something hard in the backpack—the revolver. He grabbed a bottle of water in his left hand. As he exchanged the knife for the pistol. In that moment, a tingle reverberated through his whole body. Skylos closed his eyes and held his breath as something tickled his back. The unseen hand trickled up and down his arm like Calliope was petting him. The sensation was more intense than the previous night and felt like she was touching him for the first time.

"All done here. I'd still appreciate that water if your offer stands."

The man's voice interrupted Skylos' ecstasy. When he opened his eyes the businessman's car was back off the jack. He still had the element of surprise though. Skylos slammed the door with his hip and stepped forward, the pain in his leg already subsiding. He tossed the bottle of water to the approaching man, but purposely let it fall short. It rolled away from the road into the desert.

"Dammit!" the man yelled as he chased after the bottle.

Skylos closed within a few feet, raised the gun at the back of the man's head, and squeezed. A fine red mist hung in the dry desert air and the man dropped just like in the movies. Skylos tossed the gun and spun on his heels to face the highway. Cars and trucks continued past. No one noticed. Grabbing the man's leg, Skylos dragged him beside the white pickup where he was more obscured. Skylos quickly grabbed the man's wallet and watch before moving his own luggage to the beige car.

He looked at himself in the rearview mirror. There wasn't a speck of blood on him. The gun was a cleaner, superior killing tool, but it was too loud. He realized he much preferred a stealthier approach. He slipped the wallet into the backpack with the other keepsakes and affixed the watch to his arm.

You're getting along well without my guidance, Calliope said as he merged back onto the highway.

"I'm following your signs," he said with a smile. "I can see them now. The sinners."

I'm impressed.

Skylos was pleased that his presumption was correct. Killing drew her nearer. But more importantly than that, each kill was strengthening the bond between the two of them. He could still feel her presence.

"Where do you go when you're not here? Back to heaven?" When no response came, he wondered if he'd overstepped.

I'm always with you, Skylos. A breath escaped his lips in a little moan. To hear her utter his name was music to his ears. *But I need to be anchored to communicate. It requires extensive energy.*

"And energy is released from death," he said, matter-of-factly.

Yes, she whispered.

"Then I'll keep killing for you," Skylos said enthusiastically. "I can't wait to deliver Samantha to you."

Calliope's fingers brushed across his scalp and hair and he let out another moan. Her touch faded until he could no longer feel the angel. He had so many more questions, but they'd have to wait. There were plenty of more miscreants to reinforce their bond. Reinvigorated by Calliope's visit, the throbbing in his leg faded away completely and the remaining hundred miles passed in a heartbeat.

Chapter 22

Elliot – Greenwich, CT – Sunday Morning

Elliot swung his feet to the floor and stretched. It was going to be another good day. The sky still held dark, imposing clouds that would keep construction at bay and the creative juices were already flowing. The moment his eyes opened he was ready to put his killer to work again. The chapters focusing on the detective would have to wait for another day.

He scurried to the kitchen, grabbed a protein bar from the cabinet over the fridge, and then pulled a stool from under the countertop. He angled the laptop to avoid a glare from the single shaft of sunlight piercing the clouds through the bay window at his back. Crumbs fell between the keys as he held the bar in his mouth and added to the outline Marcie forced him to create.

Last night before sleeping he'd thought about turning the killer lose on Samantha. While that was still the master plan, he had something different in mind for the interim. The killer's motives were clearer than ever—petty revenge. It was the same thing that had been plaguing Elliot himself. First a disrespectful janitor, then the pretty girl at the gym who wouldn't give him the time of day, and finally the annoying construction workers next door. Besides Samantha he had more people on his shit list: the package handler that damaged his last order and all the damn incompetent drivers on the road.

Some of the small details were already fleshed out too. From prior research, he knew of at least one real-life serial killer who'd used fake casts as a premise to lure victims. It would be a smart way to con a deliveryman into your house. The other idea needed a bit of work. Being able to single out a specific driver was logistically difficult, especially in the middle of a desert. He documented the idea anyways. Once he got on a roll, the proper direction would come.

Elliot tipped the laptop and shook the bits of breakfast to the floor and read the last few paragraphs. He loved where the story was going. Especially after finding an elegant way to get the plot back on course. Detective Laramie wouldn't have to travel to L.A. if the killer were coming to him. All he had to do was put Samantha in Louisiana. Elliot beamed with cleverness. Marcie would hate the fact he'd written Samantha into the story, but tough shit.

He closed his eyes and let his fingers fly across the keyboard at breakneck speed. Scenes started to coalesce like a movie in his head. The idea blossomed into paragraph after paragraph without effort. His killer obeyed his every command. After a brief struggle, he added the delivery uniform to his pile of spoils. He introduced a firearm. It broke the previous M.O. of using knives, but it added more versatility of the character.

Another hour later and the killer was back on the road. Starting his trek toward Samantha in the car he'd taken from the businessman. He stopped for a moment to grab a bottle of water from the fridge. Elliot sat back down and reread the last few pages. The more he read, the more the desert murder scene nagged at him. It felt too... forced. It was a shame to have to start over, but it was all part of the process. He highlighted the last two pages.

"C'est la vie."

His finger hovered over the delete key, unable to muster enough strength to depress the button. Elliot pulled his hand back and cracked his knuckles. *This isn't the first time I've had to abandon a story idea. Why am I struggling with this one?*

Elliot returned to the keyboard and literally forced his finger onto the Delete key. As the text disappeared, a sharp throbbing pain hit him behind his right ear. He swatted at his head and looked around the room expecting to find a bee. His vision blurred and the room spun.

Using the walls to keep himself upright, Elliot stumbled into the bathroom. He grabbed his EpiPen from the cabinet and jabbed it into his thigh. He lowered himself onto the lid of the toilet and took deep breaths, waiting for the medicine to reach his bloodstream. Nothing improved. He turned the injector over in his hands. It looked like the medicine had been administered correctly. Pulling himself up, he stared into the gilded, oval mirror and folded his ear forward. There were no visible marks.

He grabbed a handful of painkillers from the cabinet and swallowed them dry. Was he having a migraine? A stroke? After a few minutes, the vertigo ceased and the pain in his head lessened to a tolerable level. It was an understatement to say that he was stressed. Marcie was probably right, he needed rest.

On uneasy legs, he returned to the kitchen and brought the laptop with him to the couch in the front room. He flopped down and brainstormed aloud.

"I need to replace the businessman with another woman. It's easier to hate the villain when they're killing women." He placed his fist under his chin for a moment. "How about a slutty bartender? I could switch the location to closing time at a dive bar. Let's keep the

element where he hides the body behind a car though...
Wait. No, have him roll the body underneath."

Elliot clutched his temple and waited for another sharp influx of pain to subside. He jotted down some notes and nodded. This was shaping up better. Elliot gritted his teeth and hammered away at the keyboard again, hoping to drown out the pain.

Chapter 23

Samantha – Chicago, IL – Sunday Morning

The day's first beams of sunlight leaked through Samantha's blinds. She'd been awake for the last half an hour, struggling to dictate her latest dream using a speech-to-text app on her phone. It seemed to get every fifth or sixth word incorrect. As frustrating as it was, it beat the archaic pen and paper.

"After executing the businessman in the desert, he moved his luggage to the car and took off. The new vehicle was light tan in color, make and model unknown. A body was left behind, concealed beside a white pickup." She paused to look through Christopher's notes. "Presumably, this is the same truck belonging to the construction worker." Samantha double-checked the words for accuracy again. Close enough. She saved the notes and closed the application.

Skylos, as she and Christopher had taken to calling him, racked up two more kills yesterday. He seemed to be escalating. According to the news outlets, neither body had been reported so far. This surprised her. She expected the shipping company to investigate a missing truck and driver almost immediately. The other body was left along a desert highway. State police would investigate the stranded car within a day if not sooner.

Considering when she'd received the previous visions, and the fact that UPS didn't deliver on Sundays, she was confident both killings took place within the last twenty-four hours. Presuming the dreams came in chronological order, the first happened during normal working hours. There were highlights of red in the sky during the other murder. Which meant it either occurred at dusk last night or early this morning. If it *were* this morning, after taking time zones into account, Skylos couldn't have gotten far.

Christopher continued to be adamant about not contacting the police... But if she could point them in the right direction, they might catch him. She got up from the bed and paced around her bedroom. She had to try.

Samantha started to dial 911 and then changed her mind. Emergency services used a location system to triangulate cell phone positions and properly route the call. An anonymous tip about something in L.A. coming in from Chicago would be suspicious. Additionally, she had no information on where to tell them to look for the vehicle. She needed something more solid.

Maybe Christopher had gotten something she'd missed. The way he processed the visions was unique. Either his mind was more analytical, or they were receiving the information from different sources.

Christopher picked up almost immediately. 'Hey' was all he said.

"I hope it's not too early," she said.

"No. I'm up. My daughter will be dropping the twins off shortly anyway." The line was silent for a moment. "I presume you had them too?"

"Yeah... Two this time. Any thoughts as to why he's escalating?"

"It's difficult to say. At first, he had a type—young, promiscuous women..."

"I know. These last three have seemed random. His methods changed too. From knives to a gun. Unless... Is it possible that there's more than one killer?"

"No. That's not what the evidence is saying to me. Ever since you mentioned that name—Skylos—I've been... I don't know. Feeling it." Christopher yawned into the phone. "You'll have to forgive me; I haven't gotten any coffee in me yet. It's true that his methods have changed, but I don't think there *is* a pattern. He's killing when he needs something. The construction worker, for example, was to access his house and truck."

"That makes sense. What about the deliveryman? How does he fit in?"

"It could have been to get free reign to anything on the truck." Christopher fell silent for a moment while he thought. "Or maybe he had to kill him. It's possible he noticed the body in the pool through the window."

"After that, he took the construction worker's truck—which he'd hide the businessman's body behind later. Based on the footprints I noticed in the sand, I think he's doing this alone. Unless you count your demon."

Samantha nodded in understanding of Christopher's narrative. "Okay. That's also when he swapped cars. He's on the move and trying to stay under the radar."

"The media probably has people on high alert and he's looking for a new hunting ground. I was a betting man, I'd put my money on Las Vegas," Christopher said.

"Why Vegas?"

"Population density. On top of that, A good portion of people walking around are intoxicated at any given point. If he's killing for the sole purpose of killing, drunks make for easy targets."

"Hmm... I've never been, but I always presumed there's surveillance everywhere. I don't feel like its Skylos' style to go on a killing spree."

"I suppose you'd know better than me. However, there's no evidence so far of him dumping bodies. If he was along the highway in the desert, it's because he was en route to somewhere." The sound of a doorbell and the faint yell of the twin's voices carried through the phone. "Sorry to cut this short, but I need to get going."

"No problem. Enjoy your day with the kids."

"I'll send you pictures of my notes when I get a chance."

"Thanks."

Samantha pulled up a small map of Los Angeles. If Christopher's hunch about Vegas was accurate that narrowed things down to two major highways—I-5 or I-15. She'd have a fifty-fifty shot. Unless she called in two different tips to separate Highway Patrol offices... Scanning for numbers, she found they wouldn't open for another two hours. Time was of the essence. She'd have to settle for local police.

The cities of Devonshire and San Bernardino appeared to be ideal. They were sixty miles apart and located on the outskirts of the metropolitan area. San Bernardino was closest to Vegas, so she dialed there first, making sure to use star-six-seven to block her number.

An officer with a deep voice answered. "San Bernardino Police Department." Samantha clammed up. This was probably a mistake. "Hello?" the man repeated.

"Yes, I uh... Wanted to call in a tip about the Bud... Umm... The stabbings last week." She closed her eyes and took a deep breath. *Calm down. Relax.*

"One moment, let me transfer you to a detective." Samantha waited on hold for what seemed like an eternity. She pulled her phone away from her ear and checked the call timer. It had only been a minute and a half. Another voice came through the speaker.

"This is Detective Stanford. I understand you have some information to share."

Samantha spoke slowly and with confidence. "Last night I saw the man responsible for the L.A. stabbings. He was driving a stolen, white pickup north along the I-15. After attacking another gentleman, he stole his tan sedan."

"There hasn't been a sketch released of the subject. How do you know it was him?"

Samantha froze up again. She hadn't thought any of this through properly.

"Miss?"

She panicked and hung up. Christopher's warning from the other night echoed in her ear. Without an immediate threat, she wouldn't be taken seriously. Samantha pulled the blouse away from her skin and fanned herself. After taking a few minutes to calm down, she dialed the other station. If she didn't follow through with her original plan, the first call could have been for nothing.

A female officer answered at the other precinct. "Devonshire P.D., how may I direct your call?"

She tried to keep it vague this time. "I'm sure it's nothing, but I saw something last night while I was driving along Interstate 5 that seemed out of place."

"Please hold while I transfer you."

She took a deep breath. That seemed to go smoother. After a short wait, another officer answered.

"Detective Harris."

"I was driving north along the I-five last night. I passed a white pickup and I swear I saw a body beside it in the rear-view mirror. Probably my mind playing tricks on me, but it's been eating at me."

"Can you tell me what exit or mile marker you were near?"

"Uhh... Sorry, I don't recall."

"The dispatch officer from San Bernardino's mentioned a similar call. Are you aware that filing a false police report is a felony?"

Samantha quickly hung up. *Shit! Chris was right. Of course, Chris was right.*

Chapter 24

Skylos – Las Vegas, NV – Sunday Morning

Skylos pushed a laundry cart through the male dormitory of the Las Vegas Rescue Mission. It was still ingrained within him to be a good guest. He kept his backpack with him and slung over his shoulders. Once he wrapped up, he'd be on his way again.

Steven, a young staff member with long blonde and a cross displayed outside his flowered shirt walked beside him. "So where are you headed after this?" Steven asked while stripping another bed.

"Hitchhiking to Utah. I'm trying to locate…" Skylos threw a set of bedsheets into the cart. "A family member of sorts."

Steven freed a sheet corner from the next mattress and looked up. "I believe in the best of mankind, but that seems risky. Vegas tends to attract… an above-average number of shady characters."

"I don't know about that. I met some great people on my way here. A businessman drove me into town when my truck broke down."

"Then it sounds like you've got lady luck on your side. Your family can't pick you up?"

"No," Skylos said shaking his head. "It's been forever, and she doesn't know I'm coming. I want it to be a surprise."

Steven smiled. "I can only imagine the look on her face when she sees you."

"I know," Skylos said, an enormous grin overtaking his face. "I can't wait." Skylos glanced at the watch on his arm. It was a few after ten. "I should get going. Are you good here?"

"Of course. You've already helped out more than expected."

"Thanks." Skylos turned around and headed for the stairway.

"Good luck and safe travels, my friend," Steven called from behind him.

Skylos stopped at the office. A curly-haired brunette with a program director name tag stood beside the suitcase he'd left there. He glanced around nervously.

"Thanks for everything."

"On your way out?" she said. Skylos responded with a nod. "I understand you were a big help this morning. Too bad you can't stay, we could use more volunteers," Barbara said with a smile. "Let me grab you a bagged lunch."

Skylos grabbed the suitcase handle. "It's not necessary."

"I insist. I'll only be a minute or two." The woman disappeared from the office.

Skylos shifted his weight back and forth between his legs. He checked the zippers on the bag and tried to remember whether anything in the suitcase was suspicious. Was she calling the police now? Because of his leg he couldn't run. If cornered like an animal, he'd fight like one. He slipped the backpack off and set it on the desk.

Barbara re-entered the room as he wrapped his fingers around a pocketknife. She held out a brown paper bag. "It's nothing fancy: a sandwich, some chips, carrots, and a bottle of water."

Skylos dropped the knife and took the sack. He packed it away and closed the backpack before she could glimpse inside.

"Thanks."

Skylos hurried up the street, checking over his shoulder every so often. He followed a sign pointing to the Cashman Center he'd seen when driving to the shelter last night. It took him about twenty minutes to walk to the convention center. He smiled. The parking lot was jam-packed, which increased his chances of catching a ride. He stepped over the small metal barrier and wandered among the vehicles.

Seven tour buses sat in a line at the back of the lot, each separated by an empty space. Skylos walked down the row and inspected each. The first green bus had a locked door and no sign as to its destination. The next two black buses were also locked. The fourth bus, black with highlights of gold, had a white cardboard sign in the windshield indicated it belonged to the Salt Lake City Mission. The door and several windows were ajar, allowing the desert heat to escape. If he boarded the bus with its occupants, he wouldn't even have to search for a ride.

The folding door gave way as Skylos pushed against the hinge. He headed to the back, shoved his suitcase under a seat, and ducked down. It only took him a few minutes to realize his folly. The interior was unbearably hot. He hit himself in the head. *Why didn't you go into the convention center and try to blend in with the group as they left?*

"Hello?" Skylos froze at the female voice echoed from the front of the bus. "You're going to get heat stroke back there. Come on out."

With great hesitation, he emerged from the bus. A woman in a long, lavender dress and jacket stood by the adjacent bus with a canvas handbag bag over her shoulder. His eyes focused on the ornately carved rosary hanging around her neck.

The sister laughed when he stepped fully into view. "You thought you could sneak onto the bus and pretend you belonged?" Her face and voice lacked signs of sarcasm. The question was sincere.

Skylos shrugged, unsure what to say.

"This bus is here for the Women in Religion Convention. You would have stuck out like a sore thumb once all the sisters and nuns piled onto the bus. If you survived long enough for them to board anyway. It must be over one hundred degrees in there... Where are my manners? I'm Sister Mary Elizabeth from the Franciscan Sisters of the Atonement." Skylos continued to stare at the woman. "It's a mouthful, isn't it?"

Skylos nodded, a blank look still crowding his face. This young woman with her hair in a tight bun was too down to earth to be a sister. He wondered for a moment if she was who she claimed to be. At that moment, an unfamiliar memory played out in his head. He'd stalked a woman in a nun's habit before. He kept to the shadows, following her to a bank, and then a bakery. When she emerged, he crept up from behind and raised the brick... Suddenly the memory slipped completely from his grasp.

"I got tired of the stuffy convention floor and came out for some fresh air and to feel the warmth of the sun. I saw you skulking around and figured I'd say hello." She looked down at the suitcase and flashed him a smile. "Something tells me you're looking for a ride." Closing her eyes, she put her hand to her forehead like she was receiving a message from above. "Somewhere in the vicinity of Salt Lake City. Am I right?"

Skylos' ears perked up upon mention of his destination. He gave a hesitant nod. Did the previous vision fade because she was here to help him?

"I know what you're thinking. I talk a lot. But to make up for it, I also act a little weird and tell corny jokes." The sister stood still for a moment, giving him a chance to say something. When he didn't, she continued. "Don't be afraid to ask for help. We all require assistance at some point in our lives."

Skylos blinked. It was worth a shot. "You're right. I'm trying to find a way to Salt Lake City."

"Wasn't that easier than hiding in the back of a steaming bus? As luck would have it, I'm heading that way and would welcome the company. That is provided you can find your voice for some conversation."

"Really? Just like that?" Skylos rubbed the back of his neck.

"Whoever gives to the poor will not want, but he who hides his eyes will get many a curse." She took a step closer. "Besides, I have a good feeling about you."

"Okay."

He followed Sister Mary Elizabeth as she wove a zigzagging path between cars. Skylos narrowly avoided running into her when she came to an abrupt stop in front of an old, blue Chevy Impala. She placed her hand on the hood and turned around.

"One other condition before we go," she said, raising her pointer finger. "I want your word that you'll truthfully answer any questions I ask while we drive. It's a six-hour trip and the time will pass more quickly with spirited conversation."

Skylos nodded his head, slow at first, then quicker. "Sure," he said with a smile. Since she was a nun, or a sister—he wasn't sure if there was a difference—she might have some insight about angels. Either way, she was guaranteeing him a ride to his second scheduled stop.

The sister raised her palms. "Are you going to introduce yourself, or should I make up a name for you?"

"Sorry. My name's... Skylos."

"That's funny. Because that's the name I was going to choose." She smiled more broadly when the corners of Skylos' lips turned up. "Is that a nickname?"

He nodded. "It's what... Everyone calls me."

"Skylos it is then." Sister Mary Elizabeth opened the trunk with the car key. "Want to toss your bags in?"

He lifted the suitcase into the trunk. "I'll hang onto my backpack," he said, thumping his hand on its side. She slammed the trunk and then unlocked the doors. Skylos took the passenger seat and placed his bag on the floor. The sister placed her own canvas bag on the seat between them.

"Ready?" she asked.

"I guess so."

"You don't know how lucky you are. I should have been on that bus, but I lost track of time while volunteering at the hospital. I drove down by myself on Friday morning." She started the car and rested her hand on the shifter. "Seatbelt please."

He tightened his belt, and she left the parking lot. Skylos avoided eye contact and stared out the window.

"I see you're a man of few words. We can listen to some music until you get over your shyness. There should be a CD in my bag if you wouldn't mind digging it out."

Skylos reached into the tan canvas bag with a blue, stylized cross applique. Among the haphazard pile of postcards, pamphlets, and business cards from the convention he found a CD case still wrapped in plastic—Organ Music for the Soul. The cover featured a picture of an old woman in front of an organ.

Sister Mary Elizabeth glanced over as he pulled it out. "It was one of the goodie bag items. I hate those plastic covers. Please tell me you've got a knife in your bag to open it?" The smirk on her face made him wonder if she knew, but her focus remained on the road.

"Let me look."

He pulled the backpack onto the seat's edge and pretended to search for a knife. He slit the plastic with surgeon-like precision and removed the plastic in a single piece. 'Ave Maria' played as he pushed the disc into the player and returned the trash and empty case to her bag.

"What happened to your hand? Did you get into a fight?"

Skylos looked down and frowned at his bruised knuckles. "Yeah. Wrong place at the wrong time, unfortunately." He opened and closed his fist. It was still sore. Skylos shrugged when she apologized.

"Do you like the organ music?" she asked.

"It's okay, I guess," he said directing his attention out the window again. "I don't listen to enough music to know what I like."

"They have an interesting history. The first generation of organs were too large to be moved because they were steam powered. Do you know what they were called?" Skylos shook his head. "Calliopes."

His jaw hung open and his head snapped in her direction. "What?"

"Well, it's more elegant than 'train whistle', which is essentially what they were." The sister glanced over and gave a sly smile. "If you're impressed now, wait until you've heard another five hours of my useless trivia."

He eyed her up and down. *Is she an emissary of the angels as well?* That would explain their serendipitous meeting. "Do you... know Calliope?"

"No. I can't say that I've heard any actual calliope music. From what I understand though, they're quite loud."

Skylos slumped back down. Maybe it was a coincidence. He fell silent for a moment again before phrasing the question in a different manner. "Do you believe in signs, sister?"

"Divine signs? Of course. I see them every day in the people I meet. Although you need to be careful. If you look too hard, you'll see them everywhere." She reflected on his frown for a moment. "Does your question have anything to do with why you're hitchhiking?"

One of his eyebrows rose. Her comments continued to surprise him. Maybe she did know more than she was letting on. Either way, he promised honesty. "Kind of. I'm searching for someone."

"Then it seems like you have a spiritual journey as much as a physical one ahead of you. Any other way I can help?"

He shrugged. "You're already giving me a ride."

"So, searching for someone, huh? Is it family...or a long-lost love?" She took her eyes off the road long enough to wink at him.

Sister Mary Elizabeth waited several minutes for a response that never came. "Fair enough. But I'll break you before this trip's over." She hummed along to the last song as they passed over the Arizona state line. When the CD had played in its entirety, his stomach rumbled loudly.

"Sorry, I didn't think to ask if you needed to stop. I already filled my belly at the convention hall's buffet. I can stop somewhere for you."

"It's okay, I have a bagged lunch." Skylos pulled out the brown sack from the shelter. He held out half of the sandwich which she politely declined. With the bag resting on his lap, he ate everything and returned the trash to his backpack.

"A pocketknife and lunch. Got anything else fun in big bag of tricks?"

Skylos thought for a moment and dug through the bag again and brought out the lockpicks and practice lock.

"That's neat. Is it as easy as it looks in the movies?" the sister asked.

"I actually just picked them up and haven't had much time to practice." He pulled the plastic off the collection of different sized picks that sat inside a small, black carrying case. Following the instructions, he raked them across the pins of the padlock. It sprang open surprisingly easily.

"A recent hobby?"

"Yeah."

"I suppose that's one of those things that isn't particularly helpful on a daily basis but becomes invaluable when you need it. My junior year of college, my girlfriend and I locked ourselves out of our apartment. While I understand it takes a skillful hand to do the work, locksmith's charge an arm and a leg." Sister Mary Elizabeth fell quiet upon realizing he'd zoned out and focusing solely on the lock.

An hour or so later Skylos grew bored of the picks. He dropped them back into the bag with a loud yawn.

"Lean your seat back and take a nap. If I'm capable of anything it's entertaining myself. Throw your bag on top of mine and stretch out."

A nap did sound good. He didn't expect for Utah's scenery to be as bleak as California's. Although never having left the outskirts of Los Angeles, he had nothing on which to base that assumption. He hoped once they crossed over the Rockies that the scenery would be greener.

He placed the backpack down, making sure the opening faced him, and realized too late that the zipper wasn't completely secure. Before he could reach for the pull Sister Mary Elizabeth slammed on the brakes and swerved into the left lane. Skylos braced for impact, but there weren't any vehicles in front of them. A coyote fled off into the wilderness on the opposite side of the highway. The unplanned maneuver sent the backpack tumbling. The wallets of his victims spilled out onto the floorboard.

Sister Mary Elizabeth glanced over, swallowed hard, and then returned her eyes to the road. Skylos quickly stuffed the evidence back inside. She'd seen everything, but what could he do? He couldn't kill the woman. Not only was she in control of the vehicle, but he still wasn't sure whether she was under Calliope's influence. He looked down, watching her from the corner of his eye.

After several minutes of awkward silence, she spoke. "I'll address the elephant in the car. It looks like you're more so running *away* from something instead of *toward* it."

Skylos felt an odd pang of guilt. The carefree and cheery tone in her voice was gone. "It's not what you think..."

"It's not my place to pass judgment, but I 'd like to hear the whole story. It might even help *you* to talk about it. And remember. You made a promise."

"Okay," Skylos said, turning to face her. Technically he'd told the truth so far. He chose his words with care. "In the past, I spent a long time homeless and living on the street with no one who cared. I've been forced to do some unpleasant things to get by. These are a reminder of that." He watched her process the words.

"You think running away from it will help?"

Skylos shrugged. "Staying in Los Angeles wasn't going to accomplish anything. I need to set out on a different path so that I can put things right."

"That's admirable," the sister said with a smile. "It's important you do whatever it takes to set things right. The little voice you're hearing is your conscience. Listen to it. Can I help in any way?"

Skylos shook his head. *Everything will be perfect once I get rid of Samantha.*

"I'll be praying for you." The sister fell quiet as they drove another handful of miles until they passed a sign for a gas station.

"I'm going to stop for fuel and a bathroom break. We don't have to stay long. I know you're anxious to get on your way." Skylos stretched and faked a yawn to check the gauges. She was telling the truth.

At the next exit Sister Mary Elizabeth pulled off the highway and into a parking lot shared by a gas station and a family restaurant. Skylos glanced around as the car came to rest in front of a pump. While the rest stop wasn't crowded, it was far from empty.

Skylos' mind ran wild as soon as the sister stepped out. She acted cool on the exterior, but he wasn't sure whether he provided an adequate explanation for the stolen wallets? It was possible she'd go inside and alert the authorities. Were clergy members required to report crimes? His knee bounced on the floorboard as she fueled the vehicle. The tote bag was still in the car. He hadn't seen a cell phone in it. Did she have one tucked in her dress?

Skylos took a deep breath and decided he had to follow her. He needed to get out anyway, his leg was aching something fierce.

Sister Mary Elizabeth looked and smiled over when the passenger door closed. "Good to stretch your legs, isn't it?"

"You don't know the half of it."

She replaced the pump nozzle. "I need to use the facilities."

"Me too," he said, following on her heels. She wound her way to the back of the store, browsing the shelves of snacks as she went. Skylos ignored them, focusing on her movements. When they reached the small alcove where the restrooms were, she pushed on the door of the women's room. It was locked, so she waited against the wall and smiled at him.

Skylos checked the men's room. It opened. Knowing it would only draw suspicion if he hesitated, he rushed inside and forced his bladder empty with a speed that rivaled a racehorse. Urine dripped from the sides and bottom of the urinal. He ran his hands under the sink and gave them a quick wipe on his pants before pulling the door open again. The small hallway was empty.

Shit! She's already gone. He hurried to the windows at the front of the store. The Impala was vacant and parked where they'd left it. Turning around, he headed back to the restrooms. As he placed his ear to the metal door of the women's restroom, it swung open.

Sister Mary Elizabeth gasped as Skylos stumbled into her. "You scared me half to death," she said, resting her hands on her breast taking deep, panting breaths.

"Sorry," Skylos stammered. "I thought I'd lost you. Ready?"

"Yeah. Let me grab something to drink."

Skylos followed to coolers where the sister selected an iced tea. He picked a flavored water and snatched the bottle from her hand. "My treat. It's the least I can do to repay you." Skylos did his best to conceal the large wad of bills as he paid for their purchases and then they returned to the car.

"We have about three hours to Salt Lake City."

Skylos studied the mirrors as they re-entered the highway. She didn't seem to have called anyone, or at least they weren't being followed. While the nun wasn't as talkative as before she didn't' seem anxious. He was safe for now.

After half an hour she returned to her chatty ways. "Do you mind if I ask about your limp?" She caught the frown on his face. "If it's a painful memory don't revisit it."

"It's a bit of a long story, but to keep it short: it's called Perthes disease. I fell off a counter as a child and broke a bone in my leg." He looked back out the window. "It never got treated. From what I understand, blood flow became obstructed around my knee causing portions of the bone to die and become necrotic."

For the first time, Sister Mary Elizabeth frowned. "The neglect of a child..." she said, shaking her head. "There's nothing they can do for it now?"

"No"

"I'm sorry..."

"I've mostly grown used to the pain. Most of my childhood is a blur by now anyway." He looked up and then gazed out the window. "But it's okay. I have someone watching over me now."

Chapter 25

Elliot – Greenwich, CT – Sunday Afternoon

"Elliot Thompson," called a graying nurse in light purple scrubs with plastic framed glasses. She scanned the waiting room of the urgent care facility. When nobody budged, she called out again. "Mr. Thompson?"

Elliot stood and walked toward the woman. He was wearing what he'd thrown on after waking up—a pair of gray sweats too large for him and a plain blue t-shirt—plus a pair of dark sunglasses.

"Immediate care my ass, I've been waiting almost two hours," he grumbled, once he knew he was close enough for her to hear.

"Well, you're free to wait in the emergency room instead." The nurse lowered her clipboard and looked him in the eye. "Do you still want to see a doctor?"

He wiped the scowl off his face and nodded. "Sorry."

"Then please follow me." The woman led Elliot to an empty exam room and gestured to the table. "Someone will be with you in a few minutes."

Before Elliot could open his mouth to protest, the woman backed out and pulled the door shut. He lay down on the exam table and curled up into the fetal position. To his surprise, it wasn't long before a knock came at the door.

"Come in," Elliot said, holding his head and sitting up.

A man with a tight buzz cut in a white coat stepped into the room. He looked in his mid-twenties and fresh out of medical school. The nursing assistant sat down on the small stool and logged into the computer against the wall. "I'm going to take your vitals before the doctor sees you. Can you tell me what brought you in?"

"A migraine," said Elliot holding the back of his neck. "Pain is radiating from the base of my skull. Bright lights only make it worse. I also have vertigo and a ringing in my right ear."

The man spoke aloud while typing. "Patient experiencing migraines, light sensitivity, dizziness, and tinnitus." He looked toward Elliot. "On a scale of one to ten, how would you rate your pain?"

"Seven."

"When did the symptoms start? Do you have a history of migraines?"

"I've never had a migraine till this morning."

"Currently taking any medication?"

"No," said Elliot. "Aside from handfuls of Advil that haven't helped." The nurse cocked his head. "I've taken eight so far today."

The nurse spun around and stood up. "Let's get your temperature, blood pressure and oxygen levels." Elliot sat still as he swiped a thermometer across his forehead. "Ninety-nine," the man mumbled and proceeded to slip a cuff onto Elliot's arm and a clip onto his pointer finger. The machine inflated to a point where it felt like his circulation was being cut off and then beeped. "Oxygen saturation is ninety-seven percent. BP is one twenty-nine over eighty-two." The nurse logged the numbers into the computer.

Elliot stared at the man like he was an idiot. "Yeah, those numbers mean nothing to me."

"Your blood pressure is a bit elevated but that's expected with the pain you're reporting."

"See, how hard was that?" Elliot said under his breath.

The nurse bit his lip, locked the computer, and rolled the stool back under the small counter. "The doctor will be in shortly."

"Shortly? I have to wait again?"

"Unfortunately. It's a Sunday afternoon and we're busier than normal. If this is an emergency..."

"I should have gone to the emergency room," Elliot mocked in a sing-song tone. "So, I could wait there."

"The doctor will be with you shortly." The nurse forced a smile and left the room.

Another twenty minutes passed before the doctor, a man in his fifties with a thick mustache, entered the room without knocking. He reached out his hand and shook Elliot's.

"I'm Doctor Garner. No previous history of migraines?" the doctor asked, more so repeating the notes in the computer than asking a question. "Any recent accidents or head injuries? Have you gone scuba diving, snorkeling, or skydiving recently? Are you on any antibiotics or cancer medicine?" Elliot shook his head to each question. "Hmm... Do you have a carbon monoxide detector in your home?"

"Yes, hardwired."

The doctor stood and used two fingers to probe Elliot's neck. "Your lymph nodes seem normal. Any family history of strokes or cancer?"

"My father passed away from a stroke at age forty-one. But he smoked two packs a day for twenty years." The doctor stepped back and nodded.

"And you don't smoke?"

"No."

"What do you do for a living?"

"I'm a novelist."

"Would you say it's stressful?"

"No, not normally..." Elliot paused for a moment and swallowed the lump in his throat. "So, what's wrong with me?"

"Honestly, it's difficult to make a diagnosis without running tests. Tinnitus and dizziness are easy enough to treat but are often symptoms of a deeper ailment."

"What's the worst-case scenario?"

"Let's not speculate until we can rule things out. Migraines are most often triggered by stress, allergens, and sometimes something as small as a change in sleep patterns. Unless they become chronic, they most often abate within a day or two without any necessary treatment. My advice is to go home, take some Advil, eat a balanced meal, and then get a good night's sleep. You'll likely wake up in the morning and feel fine."

"Sleep it off?" Elliot sneered. Something in his gut screamed that something was wrong. "I've been taking over the counter pain meds all day and they haven't helped. I don't know whether I'll be able to sleep if this continues. You can't give me anything?"

Dr. Garner pulled a pad of paper from his coat pocket. "I can write you a prescription for a single Xanax pill. It should help you sleep tonight until you can see your primary doctor."

"Xanax?" Elliot raised his eyes and his voice along with it. "I waited almost two hours for you to suggest I'm having an anxiety attack?"

Dr. Garner shook his head. "I'm not diagnosing this as an anxiety attack. Xanax can be used to treat any number of conditions. First and foremost, it has a particularly strong calming effect. I think it may provide some relief. It's your choice if you'd like it or not."

Elliot shrugged and thrust out his hand. "I guess I'll try anything at this point."

The doctor scrawled an indecipherable note on a prescription pad and handed it over. "If you're still having symptoms in the morning, make an appointment with your primary care doctor. They can order blood tests to eliminate anything serious. It's important that you go to the emergency room if any of your symptoms worsen."

Elliot let out a low growl and stormed out around the doctor.

Chapter 26

Marcie Andrews – Queens, NY – Sunday Night

Marcie hunched over her tablet in the plush gray armchair in the front room of her tiny Queens apartment. The television mounted on the wall reported the local news, but it fell on deaf ears. Her finger tapped the refresh button for what was probably the hundredth time. According to the chat logs and blog timestamps, Samantha wrote almost every night like clockwork. Often on the weekends, she did little other than spend time on the site. Something had changed. She's been in complete radio silence for well over a week.

It couldn't have been the legal notice that compelled her to stop. Her last post had been days prior. She hadn't responded to the Digital Millennium Copyright Act notice either. And the takedown deadline was tomorrow. At this point, Marcie knew one wouldn't come. Something had happened to Samantha.

She clicked on the forums that she'd been ignoring until now. It quickly became obvious that Samantha's fans were just as curious about her whereabouts as she was. User activity was intense and chaotic. Moderators struggled to keep threads under control. Little lock icons filled the screen as she scrolled. Marcie investigated the most popular ones. Someone had been spamming the site with posts to an external video link.

Marcie clicked on the link, half expecting to be led to one of those disgusting revenge porn sites. Instead, she found a video claiming to show Samantha's arrest. The footage, which was a terrible, shaky mess, showed a blurred brunette figure being tossed in the back of a squad car. If it was to be believed, Samantha wasn't writing due to being in police custody. It made sense when she thought about it. Someone else had come to the same conclusion: that Samantha was somehow tied to real-life murders.

Marcie stopped in the middle of drafted a letter to the site's email address. If she were incarcerated, she wouldn't be getting it anytime soon. Either way, her inbox was probably flooded to the point where who knew whether she'd even see it. Sending an email about the emails might even make things worse. Including bringing scrutiny upon herself or Elliot. She deleted the message and redoubled her focus on scouring the forums.

In doing so she learned a few things. Firstly, confirmation of Samantha's arrest. Secondly, that the original story idea originated from a vivid dream. Was this how Elliot received his ideas? She groaned. It was hard to speculate when he never opened up about anything. Marcie crossed her fingers and logged into Elliot's cloud storage. Despite his fear of being watched, he was still backing his files up.

She mumbled and nodded while speed-reading through the documents list of tracked changes. So far it seemed he'd taken her suggestions to heart. And then things got worse.

"Elliot you stupid sonovabitch!"

He went and wrote Samantha *into* the story. Marcie ground her teeth and finished scanning the document.

The story had improved. Hell, it had improved a lot—perhaps even enough to save the story. Although, she had no idea what significance 'The Silo Killer' even had. As she feared though, there were two additional murder scenes. She grabbed a crocheted blanket from the chair back and wrapped it around her shoulders.

"Please let me be wrong about this..."

Marcie entered the details of the bartender's murder into the search engine. She sighed with relief when it yielded no recent results. Of the five murders, only the first mirrored actual cases. Maybe Elliot was right, and this was all a bizarre coincidence. She reached out to put the tablet down on the coffee table, but something inside still nagged at her. It was hard to dismiss the uncanny likeness was to the L.A. victims.

She pulled the tablet close again. It had been a few days since she checked into the construction worker's murder. When she checked again a headline jumped out immediately. *Police searching for a suspect in a triple homicide.* She opened the article and read it aloud.

"California state police are searching for the individual(s) behind a triple homicide.

"Two bodies were found early Sunday afternoon in an Altadena home. The first was identified as Thaddeus Cole. Cole, a construction foreman, was stabbed to death and dumped in the pool on his property. The body had been in the water for several days.

"The second victim was Walter Kevins, a 28-year-old UPS driver. Kevins was both stabbed and shot during an altercation inside Cole's home yesterday. The abandoned delivery truck led Police to the grisly scene.

"The remaining victim was a middle-aged man found beside Cole's truck along the I-15 roadside in the desert. So far police have not been successful in identifying the individual, but his death involved the same caliber firearm from the earlier scene.

"At this time officials have no further information regarding the suspect or his motives. The department has also not yet commented on whether these murders were related to the stabbing deaths from the previous week. Any information on the murders should be reported to the LAPD."

The afghan did nothing to combat the cold penetrating Marcie's bones. This is not what she needed to read before bed. The construction worker, Cole, was Elliot's third victim. Kevins had at least a partial foundation in Elliot's story too. Though at this point the story started to diverge. The 'Silo Killer' murdered him after purposely rear-ending him on an unpopulated desert road.

Elliot's last victim, 'a chesty blonde bartender in shorts that left little to the imagination', was a far stretch from the unidentified businessman. Marcie put the tablet down. While not unbelievable, this one had Elliot written all over it. It was purely fabricated. She wondered if Elliot realized he was going 'off script'. Despite the evidence staring them in the eye, he refused to believe something unexplainable was going on.

Marcie pulled her phone off the charging pad and called him.

"You've reached Elliot's phone. Please leave a message. If it's an emergency, text me something racy, and I'll get back to you immediately."

She hung up and dialed again. "Damnit Elliot, pick up the phone..."

The voicemail message replayed. Marcie tried his landline and received only a busy tone. She dialed one final time and left a message.

"Elliot, call me back once you get this. I'm starting to get worried. If you're avoiding me for some reason, you're so dead."

Chapter 27

Skylos – Cheyenne, WY – Monday

Afternoon

Skylos leaned against the storage rack full of propane tanks in front of the Cheyenne Walmart and waited for his ride. He looked up from the E.J. Thompson detective novel he'd bought inside and checked his watch. If they were on time, he'd have another hour to wait. It was the second time he'd hitched a ride today. Hopefully, Paul would be as nice as Dan, the truck driver who'd brought him here from Salt Lake City.

Dan, like Sister Mary Elizabeth, had radiated purity. He didn't ask any questions, a nice change. In addition to that, he'd shared his lunch and offered his phone as a mobile hotspot. With access to the internet, Skylos was able to fine tune his plans. His original itinerary had him going to Kansas City. Since Dan wasn't going that way he adjusted accordingly.

Dan also turned him onto an application for organizing ride shares among college students. This put him into contact with Paul. Paul was driving back to school at the University of Nebraska Lincoln after a family funeral in his hometown in Wyoming. This worked out even better. Lincoln had a train station within walking distance of the university. The train would get him to Chicago before Tuesday evening. No more uncertainty from trying to find a ride.

After waiting a little over an hour, a white Nissan Versa pulled into the no-parking zone in front of the store. The horn sounded and a young man in a red polo hung out the open window.

"Are you Skylos? I'm Paul. You ready?"

Skylos stood, gathered his things, and entered the car via the back driver's side door.

"Hang on, I've got to piss," said a man in a gray collared shirt from the passenger seat. He hopped out and ran into the store.

Skylos sized up the driver. He had a few dozen pounds on him and was several inches taller, at least six-foot. Errant strands of slicked down brown hair brushed against the cars ceiling. A few minutes later the other man returned. He jumped back in the car and turned around, extending his hand.

"I'm Sean, Paul's cousin."

"Skylos," he said, shaking Sean's still damp hand. He was the same size as Paul, and if Sean hadn't mentioned they were cousins, he would have assumed they were twins.

"Skylos? Is that your last name or your video game handle?" Sean asked while buckling his seatbelt.

"My name."

Paul and Sean looked at each other and shrugged.

"Alright. Once we gas up, we can get on the road..." Paul cleared his throat and rested his hand on the gear shift but didn't move the car.

"Oh. Sorry." Skylos opened the fanny pack and withdrew a fifty-dollar bill. "Will this cover it?" he asked, extending his arm through the gap between the seats.

"That'll do it," said Sean, snatching the bill and tucking it into his pocket. Paul smiled before putting the car into gear and driving to the gas station.

"Visiting your parents in Wyoming?" Sean said, turning around in his seat after Paul started pumping gas. Skylos let out a soft sigh and picked his book back up. "Not a talker, huh?"

"Sorry, I'm saving my voice," Skylos said pointing at his neck. "Sore throat." Sean let out a low snort and turned around.

Paul returned to the driver's seat and looked back at his new passenger. "Ready to go?"

Sean shook his head. "Don't waste your time." Paul shrugged, then turned the ignition key and left the parking lot.

The two college kids ignored him and alternated between talking and singing along to the radio. It was nothing more than background noise to Skylos. His eyes systematically passed over the words on the pages in his hand, but his focus was rapidly diminishing. He couldn't care less about Detective Laramie, even if the murder scenes he visited felt somehow familiar. His singular thought was getting to Chicago and burying that beautiful green blade into Samantha's throat.

Chapter 28

Samantha and Christopher – Chicago, IL –
Monday Evening

"It's a block ahead on the left-hand side," said Samantha, shutting off the navigation app on her phone. "Right here." Samantha pointed at the apartment complex. Christopher nodded and turned the minivan into the parking lot.

"So, do you know this 'psychic'?" Christopher asked.

"Not personally, I found her on an internet forum."

"There was a simpler time where you could dial an eight hundred number Instead of walking into a stranger's home and possibly getting murdered. I bet this woman won't even have a fake, sultry Haitian accent."

"You didn't have to come."

"It's fine, but if it turns out to be a scam to sell us essential oils, I'm out of here." Christopher pulled his composition notebook from the center console and tucked it under his arm.

Three four-story, gray brick buildings enclosed the parking lot in a semicircle. Samantha led the way toward the southernmost one and entered the lobby. As she reached for Five-G's buzzer, Christopher grabbed her wrist.

"I'm not expecting much more than a cold reading. Make sure you don't let her pry any information out of you."

"For someone who doesn't believe in psychics, you seem to know an awful lot about them. At least try to keep an open mind. She was highly recommended and it's not like we have anything to lose."

"Alright," he grumbled. Christopher released her arm, and she pressed the buzzer. The door groaned in response without any hesitation.

Christopher grimaced and held the door open for her. "She must have seen us coming." Samantha shook her head and turned left, following the numbers as they counted down. Christopher stopped several paces away from 5G and sniffed the air.

"Sage," Samantha said. "The occult community uses sage smudges in healing and purification rituals. When burnt, it smells like marijuana." She rapped her knuckles against the door.

"I've been around enough weed to know what it smells like."

A petite, pale blonde in a faded Metallica concert tee opened the door and motioned them inside. "Sam, right?" Samantha nodded. "I'm Deb. Please come in."

Christopher stepped in front of Samantha, sheltering her while surveying the apartment. When he saw no immediate threats, he moved aside and extended his hand. "I'm Chris, Sam's dad." Samantha gave him a sideways glance but said nothing. She started to slip her shoes off.

"Keep them on, make yourselves at home. Can I get either of you a glass of water or a can of soda?" Christopher shook his head.

"A glass of water would be great," said Samantha.

Deb entered the kitchen via an arch to their immediate right and filled a glass with water.

Christopher took several more steps into the room and took note of the exits. The entry opened into a large sitting area with a sliding patio door on the opposite wall. A fit young man with messy hair in a striped red and black shirt sat on the edge of an old couch playing a racing game. Beyond him was a short hallway that probably led to the restroom and bedrooms.

When Christopher's eyes passed over the man on the couch he jumped up, hid a colorful water pipe in front of his body, and then ducked down the hallway. Christopher shot a disapproving glance at Samantha but hadn't been paying attention.

Deb emerged from a second entrance to the kitchen bordering the dining area and set down the water. "We can sit here and talk."

They joined her at the table, Christopher taking a seat at the far side so he had a view of the entire apartment, and Samantha beside him. He set the notebook in front of him and interlaced his fingers over it. Deb remained standing on the opposite side.

"No crystal ball?" Christopher asked with a soft chuckle. Samantha hit him beneath the table.

"It's okay," Deb said smiling. "He's welcome to be a skeptic. To answer your question, crystals are expensive. A bowl of still water is an equally effective scrying device. Your email was vague. Can you elaborate on the situation?"

"We've been having..." Samantha turned to face Christopher and then looked back to Deb. "Visions, for lack of a better word. We suspect there's an otherworldly source behind them."

Deb took a seat. "Both of you?" she asked, more for her own sake, eyes darting between the two of them. "What type of visions?"

"There's different types?" Christopher said.

"Prophetic dreams? Remote viewing? Waking hallucinations? And is this the first time you've experienced something like this?"

"Uhh..." he turned his palms up and glanced toward Samantha.

"Through our dreams... If you can call them that," Samantha said. "Although we're seeing the same things, the experiences are far from identical. And no, this is something new to both of us."

"Interesting..." Deb tapped her purple fingernails on the table. "Have you seen one another in these visions?" They shook their heads. "Anyone else in the family experiencing the same thing? Particularly children? And have you had the house checked for mold? The spores of certain strains can cause hallucinations."

Christopher frowned at the thought. He knew for certain that mold wasn't behind the murderous visions, but he hadn't considered the possibility that the twins may be affected.

Deb picked up on his reaction. "I wouldn't worry about it. Children are more sensitive to spiritual activity, however since little is taboo to them, they'd probably bring it to your attention. If they were seeing something, you'd know."

"So where do we go from here?" Christopher said, eager to shift the subject away from his grandkids.

"I usually start by giving background on what it is that I do. The occult practices have as many different branches as... law enforcement." Christopher coughed into his elbow as to not betray the surprised look on his face. "My experience lies in tarot cards and aura reading. I'm also a psychic empath." Christopher had the urge to raise his hand, but she clarified before he could say anything. "Which means I'm attuned to the energies surrounding others."

Samantha nodded in acknowledgment. Christopher scratched the side of his neck.

"How about we start with the skeptic first."

Christopher shrugged. "Okay. What do you want me to do?"

"Nothing. Just sit still and relax." Deb perked up in the chair and gazed into his eyes. To combat the unsettling feeling, he furrowed his brow and stuck his tongue out. Deb didn't flinch. She turned her head and repeated the process with Samantha—who sat perfectly still.

"Hmmm..." she mumbled and shifted in her chair. Samantha sat statue-like while Deb drew her mouth together tightly and scrunched up her face.

"What is it?" asked Samantha.

"There's a small tear in both of your auras near your right ears. Perhaps caused by a misalignment with the Third Eye Chakra. In fact, that could explain the visions, though not why you share them." She paused to think some more. "Have either of you experienced any physical effects? Ringing in your ears? Sensitivity to sound?"

Ringing in the right ear? Those details were too specific to be coincidental. Christopher had been chalking it up to years of shooting practice catching up to him, not a symptom of the visions. "What exactly does this mean?" The tremble in his voice surprised him.

"I don't know. I haven't seen anything like this before. I'm not a certified Reiki healer or trained to align chakras. But I'll gladly refer you to someone who can."

"There isn't anything else you can try?" asked Samantha.

"Let's see," Deb said in her cheery demeanor. "There's obviously a strong connection between the two of you..."

Deb leaned forward and reached her hands across the table, palms facing up. Samantha scooted closer and placed her right hand atop Deb's. Christopher's sigh was masked by the chair scraping against the floor as he moved his left hand into Deb's. Deb cleared her throat and closed her eyes. Samantha followed suit. Deb's head turned from side to side, and she started humming. The noise gradually rose in pitch until it matched the ringing that he never consciously realized accompanied each vision. She winced and her fingers twitched.

Christopher leaned closer. The girl's lip was quivering but he realized the sound wasn't coming from her at all. As he started to move back, Deb's hand grew clammy. She clutched him in a death grip, her fingernails digging into the back of his hand. Samantha emitted a yelp of pain. Christopher yanked away. Deb was a hundred and forty pounds at most, yet he couldn't free himself from her grasp.

Suddenly Deb let go. At the same time, a memory of a breaking rearview mirror flashed through Christopher and Samantha's minds. Christopher fell back, nearly falling out of the chair. White discolorations marked the back of his hand, topped with four half-moon indentations. The girl across the table from him was barely recognizable. Deb's eyes watered behind dark circles on a face now gaunt and white. All of Christopher's skepticism faded when a single drop of blood splashed to the table.

"Your nose..." he said.

Deb wiped it against the back of her hand, but there was nothing.

"Are you okay? You look like a truck hit you."

"I've never experienced this kind of... sensory overload before. Like processing visual input from a dozen different eyes simultaneously. It lasted a few seconds before the pain... Whatever it was, something forced me out."

"Out of what? Did you see something?" asked Samantha.

Deb shook her head. "It hurt so much."

Samantha glanced at Christopher and he went into action. He moved into the kitchen and pulled a glass from the cabinet she'd opened when they first arrived. He filled it with cold water, set it down, and clasped his hand on her shoulder.

"It's okay. Take your time."

The color returned to Deb's face after she chugged all but a mouthful. "Thanks," she said looking up at him.

Christopher returned to his seat and opened the notebook to a blank page. He nodded in thanks to Samantha as she handed him a pen from her purse. "When you're ready, tell us anything you can. Even if it's just a jumble of shapes,"

Deb licked her lips and wiped the tears from her eyes. "I was inside a car, but everything was dark." She glanced toward the sliding glass door. "Like I was looking through a tunnel... I've never..."

"Try to focus," Christopher said as he took notes. "You're doing good."

The petite woman squinted and scrunched up her face, fighting against the pain. "There was a ditch with sparse trees out the window...and an overpass."

"Okay, so it was on the highway," Samantha said.

Christopher shushed her and then turned back to Deb. "Could you make out anything else?"

"Samantha was right. It was a highway. A divided one. I can still see a brown sign." She sat in silence for a moment. Christopher waited. "For a Pony Express Museum? There were two people in the car. No, wait... Three. I was one of them." Deb slumped back in the chair and let her arms fall to the table.

"Pony Express?" Christopher lifted the pen from the page. "You're sure about the sign?"

Deb slowly nodded.

"I've never been able to read anything within any of the visions. Even where there should have been letters or words."

"You're incapable of reading while dreaming," said Samantha.

"That doesn't sound right, I'm sure I've read things in my dreams before."

"That's your brain filling in the gaps with what it thinks should be there. It has to do with which portions of your brain remain active and accessible during REM sleep."

Deb nodded. "Samantha's right. I've done a bit of research on the subject."

Christopher shrugged, taking their word for it. He looked over the notes of everything Deb had dictated. If she were the real deal, and all evidence pointed toward that, these were the best leads they'd received so far.

Samantha used her phone to search for locations of Pony Express Museums. Several were located across the United States. Only Kansas and Nebraska bore the formal name. Samantha put her phone back into her purse when Deb started talking again.

"There's something else. There's... something wrong with the man in the back seat." Christopher and Samantha locked eyes. They didn't have to say anything. It was their killer. "I saw him in the rearview mirror before I was..." She swallowed the lump in her throat. "Ejected."

Christopher's heartbeat raced as he leaned forward. "Can you describe him? Sketch his face?"

Deb shook her head. "I couldn't physically *see* him. A void resided where he should have been." Christopher recalled the feeling of something missing from the epicenter of his visions. Deb gave her head another quick shake. "No, that's not right. It was more like something was overlapping him..." She shuddered at the recollection. "Enveloping him."

"Demonic possession?" Samantha asked. Christopher dropped the pen.

"I haven't dealt with demons before, but I don't think so. It is possible that something has leached on and is feeding off him though. Negative entities, like psychic vampires, can do this. But I understand they're rare."

Christopher spoke up. "Was this similar to the tears you mentioned in our auras?"

"I suppose, but this was far more drastic. I get the feeling that whatever this thing is, it's taking a toll on his mind." Deb finished the glass of water. "There's more."

Samantha cocked her head to the side. "Oh?"

"I didn't do this. I'm not clairvoyant and have never had a vision like this before in my life. This came *through* the two of you. Something is bestowing the visions upon you, vying for your attention. I don't know what you've been seeing, but I know they're not full of sunshine and puppies."

"Well, you're not wrong," Christopher said with a smirk.

"You said something is doing this to us," Samantha said. "Is it the same thing attached to the man in the car?"

Deb shook her head. "Similar maybe, but not the same entity. If you were to repair the tears in your auras, you may slow it down. Though this would only be a stopgap. Excuse me, I really need some painkillers." Deb stood and disappeared down the hallway.

"I owe you an apology. This was well worth our time," said Christopher.

Samantha smiled and resisted the urge to say: 'I told you so'. As Deb walked back into the room, Samantha's phone rang inside her purse. She silenced the phone after checking the display. There would be plenty of time to call her web developer back later.

"Sorry I can't pinpoint what the entities are. I've encountered guardian spirits attached to families before, but this doesn't fit the bill."

Samantha's phone beeped out a voicemail notification.

"You said entities, plural? Are we both *communing* with the same thing?"

Deb shook her head. "Not necessarily. It's believed that spirits don't experience time or distance in the same manner we do."

"Well, they have our attention. I just don't know what we can do if the information is coming too late?"

"Too late?"

Samantha turned toward Christopher, not wanting to upset him by revealing too much.

He bit his lip and hung his head. "I've been seeing bloody crime scenes. The aftermath of murders. Samantha, on the other hand, has been experiencing them firsthand as they happen. We're always one step behind the killer."

Deb's eyes went wide. "Shit! I sensed something dark but didn't expect that. I'm sorry you're going through this. How can I help?"

"You've *been* helping," pointed out Christopher. Deb offered a weak smile.

"Is there anything we can do to get more information from our visions?" asked Samantha.

"Hmm... You might be getting as much information as the spirits can give. If that's the case, nothing will help. Otherwise, try getting plenty of rest, staying hydrated, and cutting out toxins like alcohol, tobacco, drugs, et cetera. That will help if any limitations are on your end."

Samantha nodded her head. "We did hypothesize that alcohol hinders the visions. It would be nice if we could just communicate directly with whatever these things are."

"Theories about contacting spirits are similar to those about extraterrestrials." Deb looked at Christopher, anticipating the eye roll that followed. "Bear with me for one moment and I'll explain. There are three common interpretations as to why there's never been documented interactions with the spirit realm. One—spirits are so different from us on a physiological level that most people can't interact with them. Two – spirits choose not to interfere or have their own set of rules governing them. Three—they ignore us because we're not worthy of their time. This is aside from the ever-popular opinion that the spiritual realm doesn't exist, and the believers are crackpots."

"I miss that ignorance," Christopher said with a sigh. "If depressants like alcohol disrupt the visions, could stimulants or hallucinogens boost them? Not that I'm promoting LSD or shrooms... But what about something like peyote?"

"I...wouldn't recommend it," said Deb.

"Peyote is just as illegal too," added Samantha. "Unless you're of Native American descent and using it for ceremonial purposes."

Christopher raised an eyebrow. "Really?"

"Yup," replied Deb. "And there are safer alternatives. Guided meditation, exercise, and music have all been proven capable of altering brain chemistry. If anything, I'd suggest combining automatic writing with targeted binaural audio."

"Binaural what?" asked Samantha.

"Sounds played at specific frequencies designed to trigger certain portions of the brain. You can find samples on YouTube, though it might take a few tries to find something that works for you. There's a lot of crap out there. And make sure you use headphones."

Samantha picked her phone back up and fiddled with it. "You mean ones boasting warnings about awakening my inner genius aren't genuine?" Deb giggled.

"How am I going to explain a search history for 'Bi-Oral' to my wife?" Deb let out another giggle and Samantha hung her head.

"Don't encourage him," Samantha said.

Deb put on a serious face once again. "Are you familiar with automatic writing?"

"It's similar in principle to pendulums and Ouija boards, right?"

"Yes. The idea is to keep your conscious mind busy so your subconscious can freely pass along information. Some people have claimed success digitally, but I've always preferred pen and paper myself. Any other questions?"

"Have you ever heard of Skylos?" Christopher asked.

"No... What's that?"

"Line of sight to the sky?" Deb's roommate yelled from the couch. Christopher jumped. He'd forgotten the young man was there. "L.O.S. is a common abbreviation for line of sight."

"Uhh... Thanks," said Christopher. Deb shrugged.

"Well, you've helped put some things into context." Samantha looked down at her phone again. "We should get going." She stood and gathered her things.

"Yes. Thank you," Christopher said as Deb walked them to the door. After an awkward pause, he pulled his wallet from his back pocket. "What do we owe you?"

"Nothing," replied Deb, putting her hands out. She gave Christopher another large smile. "I never charge for my gift. And it feels duly wrong with what you're going through."

"We're appreciative of your help. You've done more than you know. Please accept a donation," Samantha said, pressing several twenties into her hands.

"Thanks." Deb gave Samantha a quick hug and then pulled back, leaving her arms on Samantha's shoulders. "You're tied up in something complicated. If you need anything else, let me know."

"Thank you," said Christopher, as she hugged him as well.

...

Samantha listened to her voicemail as she slid back into the minivan. "Hey Sam, it's Simon. I haven't heard back from you regarding this legal notice. Were you planning on ignoring it and seeing what happens? Give me a ring back."

What Legal notice? After fastening her seatbelt, she scrolled through a long list of ignored emails searching for legal jargon. Thirty some emails in she found the DMCA violation email. She looked back further and found another with a similar title. Samantha tapped on the email and read through it.

The email contained a standard cease and desist order addressed to Samantha Blackblood. The form was like the ones used by her previous employer, and not a phishing scam. It didn't make sense though. What was the legal department of Penguin Random House contesting? Maybe she had accidentally sent something from her personal address instead of her work one.

The legal document requested compliance within seventy-two hours from their first contact, which according to the first email, had already come and gone. Even though she was no longer employed by Windy City Publishers, she felt obligated to at least call. The least she could do was leave a voicemail. As Samantha dialed, Christopher shifted the minivan into gear.

While backing up, Christopher's own phone rang. He slipped the car back into park and pulled the phone from his shirt pocket. *Why was his daughter calling this late?* Christopher flipped open the outdated phone and held it to his ear.

"Hey Jess, is everything alright?"

"Where are you, Dad?"

He glanced over at Samantha and then moved the phone to his other ear. "Out. Why?"

"I know you're out. Mom called because you weren't answering your phone. You missed your appointment with Dr. Bayer tonight."

"Oh... No one called. I must not have been getting reception. Something came up. I'll reschedule my appointment."

Samantha began leaving a message as quietly as possible. "My name's Samantha Englund and I received a DMCA notice Friday afternoon. Please reach out to my employer at..."

Jessica's voice boomed over the cheap phone's speaker. "Englund... The girl you asked about the other day? The one I explicitly told you to *not* get involved with! What the fuck's going on, Dad?"

"Shit," Samantha said under her breath after ending her phone call. She mouthed the word 'sorry' to Christopher. He waved her off.

"It's none of your business."

"It is my business when you're hanging out with shady murder suspects. At least if you end up in a ditch I'll know where to start. What the hell is going on?"

"It's complicated and I can't explain now. I'll see you and the kids in the morning. Good night, Jess." Christopher snapped the phone shut and slipped it back into his pocket. He turned to check his blind spot and caught the horror displayed on Samantha's face. "I'm sorry about that."

"*You're* sorry? I dragged you into this. How much trouble are you in?"

"Don't worry about it. This is what happens when you have a nosy daughter who's also a police officer."

Samantha nodded and stared out the window as he drove her back to her apartment complex. After several miles, she broke the silence. "I already know your stance on this, but I'm considering filling in Agent Montgomery."

Christopher took his eyes off the road long enough to meet her eyes. "Nothing good can come from..."

"Believe me, I know," Samantha interrupted. "But we finally have something more concrete."

Christopher sighed. "You already tried calling someone, didn't you?"

Samantha hung her head. There was no lecture, but the disappointment was thick in his voice. Her stomach twisted, like she'd let down her own father. She focused on the car's floorboard. "I called in an anonymous tip to the Highway Patrol yesterday morning. I thought if they mobilized quickly enough, they'd catch him. It went as you predicted. There's no need for an 'I told you so'."

"But that's the best part of being a parent," Christopher said with a smile that put her at ease.

"I honestly feel that Agent Montgomery will be more responsive. I already attempted to tell him everything during the interrogation."

"Law enforcement officers are trained to keep an open mind and explore all potential scenarios. But this is so far outside the standard procedure manual. A month ago, it wouldn't have mattered how much evidence you put in front of me. Without living through this, I wouldn't have believed you."

"I know, but I've been thinking about what Deb said. There were three people in the car. That means two more potential victims. As of right now, they're alive...I can feel it. This is the first time we've had an opportunity like this. If a roadblock went up in time, maybe we could save them."

"Trust me. I understand the dilemma." Christopher said, stopping in front of her building. "Good luck. And if you don't mind, keep my name out of it."

Chapter 29

Samantha – Chicago, IL – Monday Night

Samantha locked her apartment door and sat down at her kitchen table to think. They'd learned a frightening amount of information. Whatever Deb experienced was different and more intense than any of hers or Christopher's.

Unfortunately, this information hadn't come without a price. Whatever Deb tapped into had been physically draining. Samantha wondered about the ramifications of that. As much as she wanted Deb's help in the future, she didn't want to doom her to their current plight.

Her mind started to race. Would Christopher and she suffer effects like that? What if Deb's actions created a link and gave Skylos a glimpse back at them? If so, all three of them were in grave danger. Calling Agent Montgomery was their best chance at putting a stop to everything.

But she had to do her homework first. She was only going to have one chance to make him believe her. Samantha picked up what she'd started in Deb's apartment and investigated the Pony Express Museum sign. She'd narrowed things down to Marysville, Kansas or Gothenburg, Nebraska. The two historic sites were less than three hundred miles apart. Taking travel time into account, both were a reasonable distance from Skylos' last known kill.

Samantha pinched her fingers apart, zooming in on the small maps on her phone. She followed a path along the highway prior to each respective exit using Google's street view. She wanted to see everything that Skylos would have. A green historical site sign stood before an overpass at both locations. The terrains were similar too. Samantha switched back and forth between Marysville and Gothenburg, looking for anything that stood out. Then it hit her. One of the things Deb mentioned was a divided highway. The highway in Nebraska was divided, where Kansas was not. Skylos had to be near Gothenburg in Nebraska!

"Woohoo!" Samantha said aloud. She pulled the creased business card from the bottom of her purse, took a deep breath, and then dialed the number.

"This is Agent Montgomery."

"Hi, it's Samantha Englund. You... uh... interrogated me a few days ago."

"Yes, I recall. I've been waiting to hear from you."

"You have?"

"I had the impression you knew more than you were letting on. Additionally, I found your number present in a couple of California Police Department call logs." Samantha kept quiet. "Don't worry, there are no plans to bring charges against you. Is there something you wanted to tell me?"

Samantha spoke slowly. "I have something I think would be worth checking into." She paused a moment to see if he'd respond. "I believe the killer is in Nebraska heading East along I-80. He passed the exit for Gothenburg roughly forty minutes ago."

"And how did you come about this information?"

"We had another vision." She winced immediately after saying the words.

"We?"

Samantha's face grew warm. "You know, the royal we."

"I don't care if there's a club of witches..."

"Coven," she interjected.

"Huh?"

"A group of witches is a coven." Her face reddened more, feeling stupid for correcting him.

"Trust me, I don't care who's involved. And the only reason I'm entertaining this is that your intel has been accurate thus far. What else can you tell me? Do you know the make and model of the car he's traveling in?"

"No. But I think there are two other passengers in the car." Under her breath, she added: "If they're not already dead."

"Okay. I-80 past Gothenburg, got it. I'll look into it. Anything else?"

"I have a feeling that he's coming after me," Samantha said with a shaky voice. She wasn't entirely sure why she said it. It wasn't something she'd given serious thought to, but at the same time it made all the sense in the world.

"Did you receive an actual threat? Or was this another dream?"

"It's a gut feeling. But you can't deny the murders follow a path toward Chicago."

"Suppose there was a credible threat, and I could put a unit on your apartment, could you even tell me who to look for?"

"No..." Her head sank. *It was still a small victory. He agreed to investigate the Nebraska highway.*

Agent Montgomery sighed. "Give me your address anyway, so I have it."

After he read the address and apartment number back to her, they said their goodbyes. Samantha slipped into bed and shut her eyes. No matter how it turned out, it was a small comfort that Agent

Montgomery hadn't immediately dismissed her. Knowing that she'd done all she could, she drifted off.

Chapter 30

Skylos – Brady, NE – Monday Night

Skylos awoke to the twilight lit horizon outside the car windows. A breeze swayed the sparse trees beyond the ditch on the side of the roadway. He rubbed his eyes. *I guess I dozed off. Where are we?* He leaned around the driver's seat to peer at the dash.

"About three hours till we reach Lincoln," said Sean, raising his head to meet Skylos' eyes in the rearview mirror. "We should get in around elev..."

Skylos' head slammed into the car window as Paul cut the wheel to avoid hitting the yellow Volkswagen that swerved into their lane. The car horn blared for several seconds until Paul finally let up.

"Christ..."

Euphoria washed over Skylos as Calliope's arms wrapped around his neck and chest. It seemed the blaspheming roused Calliope from her slumber. He licked his lips as the familiar shiver ran up his spine. It was clear what she wanted, but he held his breath, anticipating the request.

Kill them both...

"My pleasure," he said, grinning ear to ear. The boys not only outnumbered him but outweighed him too. It didn't matter. Tad was bigger than the two of them put together. All that mattered was that Calliope wanted them.

"Did you say something?" asked Sean, lowering the stereo volume.

Skylos was too busy searching for the appropriate knives to hear him. His bag held two identical wood-handled folding knives that were perfect for. One for each cousin. As he dug through the bag, a white-hot pain reverberated through his head. Skylos pressed his hands to his temples and screamed. Pins and needles raced down his extremities.

Sean lowered his phone and turned around, stretching the seatbelt to its limit. "You okay, man?"

The car slowed as Paul's foot eased off the gas. "What the hell's wrong with him?" he said, watching Skylos via the rearview mirror.

The mirror! Calliope hissed.

Her words echoed in his head for a moment, followed by a dull thud that knocked the wind out of him. Skylos' heart skipped a beat and the static electricity in the air was gone. For the briefest of moments, he was somewhere else. The faint earthy aroma of marijuana hung in the air. Instead of being in a car, he was huddled around a table with two other people. As soon as he tried to look up, they were gone, and he was back in the car.

Skylos hazily recalled Calliope's parting message. The mirror. He released his seat belt, leaned over the front seat, and drove his fist into the rearview mirror with enough force to remove it from the windshield. The brilliant pain in his head abated. Skylos slumped back to his seat and caught his breath.

"What the fuck?" Paul said, hitting the brakes. "I'm going to pull over and call an ambulance."

In the back, Skylos mumbled to himself. The aftershock of pain rippling down his spine and his already bruised knuckles meant nothing. His sole concern was for Calliope. She'd been ripped away from him. What the hell could hurt the angel of death?

He had to bring her back and make sure she was okay. The only way to do that was to deliver Sean and Paul. Skylos stretched down and grabbed his backpack from where it had fallen onto the floor. He palmed one of the twin knives and slipped the other into his pocket.

"I don't need an ambulance, but I th-think I'm going to be sick," said Skylos. His stutter had gotten worse. He needed Calliope back at his side immediately.

"Whatever you do, don't puke in my car." Paul fumbled with the controls and lowered the back window as he pulled onto the shoulder. The car rolled to a rest near a small outcropping of trees and an overpass. Skylos scooted across to the passenger side and limped away from the car.

He moved slowly, surveying the side of the highway. He couldn't have picked a better spot himself. The ditch was a perfect ambush point. He could lure the boys from the car one at a time and take them out of view. Skylos hurried forward, bent at the waist, and then made retching noises. After a moment he leaned back and fell onto his butt, sliding feet first into the ditch. The drop in elevation was at most three feet, and it easily concealed him from the road. As he lay in wait Calliope embraced him again. *Thank god she's okay.* He rolled onto his stomach and unfolded the knife.

"Help! Help!" Skylos yelled.

After a moment, a car door slammed. Sean called out. Skylos shouted again, holding the knife close to his side as the college student's footfalls came closer.

"I rolled my ankle," Skylos said, looking up at the man. He extended his left arm. "Can you help me up?"

Sean dropped to his right knee and planted his left foot near Skylos' head for leverage. Skylos shot his hand up and tugged on Sean's right arm. He was unable to move the boy. Sean lowered his other arm as well.

"Stop fighting me. I'll pull you up."

Skylos drew the blade across Sean's left wrist. Blood sprayed from Sean's radial artery. The two men jerked their arms back and forth in a bloody tug-of-war. Neither man budged. Not wanting to risk cutting himself, Skylos chose a new target, cutting deep into the boys Achilles tendon. Sean dragged his foot back, protecting it from a second strike. In doing so, he lost his superior footing and he toppled head over heels into the ditch.

"Paul!" Sean screamed on his way down.

Skylos rolled on top of him and raised the knife for another strike. The young man recovered more quickly than Skylos hoped, catching him in the jaw with a strong right hook. Skylos fell back and lost the knife in the tall grass.

Sean limped away from Skylos toward the embankment. Skylos grabbed a fist-sized rock and charged. Sean spun around and raised his fists to defend himself but was too slow. The rock caught him in the temple, and he crumpled to the ground. Skylos straddled Sean again, striking him repeatedly. He jerked his head up to the sound of a slamming car door between the sporadic roaring of cars passing. Skylos let the rock slip out of his hands and turned back toward the roadside.

When Skylos pulled himself out of the ditch he found himself face to face with Paul. He leaned on his shoulder and panted, blocking his view into the ditch. "Sean fell and hit his head while helping me up." Paul sidestepped to check on his cousin. Skylos ducked behind him, retrieving the other knife from his pocket.

"Is that blood?" Paul said pointing down to his cousin lying motionless among the weeds.

"Yes. Lots of it."

Skylos raised the knife to Paul's neck as he spun around on his heels. The motion slit his throat from ear to ear, though not deeply enough to be fatal. At the same time, an eighteen-wheeler rumbled past, its bright headlights illuminating the pair of them. Skylos leaned back quickly and kicked Paul down the embankment where he toppled on top of Sean. When the truck showed no sign of stopping Skylos jumped down, landing in a crouch within the small ditch.

Paul pushed himself up from his cousin's dead body and searched for something to defend himself. He grabbed the rock still slick with his cousin's blood and took several steps toward the crazed man.

Skylos feigned a strike. Paul retreated backward, the knife harmlessly sailing through the air. Another slash, another step. Skylos grinned broadly and made a final, showy slash. Paul, focusing solely on the tip of the knife, shuffled back once more. The rock rolled out of his hand as he stumbled over his cousin's body.

With a pounce, Skylos plunged the knife deep into Paul's belly. He withdrew the blade and thrust it forward again. Paul screamed out in pain as he tried to protect himself, blocking the follow-up strike with his left forearm. The knife glanced off the bone, preventing the blade from finding any vital organs. Paul reached out with his other arm, groping around for the rock. Pinning the man's arm to his chest, Skylos sank the knife deep into his side. The man howled in pain and gritted his teeth.

Paul grabbed hold of the knife still within his flesh. He knew it wasn't enough. Unless he switched to the offensive, he'd bleed out in the ditch next to his best friend. He abandoned the search for the rock and reached out his fingers to jab at Skylos' eyes. Skylos lifted his head and bit into the fleshy webbing between

Paul's forefinger and thumb. He pulled the knife upward, elongating the cut on his side. Paul let go of the knife and got his hand around Skylos' throat. He squeezed as tight as he could, but his strength was fading. Skylos coughed as Paul grabbed him with his other hand as well.

Skylos pulled at Paul's finger, but they only gripped tighter. His muscles twitched as a zap of static electricity prodded his fingertips. He gasped for breath and flailed his hand, looking for the knife still sticking in Paul's side. More shocks tickled his fingertips, guiding then to the knife handle like magnets being drawn together. He yanked it sideways, widening the hole in Paul's belly. Paul's hands finally fell away from his neck. Skylos rolled to the side, coughing and sputtering to catch his breath.

Calliope's fingers wrapped around his throat, overlapping where Paul's had been. it still hurt, but the euphoria pouring from her fingertips overwhelmed the pain. She lifted him to his feet. Skylos stepped around the grass slick with Paul's guts and took both of their wallets. He stripped off his clothes and tossed them in the ditch.

A car honked as a naked Skylos returned to the car. He jumped into the passenger seat, leaned over the center console, and then popped the trunk. Inside a duffel bag, he found a pair of sweatpants and a white polo embroidered with a large scarlet 'N'. He quickly slipped into the clothes and jumped into the driver's seat.

Luckily, the keys were in the ignition and the navigation software still running on Paul's phone. Sean's phone wasn't in sight. Either he'd dropped it in the scuffle, or it was still on his body. It didn't matter. He wouldn't be calling anyone. The Nissan's tires spun briefly in the gravel at the shoulder as Skylos shifted the car into gear. He could still feel Calliope's breath against his neck.

"Calliope, what happened earlier?"

She saw...

"She?" His eyes lit up. "You mean Samantha? It was her in the mirror?"

Yes.

"Are you hurt?"

No. I left to protect us.

"She'll be out of our way soon," he said, wiping a tear of joy from his eye.

Good. Calliope's fingers trailed down his arms, lingered at his fingertips a moment, and then disappeared into the night.

Three police cars roared past on the other side of the highway without their lights or sirens. Skylos maintained the speed limit for a few miles before accelerating. Samantha was proving to be an intelligent opponent. Despite being hundreds of miles away, she was right on their tail.

But they would prevail. He had Calliope, his angelic guardian, at his side. It was only safe to presume that Samantha had one of her own. Perhaps even a demonic one. How could she have spied on him through the mirror if not for dark magic? *How can I fight against a demon? And what other powers has it lent Samantha?* The car jostled against the grooves on the highway shoulder. He jerked the car back onto the road and refocused.

He'd be in Chicago in less than twenty-four hours. Until then, he'd need to be more vigilant. It would be easy to adjust his tactics to stay away from mirrors, but who knew what else Samantha was capable of.

Chapter 31

Samantha – Chicago, IL – Monday Night

Samantha cried in her sleep while witnessing firsthand the murder of the twins. As she... Skylos... climbed from the ditch, she woke. It was too late; two more were dead. Despite Agent Montgomery's willingness to listen, calling him had no effect whatsoever. She grabbed the corner of a pillow and whipped it across the room. It clattered to the floor along with the alarm clock on the nightstand.

Watching the murders was awful, but something bothered her more. There was an anger inside her hungrier than the sadness. Failing to stop Skylos stood out above the loss of the two men. She dried her eyes and placed the clock back on the nightstand. The time shown on the clock startled her. It wasn't even ten. The vision must have begun immediately after falling asleep. Maybe there was still time to catch him.

Based on when they left Deb's, the murders had to have occurred no more than an hour ago. Two at tops. Samantha stepped through what they knew.

"Deb's vision was around eight-thirty. How long had she been wrestling with the two college kids? Fifteen minutes? If he took their car and was traveling the speed limit, he'd be somewhere between fifty and eighty miles away from Gothenburg."

Samantha unplugged her cell phone from the charger and revisited the small map of Nebraska. *This would go a lot faster with a laptop. I wonder if Von's awake.* She walked across the hall and knocked on Yvonne's door. No response. She was probably tending bar. Samantha returned to her own door.

"Hey Sam, did you need something?" Yvonne stood in her doorway, a long tee-shirt barely concealing her bare legs.

Samantha smiled. "Laundry day? Or trying to find a way to maximize tips?"

Yvonne laughed. "Today's my first day off in a week and I'm playing catch up."

An older female tenant carrying a paper grocery bag turned the corner and passed between them. She grunted in disgust at Yvonne's lack of clothing. Yvonne gave her the finger after she'd passed. The old woman turned back around when Samantha laughed. Yvonne smiled, waving with her fingertips. She stomped down the hall in a huff.

"Come on inside. Away from the jealous hags."

"Sure." Samantha stepped into an apartment that mirrored her own, though was much less tidy.

"What can I do you for?"

"Would you mind if I borrowed your laptop for the night?"

"Cops still have yours?" she asked, pulling a Lenovo laptop from the shelf beneath a glass coffee table.

"Yeah, it's still in evidence. Christopher suggested I contact a lawyer to expedite things. But with all that's been going on, I haven't gotten around to it."

"Ooh. Tell me about Christopher."

"What? Oh, no. He's only a friend."

"Yeah, sure he is."

"He's married and old enough to be my dad."

"Kinky." Yvonne laughed. "I'm just messing with you. Here's you go..." she said holding out the computer. "The charger's around here somewhere."

Yvonne headed deeper into the room where she checked behind the television and lifted random piles of laundry. Yvonne scratched her head and then disappearing into the bedroom briefly. She came back empty-handed and dropped to all fours to check under the couch. Her shirt rode up revealing skimpy, red lace panties. Samantha averted her eyes. They looked all too similar to the bloody pair on Kara's body.

"Ah-ha!" Yvonne jumped to her feet and raised the cord over her head victoriously.

"Thanks. I need to do some research that would take forever on my phone."

"No problem. Keep it as long as you need it... Just Ignore any risqué pictures you come across," she said with a sly smile.

"Thanks again, I'll bring it back tomorrow. Have a good night, Von."

Back in her own apartment, Samantha sat at her kitchen table and opened the laptop. It beeped a low battery warning. She plugged in the power cord, wiggled it until it began charging, and then resumed her research.

She located Gothenburg on the map and plotted out an hour and a half's drive. "If he stuck to the highway, he'd probably be between Kearney and Grand Island." This strip of I-80 was a familiar one. This was the route she'd take to her childhood home in Missouri. In a day, two at max, Skylos could be on her doorstep.

Samantha lined up Christopher's printed notes. Maybe there was something they'd overlooked that would help. Hours ago, Deb had pretty much guaranteed they were dealing with a spirit of some sort. It was driving the murders, but they'd never thought about the reasons behind that.

"If I was a bloodthirsty spirit, how would I recruit myself a puppet?" She twirled her long hair around her finger. "No different than a cult, I suppose. I'd find someone weak, without family or friends. A person easily manipulated out of a desire to belong." A homeless loner. Those were traits they'd already incorporated into their makeshift profile.

There was still a matter of pressuring someone to kill. That didn't seem an easy task. Unless the entity held enough power to overcome someone's free will... A shiver went up Samantha's spine. Maybe that was why she was so driven to stop Skylos? Although Christopher was documenting the dreams, he didn't share the same level of motivation. Samantha took a deep breath. She was going down a rabbit hole. It was important to focus on Skylos.

A light bulb went on in her head. She was onto something when she mentioned a cult. While there was no indication of a group of people being involved, the process of joining was the same—an initiation ritual. In that context, the first murder made absolute sense. "If I could convince someone to commit murder barefooted in a diving suit, I could make him do anything." She smiled. The information may not be helpful, but it was an important clue. She was closer to understanding everything, if only barely.

Samantha picked up a dry erase marker from the ledge of the whiteboard hanging on the wall to her left. Lettuce, almond milk, and the rest of her grocery list disappeared beneath the side of her palm. She drew a thick line in the middle of the board and created a timeline based off hers and Christopher's notes. On Monday night Skylos completed the test, taking a first victim. Tom, in Union Station, with a Swiss Army Knife.

Things were silent for a few days and then he killed Kara. Samantha closed her eyes. The memories that came flooding in were as clear as when she'd originally dreamed them. The murder must have occurred after closing time. Kara wouldn't have risked being caught having sex by her boss or a coworker.

This vision began with the killer already underneath the desk. Which means he couldn't have known she'd be there. Unlike the first, this kill wasn't premeditated. So why was he there after hours? As soon as she posed the question, she realized the answer. The packages on the desk. She wrote 'Squatting?' on the board and circled it.

Exactly one week later he killed again—the construction worker. This vision she missed, so she consulted Christopher's notes again. Traces of blood and hair were found on the single step outside the door. The body had numerous puncture wounds from a discarded spear fashioned from a bowie knife and a pool skimmer. Additionally, the dog was drowned as well. Christopher surmised that he lured the victim outside into a tripwire or something where he fell and struck his head. Christopher also potentially linked the drowned dog to a dogfighting ring.

Samantha circled the word and then went back and did the same with 'Prostitute'—his first intended victim that got away. She could see where Christopher's conclusion had come from. It did appear that the entity seemed to be targeting sinners.

She stepped back and took in the board. Her detailed notes had already taken up most of the whiteboard and she was only half done. She pulled the table away from the corner and continued, writing directly onto the wall.

Saturday, two days later, he killed a UPS deliveryman. This one didn't fit the punishment theme. Another case of him being in the wrong place at the wrong time? Christopher had noted this was within the same house as the third kill. She wrote and circled 'Squatting' again. A pattern was emerging after all. The other disturbing fact about this kill was that Skylos took the man's uniform with him.

"Queue an irrational fear of deliverymen."

A second murder occurred that same day. This was the first kill while he was on the move. The truck he'd left behind led police back to the other two bodies. Again, this one didn't fit any recognizable pattern. It was either a crime of convenience or done to fulfill some murderous need.

That brought her to tonight—the college kids. Samantha wrote down everything she'd recently observed. Aside from being stereotypical college kids who probably got into underage drinking and other kinds of harmless trouble, they also didn't fit the sinner theme.

Samantha stepped back a second time. The writing that stretched across the entire wall of the kitchen reminded her of a movie scene. One where the main character is losing their mind. She looked down at her phone and realized how long she'd been at it. it was already one in the morning.

She'd gotten carried away and lost her window of opportunity to inform Agent Montgomery of the killer's position. Samantha yawned and closed the laptop. At the same time, her phone chimed an email notification. Nothing important, only spam. However, now that her brain was firing on all cylinders, it came with an epiphany.

The threatening email from the publisher in New York suddenly made sense. She and Christopher weren't alone. Another author, a professional one, was using their visions as a foundation for their writing as well. It had nothing to do with one of her clients. She was the one being accused of plagiarism. Samantha curled her fingers and looked up at the ceiling.

"How could I have missed that?"

Having Christopher's perspective helped to clarify a lot of things. The help of a third may unravel things completely. Her heart sank as reality set in. For starters, it could be days, if not weeks, before she could get through to someone in the legal department. Also, the likelihood of them believing her story and putting her in contact with her accuser was remote. With the pace Skylos had set, time was at a premium.

I'm going to have to go to them. Samantha opened the laptop again and searched for flights. There was one with seats open for tomorrow afternoon. Her knee bounced anxiously under the table. *Could I convince Christopher to come along?*

As she reached for her phone it chirped another notification—a text message from an unavailable number. *You Up?* When she replied the phone rang instantly. Upon answering she realized it couldn't have been Christopher. His number was stored in her phone.

"Hello?" she said apprehensively.

"Sorry for the late call," said Agent Montgomery. "But I thought you'd want to know what we found."

"Okay," Samantha stammered. She already knew that the college students were dead. She couldn't save them.

"Your hunch was right. We found two young men in a ditch roughly four miles west of the Gothenburg exit ramp. One had already bled out by the time the Sheriff arrived. The other is in critical condition."

"Wait... What?" Samantha asked, eyes wide with surprise.

"He has a head injury, a nicked artery, and a severed Achilles tendon..." She winced as the attack replayed with each wound the agent mentioned. "But somehow he hung on."

"Has he said anything?" she blurted out. "Could he describe his attacker?"

Agent Montgomery fell quiet. "No. He was unconscious when they arrived. Once they got him to the hospital, they had to put him into a medically induced coma. If he comes out of it, doctors say he's unlikely to even remember the attack. I thought you'd want to know."

Samantha wiped a tear running down her cheek. "Thanks for letting me know," she said with a sniffle. Her phone beeped again. An incoming call from Christopher. "I need to go."

Chapter 32

Skylos – Grand Island, Nebraska – Monday Night

Skylos passed over the Grand Island city limits, lowered the driver's side window, and then tossed out Paul's phone. Those cop cars had to be looking for him. He needed to get off the highway and ditch the car, lest Samantha tighten the noose around his neck for good.

He took the next freeway exit and followed a series of signs that led to the cracked asphalt lot of the city's bus station. There was a small handful of cars parked, but no buses. He crossed his fingers and hoped that they were still running. Skylos brought the car to rest beside a fire hydrant near the building and left the engine running. He hurried out with his luggage.

The doors of the small depot rattled as he tugged on them. A short man sat upon a stool behind the glass partition. A pack of cigarettes peered out of the pocket of his plaid, short-sleeved button-down. An askew clip-on nameplate read 'Ralph'. As Skylos stepped over, Ralph set down a book with a scantily clad elf maiden on the cover and leaned toward the speaker set in the middle of the glass.

"You can't leave your car there. It'll be towed," he said, pointing to the white Nissan.

"Thanks," replied Skylos.

Ralph picked the book up and resumed reading. When Skylos cleared his throat, the man glanced over at the car, and then back up at Skylos.

"What can I help you with?" he asked, dropping the book dramatically on the counter.

"I need to get to the Lincoln train station before twelve."

Ralph gave him a blank stare. "Why don't you drive? It's only an hour by car. A bus won't get you there before midnight."

Skylos closed his eyes and took a deep breath. Once the car was towed away there would be no evidence he was here. But if he caused a scene, it would draw unwanted attention. "I'd prefer to take a bus."

After sighing again, Ralph spun his chair and pointed to the electronic schedule board behind him. "There's a bus going that way in about forty-five minutes. But it won't get you there until one o'clock."

"There isn't anything sooner?"

The man looked up at the board again. "If it's not on the board, there's no other options."

Skylos pulled the itinerary from his pocket. It was already littered with numerous schedule adjustments. This delay would cause him to miss the train. There was another, but he'd be waiting at the station in Lincoln for a few hours. That train had more scheduled stops but would still put him in Chicago tomorrow afternoon.

"How much?" Skylos asked.

"The fare is thirty-seven even."

Ralph passed the ticket through the gap in the window and took the money. He shook his head and muttered 'psycho' under his breath. Skylos glanced back and reached into his bag. Ralph bit his lip, realizing he was heard, and brought his book up to cover his face.

Skylos pulled his hand out of his bag. As satisfying as it would have been to gut the man where he stood, he wasn't worth the risk. Skylos took a seat on the bench and stared at the insignificant little man in his glass house. To pass the time he imagined different ways to kill him. *Tad's gun would have made it so easy. Blam! A single bullet through the head.* Pictures swirled in his head and Skylos recalled taking out the man in the desert in this manner. He held up one finger, feeling the stress melting away already.

But that was low hanging fruit. He could do much better. *I could place a gift card on the counter and ask him to add it to the lost and found. When he grabs for it, I'll slit his wrists.* An unrecognizable memory surfaced. Although it wasn't his own, it was equally satisfying. Skylos raised another finger and looked over at the covered trash can. *I can start a fire and run to him asking for an extinguisher. He'd have to open the door. Then I could take my time with him. Three.*

While he sat on the bench laughing and counting, Ralph picked up his phone. Skylos straightened up. Who was he calling? Ralph shifted in the stool and turned away from the bench. Skylos relaxed a bit. If he were in real danger, Calliope would warn him. They still needed each other.

Bright headlights angled their way into the parking lot after he'd played out several dozen more death scenarios. Skylos reached for his bags, but it wasn't the bus. An old tow truck with red paint long faded to pink backed up behind Paul's car. The driver exited the cab and hooked up the white Nissan. Skylos looked back to the ticket booth and smiled broadly at Ralph. *I could slit the tow operator's throat and ram the truck straight through the building. Thirty-six.*

A large black bus showed up not much later. Fearing the large mirrors on the side of the bus, Skylos threw his royal blue hoodie over his head and drew the hood tight. He stepped onto the waiting bus. Without looking up, he handed over the ticket, slouched down in a seat at the back, and fell asleep.

...

The bus driver, a middle-aged man with glasses wearing a blue Pace jacket and cap, kicked Skylos' foot. Skylos sat up, his head darting back and forth.

"Sorry man, end of the line. I almost missed you all the way back here." Skylos rubbed his eyes and then checked his watch. It was past 1 AM. "Come on man, it's late and I'm tired." Skylos stood, gathered his bags, and slowly limped to the front. "You're welcome," the driver said under his breath.

Skylos stepped into the chilly night air and took in his surroundings. Several other buses sat vacant in the yard around him. The intermittent hum of cars on the highway nearby sang a duet with the crickets. A pair of train tracks ran parallel to the highway, but there was no station platform in sight. The bus's hydraulic door hissed closed behind him. Skylos spun around and pounded on the doors before the driver could move the vehicle.

The driver cracked the door open a few inches. "Forget something?"

"Where's Haymarket Station?"

"The train station? You slept through that stop almost twenty minutes ago. It's south along the highway," the man said pointing behind the bus. Skylos turned and looked in that direction. "It's a few miles. Do you need a cab?"

Skylos shook his head. "I'll walk." The driver closed the door and pulled deeper into the lot. Skylos walked south, following the highway.

A squad car drove past after he'd been walking for about an hour. Although it didn't have its sirens or lights on, Skylos realized how exposed he was. He left the main street, turning onto 33rd Street, following a sign pointing toward the University of Nebraska Lincoln's East Campus. It probably wasn't the most direct route to the station, but he had time to kill.

The star-dotted sky was peaceful and quiet, something the light pollution of L.A. always overshadowed. The ache in his leg grew burdensome, but he put his head down and walked through the pain. He limped past closed auto body shops and other small businesses to his right and an open field belonging to the university on the other. Not long after, he wandered into a residential neighborhood. The houses were all single-story dwellings; dog houses compared to those in Los Angeles.

Skylos sat down on the curb in front of a house with white siding desperately in need of a power washing. He dug the tablet computer out of his bag while he rested. Unfortunately, neither this house nor its neighbors had an unsecured wireless connection. He crept closer to the front of the darkened house and located the water faucet. He cupped one hand underneath and slowly turned the handle. When he'd drank his fill, he headed off.

He meandered through people's yards with his nose buried in the tablet, desperate to mooch off someone's Wi-Fi and plot a path to the train station. A faint thumping pulled him away. Closing his eyes, he followed the noise that was easily recognizable from his time at the theater. The deep throbbing of bass.

The music emanated from a three-story brick building that stood out among its neighbors. An ivy-covered wooden sign sat in the yard. A coat of arms and a series of Greek letters decorated the sign. He didn't understand the individual symbols, but their meaning was clear. They screamed of overindulgence and debauchery.

There was a reason he'd missed the earlier bus and then fell asleep through the Haymarket stop. Fate brought him here to punish more sinners. Killing again would give Calliope enough strength to keep him company through the ride. Perhaps she could share more about Samantha. Skylos looked at the watch on his arm. He still had time to stop in and look around.

He walked up to the large wooden door of the frat house and turned the handle. It was unlocked.

Chapter 33

Christopher – Chicago, IL – Tuesday Early Morning

The closet light shed a soft, yellow glow throughout the small room. It would have been picturesque had the room not been filthy, and if a naked man weren't lying on a twin mattress soaked in his own blood. From the doorway, Christopher could see a chain hanging down from a small pocketknife still lodged in the man's neck. Through force of habit rather than a necessity, Christopher stepped around the used condom draped over a pair of blue boxers with a beer stein pattern. He crouched down, walked around the bed, and even climbed on top of it. It was no use. The pillow obscured the young man's face from every vantage point.

"Dammit," Christopher mumbled in both his bed and within the dreamscape. He couldn't even sketch this man's face. It was a longshot, but there may be another way to determine his identity... Nope, no name written on the underwear. Christopher resumed his analysis.

Beer cans littered the floor and the small dresser. While it had been over forty years, he knew a frat house bedroom when he saw one. A sweatshirt or a wooden paddle had to be somewhere. He'd recognize the Greek letters and would at least know what chapter house he was in. Unfortunately, the closet light was dim. There wasn't enough light to see under the bed.

Even more frustrating, every article of clothing hanging inside was a dull gray and devoid of any detail.

The meeting with Deb made it easier to understand his forced perspective. He and Samantha were receiving visions from whatever twisted spirit had a connection to the killer. If the killer hadn't paid attention to details while committing the crime, neither could he. This scene felt more rushed than most. Either he was making sure they had as little to go off as possible or he was in a hurry.

"Son of a bitch!" Christopher yelled, startling himself awake.

He grabbed his diary and phone before slipping out of bed. A board creaked beneath his feet as he tiptoed out of the room. He paused and looked over his shoulder. Martha was still fast asleep. Holding the knob, he closed the door behind him and turned on the floor lamp beside the recliner. He flipped the notebook to the next blank page and recorded what little he learned from the vision.

The dream itself was short but carried a greater sense of urgency. Was it because Skylos was getting closer? Or was his own connection to the entity getting stronger? Christopher hoped it was the former. Deb's words stood out in his mind—*whatever this thing is, it's taking a toll on his mind*. Would he notice if he were slipping into madness?

He closed his eyes and walked back through the details. There wasn't shit there. Nothing revealed the fraternity chapter or even the school. The body could have been anywhere. He had a secret weapon though. Samantha. He only saw the aftermath, but Samantha would have watched it happen. Together, they could cobble something together. His phone illuminated as he flipped it open. It was almost two in the morning, but something told him that the vision had woken her as well.

Samantha answered on the second ring. The words flew forth from her mouth like pellets from a shotgun blast. "I missed something. I'm flying out to New York tonight. There are three open seats on the flight. Will you come with?"

"What?" Christopher said, still trying to process what she'd said.

"Only for a day. I'm planning to return Thursday morning."

"Stop! Samantha, what's going on?"

She took a deep breath and slowed down. "He's coming after me, I can feel it. The trail of bodies points to Chicago."

"If that's the case, you should be staying here, with me until we solve this."

"I got an email from a publisher in New York City a few days ago. Their legal team accused me of plagiarizing one of their writers. I didn't realize what it meant at the time..."

Christopher blinked. "Another dreamer..."

"Yeah. I can't sit here and wait for Skylos to show up if there's answers in New York."

Christopher shook his head. "This is crazy."

"No crazier than anything else that's already happened. I know it's short notice, but a third person might be what we need to get ahead of things." She paused to take another breath. "I'll be back in a few days. I'll call you as soon as I find out anything."

Christopher glanced back at the bedroom door behind which his wife slept. *Martha's going to kill me.* "I'll work something out. You're not going alone."

Her sigh of relief was audible through the phone. "Thanks." She continued without missing a beat like she'd known he'd give in. "I've narrowed down his location. Considering his travel time after attacking those college kids, I'm ninety-five percent sure that he's somewhere in Nebraska."

"Kids? Did he kill a second person in the frat house?"

"Frat house? What are you talking about?"

"When was the last time you slept?" There was a creak in the house and Christopher lowered the phone. It didn't repeat. It was either his imagination running wild or the house settling. "Sorry, I didn't catch that."

"I couldn't have been asleep for more than ten minutes. But it was long enough to watch him murder the two boys he was traveling with."

"So, you didn't see the murder in the frat house?"

"No. I nodded off early and woke almost immediately from another vision. I saw him kill the two boys Deb saw him in the car with. Since then, I've been stitching together a timeline to make sure we didn't miss something. I just got off the phone with Agent Montgomery, actually."

Christopher groaned. "Really? Are you sure he's not sending the men with the white coats?"

"No. He sent patrol cars to investigate that strip of highway near the Pony Express Museum. They found the two kids. One was already dead, but the other had a pulse. Unfortunately, it doesn't sound like they'll get any information from him."

"I've never been so glad to hear that someone ignored my advice." Christopher said, twirling the pen around his knuckles. "If you've been awake all this time, that might explain why you didn't see the most recent killing. It must have happened between then and now."

"Makes sense."

"But why didn't I see all three?" he asked.

"I don't know...but it presumably has to do with the entities giving us the information. Maybe they've figured out that we're working together and are playing to our specific strengths. We got close this time. The police were right behind him." Samantha took a long pause.

"So, you think they're watching us?" Chris asked. "Even in the shower?"

"Uhh..."

"Next time I'm going to give them a little show."

"Come on, I don't need to picture that," Samantha said with a laugh. "Thanks. I was beginning to forget how it felt to laugh. On a serious note, did you get anything useful from your dream?"

Christopher sighed. "I don't think so. At least nothing to provide any hints to his whereabouts. He killed a fraternity brother, but I couldn't tell you what chapter. Where do we go from here?" Soft keystrokes filtered through the phone interrupted by mumbling he couldn't make out. "Sam?"

"Hang on... Shit. There's a ton of colleges within spitting distance of where I expect he's at. York, Doane University, Concordia, Nebraska Wesleyan, University of Nebraska Lincoln, the list goes on."

"I've never heard of Doane University. Try eliminating trade schools and community colleges. They wouldn't have a Greek system. And he doesn't know the area, so maybe focus on ones near the highway."

"Okay. Let me narrow my search..." More tapping noises came across the phone. He was definitely on speakerphone. "That leaves the Universities of Nebraska Lincoln and Nebraska Omaha. Wait... The N on the polo shirt he pulled from the kid's bag. If they were driving him, it was probably back to their school. It's Nebraska Lincoln! I need to start taking better notes like you.

"Speaking of, I think I found a pattern. There are several instances of him squatting, either before or after the kills…"

"He's too smart to risk staying at the fraternity house," he interrupted. "Unless he somehow managed to take out everyone inside."

"I agree, but that doesn't rule out somewhere else on campus. He could break into a lecture hall or sleep in a study room at the library."

"Hmm… That's a plausible theory. But it's also plausible that he'd steal another car or continue to hitchhike here."

"True. Did you see car keys in the room?"

"I don't think so, but I wasn't specifically looking for them."

"I'm going to check in with Agent Montgomery again. If we've narrowed him down to the University of Nebraska, Lincoln, I think it's worth it. Do you want to stay on the line?"

At this point, what could it hurt? "Why not," Christopher said with a sigh.

The line rang as Samantha conferenced in agent Montgomery. "I'll book your flight for you. It leaves at seven P.M." The phone rang until the agent's voicemail picked up. "I talked to him not too long ago. Let me try again."

Agent Montgomery picked up the second time. "Sorry, I've got my hands full right now. I'm trying to coordinate the lockdown of the University of Nebraska Lincoln remotely and have been getting more pushback than anticipated." Christopher's jaw dropped. Somehow the agent was one step ahead of them. "One of their fraternities reported a body about half an hour ago."

"I know," Samantha said. "I was calling to tell you that…"

Even though Samantha knew the kid was already dead, the disappointment was clear in her voice. Christopher wanted to console her. To tell her that she couldn't and wasn't expected to save them all.

"Anything else you have that might help? I have a lot more work to do."

"We're... I'm going out of town for a day or so," said Samantha. Christopher closed his eyes and held his breath. "Do I have to tell you that?"

"No. You're not a suspect. Is this because you still think he's after you?"

Christopher bit his lip as Samantha fell quiet. He heard Jessica's warning in his head, telling him not to get involved. The FBI Agent had proven sharp and could handle this... But he was already involved.

"There's a third person who's sharing the visions," Christopher spat out.

"I was wondering when the third party was going to speak up," Agent Montgomery said matter-of-factly.

"City of Chicago Homicide Detective Christopher Reyes... Retired."

"Reyes? Any relation to the officer who assisted bringing Miss Englund in for questioning?"

"My daughter," confirmed Christopher.

"Interesting. And you're having these visions too?"

"Yeah... One last case I guess." The slipped disc in his back sent a tinge of pain down his leg. It was almost as if it hated hearing him say it aloud as much as his ears did.

"Alright. Well, I'm sure we'll be in touch soon."

"Thanks for your time," said Samantha before the agent dropped off the line. "The red line's a five-minute walk from my apartment. Meet me here around four?"

"Red line, four o'clock," Christopher confirmed. "I've got it. Now try to get some sleep."

"You too. Have a good night."

Christopher closed his phone and crept back to the bedroom. As he reached for the doorknob it swung open of its own accord. Martha stood in front of him, arms akimbo. Her nostrils flared and her chin was raised high.

"Is now a good time to clue me in to whatever the hell's going on."

He expected to have at least a few hours to come up with an explanation for jetting off to New York on a moment's notice. "What exactly did you hear?"

"Presume I heard everything but explain like I heard nothing."

Christopher swallowed hard. "There's an urgent FBI case that I'm being asked to consult on..." *Technically not a lie.* "They need me in New York ASAP."

"New York? Tomorrow is when I change rotations. You expect me to work from nine to seven in the morning and then watch the boys all day?"

"Shit, that's right..." Christopher sighed and looked up at the ceiling. "I wouldn't ask if it wasn't an emergency. I'll be gone a day at most."

Martha eyed the notebook clutched at his side and pointed at it. "Does this have to do with that?"

"In a way," he said, nodding. He wondered if she'd read it without his knowledge. "You wouldn't believe me if I told you everything."

Martha stepped forward, wrapping her arms around her husband. "If you have to go, I'll find a way to make it work. I don't know what you're involved in, but promise you'll be careful."

"Of course. You know me."

Chapter 34

Skylos – Lincoln, NB – Tuesday Early Morning

The massive headlight atop the shiny silver California Zephyr blinded Skylos as it pulled into Haymarket station. He was still a block or two away from the platform but could make out a handful of people boarding. The lone ticket collector shone a flashlight up and down the platform and then ducked back inside. Skylos did his best to hurry. Killing the frat boy had drawn the pain away from his leg but he could only move so fast.

"Wait!" Skylos yelled.

The railway employee leaned out again and caught sight of Skylos limping toward the train. He stepped onto the platform and waited.

"Thanks," Skylos said, panting after he'd caught up to the man with bronze skin and a thick mustache.

"Looks like you needed a break," he said in a thick middle eastern accent. The man pointed down at Skylos' knee. "Your leg alright?"

"An old injury. This train goes to Chicago, right?" When the man nodded Skylos climbed aboard, pulling the roller bag behind him. He headed toward the back of the train until the ticket collector cleared his throat.

"Did you make a reservation online, sir?"

"No," Skylos said shaking his head. "Can I buy a ticket from you?"

"There are plenty of seats available in coach and one vacant Roomette. From here to Chicago the fare would be..." he looked at a small book in his hands. "One sixty for coach or three hundred twenty for the suite."

Skylos' handed over two hundred-dollar bills, courtesy of the sale of Tad's equipment. "Coach, please."

"Would you like me to stow either of your bags?"

"No."

"Suit yourself." The man handed Skylos his change and a receipt. "The second floor is all reserved, so take anything down here. Have you been on a California Zephyr before?" Skylos shook his head. "Would you like a quick rundown of the amenities?"

"Sure."

"Every seat reclines and has its own outlet and a fold-down table. Bathrooms are located at both ends of almost every car. The dining car opens at six-thirty for breakfast. There's a quiet car at the back of the train, though at this hour we ask that you keep the noise to a minimum outside the quiet car as well."

"Wi-Fi?" Skylos asked looking around.

The man nodded. "Your browser will give details on how to connect."

Skylos thanked the man and continued to the back of the train. The ticket collector continued his rounds in the opposite direction. Aside from a few individuals reading via an overhead lamp, everyone on the train slept. Finding no seats in an empty row, he moved to the next car. There was an opening in the first row. He stepped over a sleeping teen with headphones on and settled into a vacant window seat on the right side.

Skylos stuffed the suitcase beneath him and watched the scenery fly past the windows. He clutched the backpack in his lap like an infant and reclined the seat. Before he could close his eyes, the windows lit up with flashes of red and blue. Skylos sat back up and pressed his face to the window. He recognized the bus depot he'd left several hours ago. Two police cars sat in the parking lot.

Skylos' eyes smoldered while he chewed his nails. This was Samantha's doing. It was likely that the police were all over the university. And they may have even found the man in the frat house. Did they have the authority to stop the train? If not, would he find them waiting in Chicago?

He looked down at the backpack full of incriminating evidence. If he were smart, he would have dumped the wallets after Sister Mary Elizabeth had spotted them. Skylos checked the windows, looking for a seam or a handle, but they were a single, solid piece. He twisted in his seat and checked the windows flanking him. None of them opened. There was no way to dump the bag out the window.

His head scanned the train car from front to back. He was one of only a few people awake on the car. It wouldn't be too difficult for him to distribute the knives and wallets among the other passenger's luggage. The only other thing incriminating him was the itinerary in his pocket. The papers could be easily flushed or swallowed as a last resort. Provided the police didn't resort to detaining and fingerprinting every passenger, he had a way out.

Skylos sat on the edge of the chair watching mile markers beside the tracks pass by. He checked his watch, noting the time when they passed each. It remained consistent. The train wasn't slowing. He leaned back and wiped the sweat from his brow. Maybe Calliope had intervened somehow. Either way, he'd be in Chicago in about ten hours. Then he'd finally be within striking distance of Samantha.

Too worked up to sleep, Skylos connected the tablet to the train's network. He checked Samantha's blog. It seemed she was finished writing. Of the half a dozen people he killed last week, she hadn't written about any of them. *She must have figured out I was on to her.* It was stupid making a post on the forums. And then he saw the icon at the top of the screen. There was a private message waiting for him. He clicked on it.

The name of the woman you're looking for is Samantha Englund. She lives in an apartment building on Blackhawk in the Goose Island neighborhood. Feel free to ruin her life as she did mine.

Skylos pinched himself. He wasn't dreaming. When he henpecked the name into a public record search a smile spread from ear to ear. This was the best possible end to the day. He had both her name and address now. After traveling halfway across the country his plan had fallen into place.

As he closed his eyes in another bid for sleep the kid next to him shifted, causing his head to fall against Skylos' shoulder. With a snort, the boy started snoring. Skylos pressed his finger to the kid's forehead and shoved his head in the other direction. He longed to straddle the chair and cut his throat out. That would surely stop the awful nasal sounds in an instant. But he had to behave himself.

Skylos rested his head against the cool glass of the window and let his thoughts drift to Calliope. The quiet hum of the air circulating the train, the faint clicking of the tracks, and the boy's snoring all faded away. It was only him and Calliope. His eyes fluttered shut and his back arched as she entwined herself around him. Every inch of his skin tingled. His lips curled up and his pulse quickened. He opened his eyes hoping to get a glimpse of her.

"I'll bring you Samantha soon. I know who she is now," Skylos whispered. He slipped his hand under the backpack and unzipped the fanny pack to finger the curved knife.

I know...

Calliope's lips brushed up against his and he moaned. He fought to keep his eyes open. There would be plenty of time to revel in her touch after he'd dealt with Samantha. Business before pleasure.

They won't stand a chance.

"They? She's not alone?" The euphoria faded. It seemed there were more barriers between him and his love than he realized.

No. There are others.

"I'll kill them all. Tell me how to find them."

Eliminate Samantha and the others will fall. Calliope's voice and warmth faded as she pulled away.

He reached out, desperate to cling on to her. Though she felt more and more real, Calliope was a specter. Once Samantha and the others were out of the way this too would change. He closed his eyes and slipped his hand into his pants.

Chapter 35

Elliot – New York, NY – Tuesday Afternoon

Elliot crept around the corner from the elevators and ducked behind cubicles on the way to his temporary office. Marcie spotted him anyway. He felt foolish; she would have figured out he was there sooner or later anyway. He rose to full height and half-jogged toward the office door.

"Elliot, what the fuck?" She called, plotting an intercept course. "Did you forget how to pick up a phone?"

He put his hands over his ears and winced. "I would have fared better with the construction," he mumbled, stepping around her.

"Don't walk away from me!" Marcie said, raising her voice. A few people milling about the office stopped to stare.

"Seriously Marcie, not now."

She stopped. He never used her real name. Something was wrong. Marcie hurried and caught the door before it swung shut. Elliot sat slumped in the chair in the dark. He shielded his eyes with the back of his hand when she flipped the light switch.

The fluorescent lighting brought out the large black circles under his eyes and the pallor of his face. Her face softened. "You look like shit. Are you hungover?"

"If only. I've been in and out of the hospital since Sunday."

"And that isn't something you thought I'd want to know about, Ell? Are you okay?" She sat down and reached across the desk for his hand. Elliot flinched away.

"Far from it. There's a near-constant ringing in my ear. And I can barely sleep or eat because of this pain in my head. Bright lights and sounds make everything worse. That's why my phone's been off." Marcie reached back and shut off the lights. "Thanks," he said, lowering his hand.

"You drove here like this?" Marcie sat up in the chair, drew her hands back and interlaced her fingers. "What did the doctor say?"

"Doctors, plural. I've been poked and prodded by half the doctors in New York. They've put me through the wringer: spinal taps, a dozen blood draws, and all the abbreviations—EEG, EKG, CT, MRI. Even after that, nobody can figure out what's wrong with me."

"Oh my God... Is there anything I can do?"

"No," Elliot said shaking his head. "Unless you can get me some more Xanax." Marcie raised an eyebrow. "One doctor gave me a prescription for a single pill. A single, magical, pill. It's the only thing that's helped. It took away all the symptoms and I was able to write again. At least for a few hours."

"They won't give you more?" Marcie asked.

"Not until I undergo a full psych exam." He cocked his head and held up a finger. "Not one word."

"There's no shame in seeking psychiatric help. If it's that bad just go."

"Nothing is wrong with my head. I have an appointment with an acupuncturist later."

"Acupuncture? You'd literally rather have someone stab you with needles instead of expressing your feelings? Unbelievable." Marcie sighed and shook her head. "Lord knows I can't force you to do anything against your will…but go talk to the shrink. For me."

"I'll consider it." He pulled the laptop from his bag and placed it on the desk.

"What are you doing?" she asked.

"I'm going to try and work through the pain."

"You should be at home resting."

"Impossible with the construction."

Marcie lingered in the chair for a moment before slowly standing. She wanted to wrap her arms around him but knew better. "Can I at least get you a coffee or something?" Elliot shook his head and pulled the laptop from his bag. She rested her hand on his. "Look, I know we have a complicated past, but you know I'm always here for you."

"Uh-huh," Elliot said, pulling his hand away. He clicked away as Marcie walked out.

Chapter 36

Skylos – Chicago, IL – Tuesday afternoon

Skylos was the first person at the doors when the California Zephyr came to rest in Union Station. He only made it a few steps into the terminal before stopping. The scale of the place was immense. Dozens of tracks and thousands of people milled about. It put the handful of tracks he'd left in Nebraska to shame.

He stumbled forward as the kid who'd been seated next to him pushed past. "Get outta the damn way."

"I should have killed you after all," Skylos mumbled under his breath. Unsure where he was going, he followed the mass of sheeple. They passed by the ticket counters and entered the Great Hall. The marble-floored space was supported by massive carved columns and illuminated via both standing brass lamps and natural light from the vaulted glass ceiling.

Skylos pushed through the crowd to reach one of a dozen benches resembling church pews. He sat and took a moment to think. Since receiving Samantha's address earlier that morning, he had only put together a loose plan. Foremost would be scoping out her place. It would be foolish to strike before he was fully ready, and he couldn't rule out that Samantha was the anonymous contact trying to lure him into a trap.

The tablet connected to the station's free wireless connection, and he began his search. He would need somewhere to stay in the meantime. A huge city like

Chicago would have at least as many homeless shelters as L.A. Although if Samantha, and her accomplices, knew he was coming it would be the first place they looked. Skylos clicked his tongue while thinking of an alternative. Killing Tad and squatting in his house for a few days worked out well. Altadena was a small neighborhood though. Chicago was jam-packed with people.

If he couldn't rely on a shelter, maybe he could take advantage of another program designed to cater to the less fortunate. Habitat for Humanity mainly focused on families. And that meant too many people to control. Subsidized housing would be easy to locate. Though it too had its fair share of families.

Then it hit him. Meals on Wheels catered to elderly or disabled individuals without anyone to care for them. Having assisted in their kitchens back in California, he knew the operation. The organization was always desperate for volunteers. While positions as delivery drivers required background checks, nobody else was vetted. It would be easy enough to get a peek at the delivery list. After a quick query, he found the Meals on Wheels headquarters a mere two miles from the train station. Coincidentally, it was in the same general direction as Samantha's.

Daily deliveries typically went out at noon. He slumped back against the wooden pew. He'd have to wait till tomorrow. Unless he checked other avenues... Community outreach centers and churches often fulfilled the same needs for their members. Serving a smaller clientele gave them different timetables.

He changed his search criteria. Icons representing churches and community centers littered the map. He tweaked the results to only include the two-mile radius around Samantha's apartment building. Results were limited to a few dozen. Skylos wrote down turn-by-turn directions to the first several on a piece of paper and gathered his things.

Skylos sat for a moment on the bench and formulated a plan. First, he'd visit the churches and try to find a place to hunker down for the night. Next, he'd recon Samantha's apartment building. Once he knew what he was dealing with and had gotten a good night's rest, he'd finally take her out of the equation.

"Heh." For almost a week, hunting down Samantha was his singular focus. Not once had he stopped to consider what he'd do afterward. Though now he knew Samantha wasn't really the end. There were two partners to eliminate as well. Calliope said they wouldn't be a problem, but better safe than sorry. Once it was over, he could finally be with Calliope.

Skylos stopped and looked over at the massive stairway that led up to street level. As he stood and grabbed the handle of the suitcase he thought about the panic-filled moment on the train. Dragging a suitcase through the city would slow him down and make him stand out. He hurried through the sea of people to the restroom where he locked himself within the handicapped stall. He consolidated the essentials into the backpack: the UPS uniform, the boot knife, and the other miscellany he'd ordered. Although it took up a lot of space, he kept the blue hoodie. It was his one reminder of home.

He emerged from the stall, dropped the heavy bag of knives into the garbage can and pushed the suitcase under the sink. With a lighter load, Skylos headed out into the Windy City.

...

The three churches at the top of his list were a bust. Neither the first nor second had community centers. While the third did, it was vacant. He followed the directions to the last church. The exterior looked promising. A modern white-brick community center stood beside a gothic style church. Skylos entered the doors and followed placards to a large meeting room. Long tables devoid of chairs filled the space. Steaming coffee carafes and a box of pastries sat on a counter against the wall where he entered. A man gave him a nod and walked past carrying a white cardboard box in both hands. On the other side of the room, individuals came and went from the attached kitchen. They placed plastic containers into the few remaining empty boxes. He smiled. This is what he was looking for.

Skylos walked over and glanced inside a box. Three circular aluminum foil containers with clear lids lined the box. Each held green beans, mashed potatoes, and a thick slice of meatloaf. A sticker with the name and address of their intended recipients were stuck to the lids. This box contained meals for Gretchen, Harold, and Betty.

A woman with curly brown hair and a flowery blouse approached him. "Can I help you?" she asked in a southern drawl.

Skylos kept his head down, memorizing the first address. *Gretchen Ross, fifteen oh-seven North Clybourn Avenue. Apartment six-fifteen. Six-fifteen?* The apartment number was his birthday. Another sign.

"Excuse me, sir?" the lady said again when she reached his side.

He'd only memorized one address. However, he knew it was the *right* one. Skylos smiled at the woman. "Looks delicious. Do you cook everything here?"

The lady gave a faint smile and nodded. "We sure did."

"Sorry," said Skylos, holding his hand out for her to shake. "I'm Sky. I'm new to the area and looking for opportunities to volunteer."

"I'm Josephine. And we could always use another hand. Will you be joining our congregation as well?" Josephine's smile broadened when he nodded.

"Excuse me," said a teenage girl with pigtails in her blonde hair. She stepped between them, placed two more containers in the box, and carried it away.

"You've caught us at a busy time. We're getting ready to deliver dinner to ill congregation members. If you still want to help, I'm sure you could help clean up in the kitchen."

"Sure." Skylos had gotten what he came for but didn't want to raise suspicion by leaving abruptly.

"Come on, I'll introduce you."

He followed Josephine to a cramped galley kitchen where a couple shuffled around each other. A tall mustached man in a tucked in gray polo and pleated pants tied off a garbage bag. The other occupant, a blonde woman in a long, yellow summer dress, placed canisters of spices and other ingredients back into cabinets. They both looked up when Josephine entered.

"Justin, Rebecca, this is Sky. He's new to the area and looking to volunteer. I know we're almost done for the night, but I thought he could still help. I'll leave him in your capable hands." Josephine excused herself.

"Pleased to meet you," said Justin. He hoisted two large black bags over his shoulder and nodded toward Rebecca. "You can help my wife with the dishes."

Rebecca slipped on a pair of green, rubber gloves and filled the sink with water. "I'll wash if you'd like to dry."

Skylos stared at the woman but failed to process a single word she'd said. The blond hair. The rubber gloves. He flashed back to the restroom in the L.A. train station. When he'd failed to kill Candy. He instinctively grabbed a dirty knife from the cutting board next to Rebecca. Bits of translucent onion stuck to the blade, but it would suffice.

"Sky? Did you hear what I said?"

"What?" he said looking up.

"Would you mind drying those wet dishes?"

Skylos shook his head clear. "Yeah. Sorry." He slipped the knife and cutting board into the sink and moved to her other side as her husband re-entered the kitchen. After setting his backpack off to the side, he picked up a towel. She made small talk while scrubbing pots and pans. He politely responded to her questions, keeping his answers brief. Once the sink was empty Skylos wet the towel and wiped down the countertops.

Rebecca nodded, impressed. "Thanks. That should be it for tonight."

"Good night." Skylos swung his pack back onto his shoulders and turned to go.

"There's a group of us here every night. If you ever get the itch to help again, don't hesitate to come back. Especially if you enjoy cooking. I find it a chore."

He sidestepped as Rebecca moved toward him. She shifted her movements to match his in an odd little dance, then wrapped her arms around him.

"Sorry, we're huggers here,"

Skylos' hands remained limp at his side. Rebecca was warm and smelled like lavender but paled in comparison to Calliope's embrace. He broke free from her grasp and returned to the meeting room. The tables were folded and shoved into large closets. As he grabbed a donut, the lost and found caught his eye. Skylos glanced over his shoulder. Rebecca was still in the kitchen tidying up with her husband, but otherwise, the building was empty.

The blue plastic bin held nothing of real value. However, beneath a purple shawl was a blue ball cap that caught his eye. Skylos removed it and pushed the top right side out. The front bore an orange embroidered 'C' with white highlights. Aside from the chewed-up plastic band, it was in good shape. He slipped it onto his head and grabbed his tablet again. Fifteen oh-seven North Clybourn was about a mile away, and roughly equidistant to Samantha's. He plotted a route that took him past Samantha's building; he'd have to waste some time since a delivery was headed to Gretchen's. Skylos followed the digital map away from the church and toward the bridge over the river.

...

The fleeting sun left the sky a deep shade of crimson. One of the windows of the high rise in the distance was Samantha's. He traced a line east along the horizon. The smaller, red brick building had to be the senior housing development.

His stomach growled as he walked past rows of apartment buildings stretching down the right side of the street. His side, however, was dotted with small shops and restaurants. He left the main street and looked for a place to eat.

After a bit of wandering, he came across a small Thai restaurant. A chime sounded in back when he stepped through the door. The restaurant was charming and decorated with the typical eastern flair. To his left, a large carved elephant supported a circular tabletop that held a bowl of mints and carry-out menus. Lucky Cat and Buddha statues sat on the shelves behind the bar. Only two of the dozen tables were occupied, both by couples.

A young Asian woman with long black hair walked out from the doorway behind the bar. "Table for two?"

Skylos shook his head. "Only one." She smiled, grabbed a menu, and headed toward a table by the wall. He pointed. "Window, please."

"Pick any table you want." She waited as he removed his backpack and cap and then took a seat at the table closest to the door.

Only the top few stories of Samantha's building glinted through the slats of the bamboo blinds. It lay just out of reach, shining like a beacon in the sunset. Butterflies flitted around in his stomach.

"Can I get you something to drink?"

He turned his head only far enough to keep the building in his periphery. "A water, please." She nodded and retreated behind the bar. She returned a moment later. After setting down his drink, she leaned over and looked out the window. Finding nothing of interest, she returned to full height.

"Ready to order?"

"Huh? Oh..." Skylos opened the red plastic bound menu. He'd never had Thai food before, and the names revealed little of the dish's content. Pad Si-ew? Lard Nar? Bamee and Wonton? His finger traced down the sheet looking for something he understood. "Pork fried rice." The woman bowed her head slightly, took the menu, and then walked away. Skylos watched the building until it eclipsed the sun.

The waitress returned with an overflowing silver platter of rice. She cleared her throat until he acknowledged her presence. "Can I get you anything else?" Skylos shook his head and dug into his meal. She checked on the other two tables, left a check with one, and then disappeared again.

"Would you like me to wrap that up?" the waitress asked after he'd put the fork down and scooted his chair away from the table.

"Please." He hadn't even finished half and had nowhere to store it, but it could serve as a useful prop. He stood and moved to the bar while he waited for her to package his leftovers. She placed a plastic bag with his leftovers on the counter.

"Keep the change," Skylos said, handing her a twenty. Her eyes lit up.

"Thank you, you're very generous."

Skylos donned his backpack and moved to the door. Watching the waitress from the corner of his eye and stalled. He put the cap back on, situated it just so, checked the zippers on his bag, and then unwrapped a mint from the bowl. When the waitress ducked into the kitchen, he grabbed the entire stack of takeout menus and left.

The streetlamps flickered on one at a time as Skylos walked up the street to Samantha's building. Sweat beaded up on his forehead and his legs grew heavier with every step. He unzipped the pouch around his waist and wrapped his hand around the emerald-green knife. His breathing evened out. It wouldn't be long now.

Skylos hurried to Blackhawk street and traced his eyes up the glass building reaching twenty-some stories into the sky. He walked parallel to it on the opposite side of the street. The entrance at the far end of the building face was flanked by half a dozen massive concrete pillars. His heart beat faster as he approached.

Cars littered the streets around him, leaving a gap only at the building's entrance. A dark sedan sat by itself on the opposite side of the street, blocking a fire hydrant. Skylos slowed his pace, his eyes darting side to side. Something felt off. As he got closer, he noticed a lone occupant inside. He pulled the cap lower and faced the opposite direction as he walked across the street. With his bag of leftovers and a fistful of menus in hand, he entered the building.

Vibrant abstract paintings and low-backed leather couches made the lobby look more like a museum than an apartment building. Two men in white shirts and vests stood behind podiums chatting with guests and residents. The gentle sound of flowing water resonated from a textured stone waterfall behind them. Skylos glanced up and noticed at least two video cameras.

This complicated things. The entire place was under watch twenty-four seven. Skylos kept walking past the concierges and through the rest of the lobby. He walked past a large mailroom and a stairwell. He circled around the twin elevators in the center of the space and by a hallway with a pair of restrooms. As he continued around, another corridor led to a second tower and the rental office.

Skylos doubled back to the restroom. He set the backpack under the sink and stuffed the bag of leftovers inside. To a casual observer, he'd look like he completed a delivery. When he returned tomorrow, he'd be wearing the other delivery costume. Skylos dabbed the sweat glistening on his brow with a paper towel. It was then he realized his mistake.

"Shit!"

Skylos balled his first and threw all his weight behind the punch. Bloody shards of the mirror rained to the floor and countertop. He pressed a handful of paper towels against his knuckles and hurried out the door.

The familiar ache settled into his leg as he moved through the corridor to the other building. Skylos made a beeline to the exit and reached the intersecting street. Following the map in his head, he hustled to the next cross street and turned right. Looking over his shoulder, he wound up and down streets, snaking his way toward Clybourn. When he was certain no one was following, he lifted the paper towels. Cuts between his already bruised knuckles oozed a slow but steady stream of blood. He folded the bloodied paper several times and kept walking.

The twin buildings of the senior housing facility were a far cry from the architectural masterpiece he'd just left. Rusty air conditioning units desperately hung onto the faded brick exterior. The windows were so hazy that even if the sun were high, he wouldn't have to worry about shielding his eyes from any glare.

He followed the tree-lined drive to a parking lot with room for only a handful of cars. Behind the lot, a gazebo stood between plots in a vegetable garden. Although a bit dilapidated, it looked like a nice community. As he stepped closer, he realized the reason for the small lot. There was no first floor to the building, it was raised to house parking below it.

"Fifteen oh-seven North Clybourn," Skylos said aloud while looking back and forth between the two buildings. They bore the same address. The building to his left was 1507A and the other 1507B. He sighed. The plastic lid didn't specify.

Since the ringing and Calliope's whispers were always strongest in his left ear, he checked that building first. He studied the names beside the panel of door buzzers. The sticker for apartment 615's said R. Alberts. He was in the wrong place but decided to rest for a moment and attend to his injuries. Skylos pulled the first aid kid from his backpack and bandaged his hand with gauze and tape.

The opposite building had apartment 615's resident listed as G. Ross. The buzzer sounded a flat tone as he pressed it down. No response came. He pressed again and counted to three before releasing. Still nothing. He ran both hands down the panel, triggering every buzzer in the building.

One elderly voice hungry for a visitor after another flooded the static-filled speaker. Skylos kept quiet and waited. When the door let out a deep growl, he slipped inside. The voices faded as the elevator doors closed and it rose. He removed the leftovers from his bag and held onto them. The ploy had worked once before.

The sixth-floor hallway was quiet and empty. It had that unquantifiable smell of old people. A knock on Gretchen's door received no response. He grabbed the lock pick pouch and slid out a tension wrench and an S-shaped pick. If she were asleep, his job would be even easier. Skylos took a knee, slipped the metal implements into the keyhole, and did as he'd practiced on his journey here. Applying slight pressure to the tension wrench, he raked the pick across the pins.

They recessed and stuck in place. He put more pressure on the wrench, but the lock held fast. The wrench slipped in his fingers and the pins reset.

Another attempt resulted in the same failure. He sighed. The practice lock with visible internals made things too easy. He wished he'd have taken an opportunity to use them on an actual lock. He stood up and kicked the door. After a deep breath, he took a knee and dug out a differently shaped pick.

The fifth time he jiggled the pick back and forth there was an audible click. Skylos clenched his fist and shook it in celebration. The door swung inward, the security chain snapping taut.

"Is someone there?"

Skylos looked up. An elderly woman with a yellow shawl wrapped around a white nightgown peered out through the crack. Tubes from her nose down to an oxygen tank on wheels. He got to his feet and smiled. "Good to see you, Gretchen. Sorry that I'm so late..." He lifted the plastic bag. "But I brought dinner."

"Who are you?" Gretchen asked, leaning her face into the gap.

"Sky. From church," he said, raising his voice. "I've brought dinner." The plastic bag crinkled as Skylos shook it in his hand, hoping to draw her attention.

The old woman smacked her dry lips. "I already had dinner. Someone was here a few hours ago. Tim or Richard or someone."

Skylos shook his head. "I know, but Justin asked me to swing by. He was stuck in the kitchen all night. We're cousins."

She smiled. "I remember Justin. He's a nice young man and has such a pretty wife." The door closed and metal rattled as she unhooked the chain. Skylos yanked the metal picks from the knob and dropped them back into their pouch before the door reopened. "I'm not hungry, but I wouldn't mind some more company." She stepped aside, letting him in.

"I'll put this in the refrigerator for later, then." Skylos dropped his bag and glanced around the small apartment on the way to the kitchen. Unless someone was behind the shut bedroom door, they were alone.

Skylos put the plastic bag in the refrigerator. As he returned to the front room Gretchen smiled up at him from a plastic-covered couch with a white and green fleur-de-lis pattern. He stood in front of her and pondered how to proceed. Family members and nurses could frequent the halls. He'd have to be careful and keep the blood and screaming to a minimum. The woman looked like she'd had a long life and deserved a quick death.

"Something wrong, dear?" Gretchen asked.

"No..."

Gretchen shivered as a cool breeze swept through the apartment. "There must be a draft." She tightened her crocheted around her shoulders.

A tingle resonated throughout Skylos' body as Calliope enveloped him. Jealousy prevented him from enjoying it. The old woman had reacted to her presence too. His eyebrows lowered as he stared at the old bag.

Calliope was his and he couldn't bear to share her with anyone.

"I'm sorry, but I'm suddenly not feeling well," Gretchen said with a tremble in her voice. "I'm going to make some tea and go to bed."

Be a gentleman and get her the kettle, whispered Calliope's as she brushed the hair over his left ear.

"Yes, my love," Skylos whispered. He turned back toward the old woman. "Let me put the kettle on for you."

Skylos ducked into the kitchen and looped his fingers through the handle of the stainless-steel kettle on the stove as if it were a pair of brass knuckles. When he returned to the front room, Gretchen had moved near a small bookshelf by the bathroom door. Her hand rested on the telephone's receiver. She turned around and faked a smile when he approached.

A dull thud resounded through the apartment as the kettle came down upon Gretchen's temple. Her body crumpled to the floor, sending the oxygen tank sprawling to the side.

Skylos dropped to one knee beside her body and placed his hand on her chest. Albeit slowly, it still rose and fell. He grabbed a blue throw pillow with an embroidered calico cat and held it over her face.

Chapter 37

Samantha and Christopher – New York, NY – Wednesday Morning

Samantha stared out the cab's window. The traffic, pedestrians, and sprawling buildings didn't register; she only saw the face of an old woman being bludgeoned and then suffocated. This one upset her the most out of all the dreams thus far. They'd done everything right, but Skylos continued to elude them. To make things worse, the death told them nothing useful. The small, featureless apartment room could have been anywhere. The City of Chicago was enormous, especially when including the surrounding metropolitan area. Retirement communities were abundant, even within spitting distance of her own apartment. She blinked away a tear in the corner of her eye.

"I know it's hard, but you can't form personal attachments," Christopher said, placing his hand on her shoulder.

Samantha nodded. He was right, of course, but she couldn't help but feel like she'd failed in her duty.

The taxi pulled to a stop beside the skyscraper the Penguin Random House offices called home. Samantha paced outside the front doors while waiting for Christopher. After paying the driver he extracted himself from the car with a groan and joined her side.

"Do you think they'll see us?" she said with trepidation in her voice.

"We're not giving them a choice. I'm not leaving without answers, even if it takes calling in every marker I've built over forty years in law enforcement."

The edges of Samantha's lips curled up in a smile. Christopher always seemed to know what to say, even if it was usually an awful pun. Imbued with more confidence, she pushed through the revolving door. Bookshelves lined the walls, giving the appearance of a bookstore rather than an office lobby. Chris inspected displays of award-winning novels while Samantha continued to the reception desk. A young clean-cut man in a suit looked up from behind the desk adorned with fresh-cut flowers.

"Good morning. How can I help you?" he asked.

Samantha looked down at the man's name tag and smiled back. "Hi Gary, could you please ring someone from the legal department for me?"

Gary smiled and glanced at Christopher picking books off the shelf. "Can I have your name?"

"Samantha Englund." Gary clicked the mouse several times. Her heart sank. She knew what was coming next.

"I'm sorry, I don't see any appointments under that name. I'd suggest calling your party directly and making an appointment. They have better control of their schedules than I do. Otherwise, I can't fit you in for another week."

"I flew in from Chicago to resolve an important matter in person. I received a legal notice but haven't succeeded in reaching anyone. There's isn't anyone I can meet with?"

"I'm afraid not."

Samantha brushed her hair over her ear and leaned forward. "I'm an editor for Windy City Publishers in Chicago. Could you extend me some professional courtesy, Gary?"

There was a loud bang as several hardcover books fell to the floor. Samantha and Gary looked over. Christopher picked them up, stacked them on top of each other, and placed them back on the shelf. He walked over to her side and whispered, "Let me borrow your phone."

Without saying a word, she pulled it from her purse, entered the unlock code, and handed it over. He walked away while tapping at the screen. Samantha hoped he was calling in one of the favors he mentioned. Gary turned back to the computer for a moment.

"I'm sorry that you've traveled all this way, but I'm afraid I can't fit you in today. If you're still in town next week I can arrange something for you."

"Please. I'm begging you." Samantha batted her eyes at the young man. Unfortunately flirting was never her strong suit, and it came across like something caught in her eye.

"If you leave your number, I'll let you know if something opens up."

Samantha frowned and was about to recite her number when something poked her in the back of her right arm. She turned to find Christopher holding out her phone.

"Excuse me," she said taking it and stepping away from the counter.

A picture of a cute brunette with an upturned nose took up the screen. Samantha zoomed out and scrolled over a networking site profile for Marcie Andrews—a senior editor for Penguin Random House. She glanced back at Christopher.

"Worth a shot," he whispered with a shrug of his shoulders.

Samantha returned to the counter. Gary flashed the fake smile of customer service she knew well.

"Would you like to leave your phone number now, Miss Englund?"

"Could you please ring Marcie Andrews first?" She crossed her fingers below the counter. "She should be expecting a call from Samantha Englund on behalf of Windy City Publishers. Tell her it's related to the California story."

Gary studied Samantha while she held her breath. "I'm not sure whether she has any availability."

"Could you please ring her? She'll make time for this."

He placed his hand on the phone for a moment, then let out a little sigh. "One moment please."

"Miss Andrews, Samantha Englund from Windy City Publishers is in the lobby. She wanted to discuss... Sorry. Yes, I'll check your calendar."

"Samantha Blackblood!" Samantha yelled, leaning over the counter. Gary lowered the phone and covered the receiver with his hand. She lowered her voice. "Sorry. Tell her my last name is Blackblood."

Gary lifted the phone back to his ear and raised his eyebrows. "Yes... That's what she said. Yes, Miss Andrews." Gary hung up the phone and cleared his throat. "She'll be expecting you on the fourteenth floor."

Samantha wrapped her arms around Christopher when they got into the elevator.

"That was brilliant! How'd you know?"

He shrugged and gave her a coy smile. "Detective stuff. People share too much online. I figured we'd have a better chance if we could find an actual contact outside of the legal department. It's like the three bears. The editor-in-chief wouldn't have made time for us. An associate editor likely wouldn't know jack. But a senior editor? Just right. Something told me she'd be the one."

Marcie, in a black pencil skirt and red blazer, was waiting for them as soon as the elevator door opened.

"Samantha, I've been trying to get in touch with you. Who's this?"

"Christopher Reyes," he said reaching his hand out. Marcie ignored it.

"Hurry up," she said, turning away from the elevator and leading them down the hall. Christopher and Samantha looked at each other and then hurried to catch up. "I'm dying to hear how you found your way here and what the hell is going on. But first, we need to get Elliot to see the light."

They passed several workspaces. Samantha looked in awe at the sea of editors. Each of their stations had convertible standing desks, several monitors, and comfy-looking ergonomic chairs. The number of people milling about on this floor alone was greater than everyone at her previous employer. Marcie pulled open a door to an office and entered. Christopher and Samantha followed.

A dark-haired man with a receding hairline wearing sunglasses sat behind a desk in the room. He continued talking to himself under his breath while he worked. The muscles on his face contorted as if each keystroke brought him physical pain.

"Elliot, meet Samantha Englund."

"Any relation to Robert?" he asked, still not bothering to look up.

"What?" Marcie asked. She looked back at Samantha who shook her head. "No. I don't think so."

"Then what does she want?"

Marcie stepped forward and slammed her fist on the desk. Elliot covered his ears.

"You don't understand. This is Samantha Blackblood."

He rose from the desk. "So, you're the bitch that's been passing my work off as her own? Did you bring your geriatric boyfriend along as a scare tactic?"

Christopher puffed his chest out and took a step forward. Marcie beat him to it.

"Shut your mouth, sit down, and listen for once!"

Elliot winced and sat back down. "Come on. My head's killing me."

"Please Elliot, stop typing and listen for five minutes."

"I can't. The ideas are finally flowing again." He looked up long enough to say: "Don't worry, I can multitask. Now, what the hell does she want?"

With a sigh, Marcie turned to Samantha and smiled. "That's the best we'll get. Go ahead."

Samantha paused a moment. She didn't think they'd make it this far, much less thought about what to say. "We flew here from Chicago to get some answers. Christopher and I are having the same visions. Skylos has killed at least nine people and now he's coming after me. I don't know why the three of us were chosen, but I think it'll take all of us working together to stop him."

Elliot laughed. "Did Marcie put you up to this? The only unnatural thing going on is that you thought you could get away with this. You ought to be locked up alongside your crazed lacky that's reenacting the killings."

Marcie spoke up again. "Look at her site. She hasn't written in a week. I keep telling you this. I've researched each killing and they line up."

"The first few bear a resemblance; I'll give you that. But the rest don't. Your theory that the killer's real and we're independently writing the same thing is insane. What do you think, we have the same Muse?"

Marcie's jaw dropped and Samantha mouthed the word again. Muse. Elliot failed to make the connection and waited for someone to defend their position. Christopher snorted before walking forward and holding his notebook out to Elliot.

Elliot stopped typing and snatched the book out of his hand. He chuckled as he flipped through the first few pages. "All this proves is that you're a shitty caricature artist... I don't know what you expect me to see." He kept flipping pages.

Samantha glanced nervously back at Christopher. "The faces aren't familiar?"

"No. Why would they..." Elliot's eyes darted across the pages as he read on. After the first few pages, the notes stopped matching his story, but they were still familiar somehow. The notebook fell from his hands as he recalled the original inspiration for his later chapters. The ringing in his ear and the pain in his head ceased.

It wasn't possible, but the scribblings mirrored his initial ideas.

The ambushed UPS driver, the businessman with the flat tire, the college kids. All the raw ideas before he transformed them into something usable were in the book. A shiver ran down his spine. Christopher couldn't have captured those details unless he had a direct line to his thoughts.

Elliot flipped to the last page and found the proverbial nail in the coffin. The center had a sketch of an elderly woman. Like the others, the face was unfamiliar, but the narrative he knew intimately. The plastic-covered couch, tea kettle, and the pillow were still fresh in his mind... the very details he was presently preparing for print.

He looked up at Marcie, dumbfounded. Her mouth twitched in the faintest of smiles. Marcie was right.

Each death he'd concocted represented an actual person. Elliot spun the notebook to face the group and tapped it several times before he could summon any words.

"How? How is any of this possible?"

Chapter 38

Skylos – Chicago, IL – Wednesday Afternoon

Skylos laid the wrinkled UPS uniform on Gretchen's couch and searched through the closet. On the top shelf, next to a box full of old towels, was a dusty iron. He took it to the dining room table and after a couple of passes had the outfit crisp and professional looking. Skylos slipped it on over his own clothes. With the hat and signature pad, nobody would give him a second look.

He ran through his checklist again. *Directions, uniform, bag, knife.* The prep was done—he had Samantha's real name and address. He'd dug further and confirmed that she had no significant other and that nobody else was registered at her address. While it didn't rule out an overnight guest, he'd manage. He had the sheath with the boot knife strapped above his right ankle as a backup weapon.

The only thing left was a box to complete the disguise. He checked each room of the apartment and found nothing suitable. After gathering all his things, he headed to the parking garage. He lifted the lid of a dumpster near the stairs and peeked inside. A rectangular box about two feet long sat wedged beneath two garbage bags. Skylos leaned forward and pried it out. Aside from a wet stain, the box was in a decent condition. He pulled pieces of duct tape from his fanny pack and folded them over, resealing the box from the inside.

As he walked back to Samantha's building, he kept an eye out for dark sedans. The coast was clear. Since all his prior attacks were at night nobody would be looking for him during the day. He raised his head confidently and strolled past a concierge giving restaurant suggestions to a young couple. He was invisible.

A shiver cascaded down his spine as he tapped the elevator button. A shrill alarm sounded from the fire panel between the elevators and every warning light glowed for a fraction of a second. His knees buckled as Calliope's hand ran up his thigh. Skylos bit his lip and drew blood. He had to focus. There would be plenty of time to savor her presence once he finished.

"We're nearly there," Skylos whispered. She said nothing in return, but he felt her fingernails scratch down the small of his back.

Skylos let out a moan as a boy in his early teens wearing a jersey and ball cap walked up with his dog. The boy struggled to hold back the basset-corgi mix as it barked and lunged at the air next to him. Skylos held his breath.

"There's nothing there, stupid," the kid said.

The elevator to his left dinged and three people got off, all of them giving the dog a wide berth. Skylos stepped inside, keeping an eye on the still barking dog.

"I'll wait for the next one," said the kid. Skylos smiled and pressed the button for the fifth floor. "What the hell is wrong with you?"

When the doors reopened, Skylos followed the exit signs to the stairs and took them up one more floor. He left the backpack in the stairwell, licked his lips, and found her unit near the end of the hall. The Karambit was cool against his skin as he slipped his pinky through the ring. The blade sprang open with a satisfying click. He hid the knife behind the empty box and knocked on the door.

There was no response. He slammed his fist against the door in anger. One of the cuts on his knuckles opened, leaving a small smear of blood behind.

It's okay, he tried to calm himself. I *can go back to my bag and get the lockpicks.*

As he turned, he caught faint singing through the door on the opposite side of the hall. Skylos pressed his ear to apartment 601. A woman sang along to a song unfamiliar to him. He smiled. The apartment across the way would be an equally convenient place to stage an ambush. Hell, maybe her neighbor was one of the two people hunting Calliope. Skylos folded the Karambit and slipped it back into the fanny pack before clearing his throat and knocking. After a moment, both the music and singing stopped.

"Hello?" called a voice through the door.

He played up his stuttering. "I was trying to de-deliver a pa-package to your neighbor. Could you sign?"

"Uhh..."

Skylos backed up and lifted the box up so she could see it through the peephole. A chain clinked against the doorframe as the door opened. A redhead in fleece pajama pants with skulls and a tight pink tank top exposing her midriff stood inside the doorway.

"Sorry, I didn't want to leave it," he said, lifting the box in his hands. He raised to his tiptoes to scan for signs of other occupants inside. It looked empty.

She narrowed her eyes at him. "You could have left it in the mailroom."

"There's been a lot of reported thefts recently." He quickly added, "It feels like a laptop."

"A laptop?" The woman's eyes raised slightly.

"Can I set it down and grab a signature from you?" He smiled. "I'm Walter, by the way."

She returned the smile with a mouthful of perfect teeth. "Sure." She stepped back, allowing him into the entryway. "I'm Yvonne, nice to meet you, Walter. Samantha will be ecstatic."

"Oh?"

"Yeah. She... uh... lost her laptop." Skylos handed her the digital signature pad and carefully placed the box in the corner. Without looking, Yvonne scrawled her name on the surface. Skylos angled his body away from her and slipped the boot knife from its sheath. He stood, keeping the blade concealed behind his leg.

Yvonne returned the device and pulled her phone from her pocket. "Thanks, Walter, have a good day."

Skylos stared at the phone and stayed his hand. He couldn't pass up an opportunity to pry for more information. "Were you going to call her?"

"What?" Yvonne said. Her face twitched and she took a small step backward.

"This may sound odd, but would you mind if I listened in? I take great joy when people get what they've been waiting for."

Her lips parted in a smile again. "That's actually kind of sweet. You don't see many people who take pride in their work these days."

Yvonne dialed and Skylos shivered as Calliope's hand touched his wrist beside the large knife. It wasn't Samantha, but it would do for now.

Chapter 39

*Samantha, Christopher, and Elliot – New
York, NY – Wednesday Afternoon*

"And that's what led us here," said Samantha, finishing the recap of the last week. To everyone's surprise, Elliot managed to keep his mouth shut throughout the entire exchange. The office fell quiet for a moment. No one knew what to say next.

Samantha's phone rang in her purse, breaking the silence for them. She grabbed it and checked the display. It was Yvonne. *She knew I left town. Is something wrong?*

"Sorry, I'm going to take this quickly." Samantha put the phone to her ear and pulled the office door open.

"Hey Von, I'm still in New York. Is everything okay?"

"Yeah. Everything's fine. I figured you'd want to know that the UPS guy is here with your new laptop. He's leaving it with me."

"Laptop? I didn't order a laptop. Is my name on the box?"

Yvonne paused. "I don't know."

The color drained from Samantha's face. He was in their building. Across the hall from where she'd been not more than twenty-four hours ago. "Yvonne, get out of there now!"

All eyes turned to Samantha, who shook in fear. Christopher bolted out of his chair, wrapped an arm around her for support, and grabbed the phone. He hit the speaker button. Marcie and Elliot froze in place.

"Yvonne?" Samantha called again.

A loud bang came through the speaker; the sound of a phone hitting a hard surface. Grunts of a struggle followed, then a piercing scream, and finally silence.

"You son of a bitch!"

The line was quiet for a moment and then heavy breathing came across the speaker. "We'll see you soon, Samantha." The call ended.

Marcie held her hand over her mouth. Elliot began typing again.

Samantha wiped her eyes and pulled free from Christopher's grasp. He flipped his phone open and dialed. Makeup, change, and other personal items flew through the air as Samantha dug to the bottom of her purse. Her trembling hand came back with Agent Montgomery's creased business card. She let the purse fall to the floor as she dialed.

"He's in my apartment building!" Samantha yelled as soon as the line picked up.

The agent spoke in a calm voice. "Are you still inside? I want you to lock the door and barricade it if possible."

"No. I'm in New York. But Yvonne... my neighbor. She..."

"I'm already on my way. Do you want me to stay on the phone?" Samantha got choked up again and couldn't respond. "I'll take care of it. Have Chris call with your flight information."

Christopher took the phone from her again. Without missing a beat, Marcie rushed to her side and helped her back to the chair she'd been sitting in earlier.

"Agent Montgomery, it's Detective Reyes. We'll be on our way back as soon as possible. Let me know if you need anything else." Christopher gave him his own cell number and then picked up Samantha's purse and slipped her phone back inside it.

Samantha sobbed. "Yvonne's my neighbor..." she said, her voice muffled by her hands. "If I..."

Marcie knelt by her side and placed her arm around her. "I'm so sorry. None of this is your fault."

Christopher paced in the small room. "How did he figure out where she lived?"

"I may have sent him." Elliot hung his head.

"What!" screamed Christopher. He reached over the desk and grabbed Elliot's collar in a vise grip. Elliot gasped and raised his hands to protect his face.

"Chris, stop," said Samantha, drying her eyes with her sleeve. "I want to hear his explanation." Christopher freed Elliot and loomed over him, cracking his knuckles one at a time.

"I was pissed about you stealing my work. So, several nights ago I wrote you into my story. I was the one directing Skylos to Chicago after you. I... didn't think this would happen."

"What did you think would happen?" yelled Christopher as he balled his fist again. He relaxed when Samantha chuckled.

"If that were the case, I would have forced him to turn himself in. It wasn't you. You didn't even know my real name or that I lived in Chicago until this afternoon."

"What are you writing now, Ell?" asked Marcie. "Were you trying to undo this mess?"

Elliot turned the laptop around to face the group. The browser showed an electronic receipt for airline tickets back to Chicago.

"I'm sorry about your friend. This is the next available flight. It boards in three and a half hours."

"Thank you." Samantha sniffled.

Marcie also locked eyes with Elliot and mouthed "Thank you".

"It's the least I can do. And I'll just expense them."

Marcie growled at him.

Samantha wiped her eyes again and straightened in the chair. "Okay. We have a limited amount of time before we have to get to the airport. Let's make the most of it. How do we stop him?"

"Stop him?" said Elliot. "How's that *our* job? With the amount of evidence he's been leaving at every crime scene, the police should be all over him."

"But they're not," said Marcie. "So where do we start?" Samantha looked up at Christopher who was still staring down at the desk with rage in his eyes.

"We can't follow normal police investigative procedures. Even with our detailed visions, we can't fully investigate the scene. Even if I had the clout, the case became the FBI's jurisdiction once he crossed state lines. The three of us—no offense Marcie—are the closest thing we have to witnesses." Christopher scratched the stubble around his jaw. "We'll have to piece together whatever we can."

"I have something that might help," Marcie said, grabbing her tablet. "I put together a comparative analysis of both your stories. Though since Samantha stopped writing after the second murder, it's not much." Elliot stared at her. "What? I've been trying for the better part of a week to convince you that this wasn't a coincidence."

"Go ahead," said Christopher after grabbing a pen off the desk and opening his notebook. Marcie's eyes darted across the surface of the tablet.

"Both story's murder scenes are identical. Almost word-for-word. Samantha's 'Bud-K Killer' is never described physically. Elliot, however, paints him as a tall, mocha-skinned man in his early twenties bearing a pronounced scar on his cheek."

"You can ignore that," Elliot said as Christopher began sketching. "I completely fabricated his physical description. It wasn't inspired in the same manner as the other aspects."

"I never got a look at him since I see everything from his point of view," added Samantha. "All I know is that he has a handicap—some sort of injury to his leg."

"It could be faked," said Elliot. "Several of the more notorious serial killers and mass murderers would fake limps as a tactic to appear less threatening. Or to lure people."

"I don't think that's the case. It was pretty evident in his last few kills. The limp was more pronounced during the attack on the highway."

"Okay. It's not much, but it's a start," said Christopher as he jotted the information down. "Anything else, Marcie?"

"The other major difference is the killer's motivation. Samantha had him being manipulated by an unnamed demon. Elliot chalked it up to a mental illness manifesting as a voice called Calliope who coerced him to kill." Christopher put the pen down.

"Calliope?" Samantha said. The name wasn't overly familiar, but she'd heard the name before. Maybe she'd muttered it while seeing through Skylos' eyes.

"If I'm not mistaken," said Marcie. "Calliope was one of the Muses." She fiddled with the tablet again. "Yup, Calliope was the Muse of epic poetry and the wisest and most assertive of the Muses. It says here that by some accounts, she was one of Ares' lovers. That may explain her lust for violence."

"Ares? As in the god of war?" said Christopher. Marcie nodded.

"Seriously?" Elliot blurted out, scanning the room for a reaction. "We're pinning all the deaths on a mythological being?"

Without hesitation, Samantha nodded. "I'd bet my firstborn on her being the inspiration behind the killings. Which means it may be a different Muse making us write about it."

"I... Umm..." Elliot shook his head, failing to come up with a more convincing argument. He threw his hands in the air and nodded. "Okay."

"What else do we know about the killer?" inquired Christopher. "Why did she choose him? Hell, why did they choose us?"

"Maybe we're both right about our motives," said Elliot pointing back and forth between Samantha and himself.

"What do you mean?" asked Marcie.

"Samantha wrote about a killer who heard a demon, and I wrote about a man whose mental illness manifested as such. What if his mental illness allows him to communicate with Calliope?

"I've done a lot of research on serial killers during my career. There is some science behind who becomes a killer. A neuroscientist from the University of California studied the brain scans of several serial killers. After comparing to his own scan, he found a large number of similarities..." Elliot made circles with his hand as he tried to recall the details. "Certain indicators in the orbital cortex or something. Those markers signaled a predisposition toward sociopathic tendencies. Not that everyone who shares the trait becomes a serial killer..."

Samantha held up her hand. "Are you trying to say that voices heard by mentally ill people aren't caused by the illness? Instead, it makes them susceptible to hearing actual demons or spirits? That's...even more disturbing."

"So, the three of you happen to have," Marcie made air quotes. "Serial killer brains. And it's made you susceptible to manipulation by a Muse?"

Christopher shrugged. "The psychic we met with did say something to a similar effect. Not everyone has the ability to see or commune with spirits due to how they're wired."

Elliot stared past the group at the wall, his mind churning. "Holmes, Jack the Ripper, the Freddy Krueger Killer. How do we know Calliope wasn't puppeteering them too?"

Marcie shook her head. "An interesting theory, but it doesn't help us. We need to focus on this subject. Do we know anything else about who he is?"

It was Elliot and Samantha's turn to say something in unison. "Skylos," they mumbled.

"Skylos?" repeated Marcie. "That's close to the name you used... But it never appeared in Samantha's story."

"Because it's a stupid name," said Elliot. "But if we both knew it, there must be something to it. Unfortunately, it's got to be a nickname or an anagram, which doesn't help us identify him."

Marcie's fingers flew across the tablet. "How about the Greek word for dog?"

"It's not his name; it's what she's made him," Samantha said. "It may not help, but it points back to the Greeks. Which further reinforces our Muse theory."

"Yeah, but it still doesn't put us any closer to stopping him," said Marcie. The group sat in silence for a few minutes until Samantha spoke up again.

"I have an idea to get ahead of him... There are three of us. If we each take a different eight-hour shift, we can have someone sleeping at any given time. That would at least allow us to be more reactive when we have the dreams.”

“I don’t think that’ll work,” said Elliot. “I haven’t been dreaming. My ideas just seem to pop into my head randomly.”

Christopher leaned over to Samantha and whispered. “Do you think he’s being influenced while he’s awake? Like Skylos?”

“I’m sitting right here...” Elliot said, standing up from his chair. “This may be an unpopular suggestion, but what if we give him what he wants? Use Samantha as bait.”

Marcie punched him in the shoulder with all her strength.

“Ow!”

“We’re all involved in this, Ell. What if the killer’s after Sam because Calliope knows her visions are the strongest? If we offer her up what’s stopping him from coming after Chris next? Or you?” Elliot lowered his head. “For all we know, I’m likely on the shitlist as well.”

“I wasn’t suggesting we sacrifice her,” Elliot said, rubbing his shoulder. “Just use her to lure him out.”

“We’re not taking that risk,” said Christopher.

“Fine. I guess we don’t know what a Muse is capable of anyway. Hey, if we do stop Skylos, who’s to say Calliope doesn’t convince someone else to go after Samantha?”

Marcie gave him a glare that would have melted glass. Elliot looked like he wanted to say more but shut his mouth.

“Come on Samantha, we’d better get going so we can make our flight,” Christopher said through clenched teeth.

“I’ll walk you out,” said Marcie. She mouthed the word “asshole” to Elliot before following their guests out.

"Can you answer something for me before you go?" Elliot asked. Samantha's curiosity got the better of her and she turned around. "That stuff you do online. Writing in real-time with an audience. You've found people who enjoy that? No offense, but it sounds boring as hell."

Samantha sighed. "I'm sure it's not for everyone, but enough people seem interested. It's no different from live-streaming."

"Huh."

Marcie led Samantha and Christopher back to the elevator, stopping to retrieve their boarding passes from a printer. She rode down to the lobby with them in silence. When the doors opened again, she had Gary call a cab.

"I'm sorry about Elliot. He's... Well, I won't sugarcoat it. He's a selfish bastard. But he means well. Sometimes."

"I don't understand how you can work with him," Samantha said.

Marcie chuckled. "Believe it or not but we used to date. It quickly became clear who the most important person in the relationship was and things didn't last. I still try to keep him in line as much as possible."

The group exchanged contact information and Marcie waited with them inside the building until the taxi arrived. When it pulled up, she gave Christopher a quick hug and held Samantha in a long embrace.

"Stay safe," Marcie whispered.

Samantha looked out the back window as the taxi pulled away. Marcie stood on the curb watching them drive off. When she couldn't see her any longer, Samantha turned back around.

"I wouldn't wish this upon anyone, but I'd prefer Marcie was involved instead of Elliot."

"In a way, I feel she is," said Christopher.

Chapter 40

Skylos – Chicago, IL – Wednesday Afternoon

Skylos smiled through the pain from his aching groin and chest as he jogged down the stairwell. Fresh blood—his blood—trailed down the three parallel lines stretching from his collarbone to breast. The harpy had attempted to claw his heart out. In exchange, he'd nearly decapitated her. She deserved every bit of it.

Samantha was in New York, possibly meeting with a co-conspirator. But there was real fear and anger in her voice. The death of her friend would likely cause her to rush home. Unfortunately, it wasn't safe to stick around her apartment and give her a warm welcome.

Skylos pulled the shirt collar tight and broke into a brisk walk as he crossed through the apartment lobby and out into the street. He kept his head down and slowed to a normal pace. There was a good amount of blood on the uniform, but the dark brown color hid it from a cursory inspection. It bought him a little bit of time. There was a coffee shop that he passed the night before. It offered a clear view of the street and had complimentary Wi-Fi.

Two squad cars raced up the street as soon as the glass door closed behind him. Skylos didn't look back and locked himself in the single-stall bathroom. He crawled along the floor, keeping below the mirror, and wiggled out of the brown uniform. After wrapping the clothes around the signature pad, he discarded the entire bundle in the garbage can. While putting gauze over the injury on his chest, someone knocked on the door.

"One minute."

Skylos flushed the toilet, crawled to the sink, and pulled a wad of towels from the dispenser. He wet them in the sink and wiped down his face and hands. After throwing on his blue sweatshirt and pulling the Cubs hat over his brow, he opened the bathroom door. "All yours," he said to a woman juggling a bulky diaper bag and a squirming infant.

"What can I get you?" the middle-aged brunette behind the counter said with a smile.

"A turkey sandwich...and lemonade, please."

"Would you like the sandwich toasted?" she asked, pulling it from the glass case between them.

"Cold's fine." He handed over a gift card and then stuffed a five-dollar bill in the tip jar. With food and drink in hand, he grabbed a stool at the counter alongside the window. He unwrapped his sandwich and grabbed the tablet. If he could find a house for rent nearby, he'd be able to stay close and strike after Samantha returned and things died down. While eating, he pecked 'temporary housing Chicago' into the browser. There were two rental properties within walking distance. The closer host had a private room available for just under two hundred dollars a night.

Skylos thumbed through the wad of money in his pouch. He had enough cash to cover a single night, but reservations through the site required a credit card. The second problem he ran into was that the address wasn't listed. An exterior photo of the building, however, was available. He compared that image to those from Google's Street View map and narrowed it down to one of three condominiums. Close enough.

He returned the tablet to his bag. As he zipped up the bag his eyes followed a familiar black sedan speeding up the street. While he couldn't be certain it was the same car from the other night, he recited the few letters he'd caught.

"N-O-A. N-O-A."

The man beside him sipping coffee lowered the paper and looked up. Skylos smiled and raised his lemonade in a salute before taking a sip.

Once finished with his meal, Skylos walked to the vicinity of the rental property. The block was filled with a group of all-brick rowhouses. Kids shouted in glee at the baseball diamond across the street. Skylos looked at the identical two-story homes, palmed his remaining silver pocketknife, and approached the unit in the middle. The front stoop served the doors of two units, each protected with a barred metal gate. He pressed the doorbell on the right.

After a moment, the barely audible cracked speech of a woman called through the door. "Who is it?"

"I'm he-here about the rental."

"The what?" she responded.

Skylos raised his voice and repeated himself. "The rental."

"Who?"

The door next to him opened and a young man addressed him through the bars. "You're looking for the couple on the other side," he said, pointing to his left. "One more door over."

"Thanks," Skylos said.

He pulled on the metal gate of the next stoop. It was locked. Shortly after ringing the bell a petite redhead in a blue and white polka-dot dress answered the door.

"Hello?"

"Are you the one with the room for rent?" Skylos asked.

"Uhh..." She turned her head to the side. "Honey?" A tall, bearded man sporting thick-framed glasses in red flannel and blue jeans joined her side. He pulled a cell phone from his shirt pocket and pawed at it.

"I didn't receive any notifications about a reservation," he said to the woman.

"Sorry. We don't have anything scheduled. Maybe there was an issue with the site. Do you have a confirmation number?"

"I don't have a reservation. Can't you pencil me in?"

"No. You have to make a reservation online," the man said.

"But I'm here now, and I have cash," Skylos said, pulling the remaining large bills from his fanny pack.

The man shook his head. "I'm sorry, you have to make a reservation online. Using a credit card."

Skylos patted his pants pocket and raised his empty hands. "That's the problem. I'm visiting from out of town and was pickpocketed earlier. This is my emergency stash and it's all I have."

"I feel bad for you, but we can't accept cash. It's a violation of AirBnB's terms of service." After noticing the scowl on Skylos' face, he added, "The rule's there to protect you as much as us".

Skylos glanced at the bars separating him from the couple. The gaps were wide enough to reach through, but there was no way he'd be able to take them out simultaneously. One of them would get away and make a call. As much as he wanted to make them regret their decision, it would be a bad idea.

The woman looked up at her hipster fiancé, unsure what to do with the stranger lost in his thoughts on their doorstep. "Sorry... Good luck," she said and then closed the interior door.

A deafening pearl of thunder shook the house as Skylos stepped off the stoop. The sky opened up. He was left with limited options. The next rental property was half a mile north, but he'd likely face the same rejection. The train station was over a mile away, but he couldn't sleep there, especially if they'd found the suitcase or bag of knives. After Yvonne's murder, the authorities may have made a connection between the two. Gretchen's apartment would be risky too.

A group of kids carrying soccer balls ran past, catching his attention. If not for the rain, they'd still be playing in the park. Even if the weather quickly abated, they'd be heading in for dinner. Either way the park across the street, and others in the area, would be empty until morning. He stutter-stepped upon the realization that he could stay within spitting reach of Samantha's by sleeping in a baseball dugout or even in a port-a-potty at a construction site.

The rain left dark splotches the size of quarters on his sweatshirt as he wandered back toward Samantha's block. He closed his eyes and retraced his steps from the previous night. The block that backed up to the west side of her building housed an elementary school. He didn't get a good look at it, but it should have a playground he could take cover in. Thunder growled once again, and he quickened his pace.

Skylos kept an eye on Samantha's apartment building as he walked along the sidewalk. Distracted, he stumbled over a small black fence protecting the parkway's flower bed. He failed to regain his footing and stumbled over the opposite fencing parallel to the curb. He threw up his hands to protect his face but slammed into a red hatchback. The vehicle's alarm blared as he struggled to his feet.

"Are you all right?" a voice called from across the street.

Skylos glanced up at a tanned, well-built man closing the door of a black sedan. He wore a bulky overcoat. One big enough to conceal a gun. Skylos shifted his eyes to the back end of the car. It was the same plate he'd noticed racing up the street after he killed Yvonne—'N-O-A'. Unfortunately, he couldn't be sure if it were the same one parked outside when he'd first scouted the apartment. The plainclothes officer approached and offered his hand in help.

"I'm fine," Skylos said, declining the hand. "One too many drinks, but I'm not driving." Skylos avoided eye contact and brushed the dirt from his pants while backing away. He leaned against the tree for a moment before shuffling forward a dozen steps. Skylos glanced back, checking to see if he was being followed.

The officer pulled a ringing cell phone from his pocket. "Be careful," he said, pointing directly at him.

Skylos gave a thumbs-up and took the long way around the building. Once out of sight, he hurried down the block. He looped around and made his way through the unlocked gate around the schoolyard. The wet recycled tire mulch spilled into his sneakers as he walked through the playground. A small metal bridge designed to wobble when walked over connected two tube slides together. A separate section had an uncovered metal slide connected to a smaller platform with rusty monkey bars.

Skylos crawled into the blue, twisting tube. As he shimmied upwards, static electricity raised the hairs on his arms. It reminded him of the first time Calliope had manifested before him. That felt ages ago, he thought as he wedged himself in place.

He pulled a Mylar emergency blanket from the first-aid kid. With a bit of difficulty, he managed to unfold it and cover himself. The slide was dry but wasn't particularly comfortable. Still, he'd slept in worse places and would undoubtedly wake before the school day began. The rhythmic dripping of raindrops on the hard plastic soon caused his eyelids to grow heavy.

"I love you, Calliope," Skylos said as he drifted off to sleep.

Chapter 41

Jason Montgomery – Wednesday Evening

"Agent Montgomery," Jason said into his phone as he watched the sloshed man stumbling down the street. It was broad daylight, but he had bigger fish to fry than public intoxication. "What do you have for me?"

"The airlines confirmed that Samantha Englund and Christopher Reyes are aboard flight 359 to O'Hare. The plane is on-time and scheduled to land at half-past eight, local time. Do you want us to send a car to pick them up?"

Jason pulled the phone away from his ear briefly to check the time. There was more than enough time to reach the airport, even if he stopped for a quick bite. "No thank you. Ms. England is expecting me. I'll pick them up myself."

He ended the call and slipped the phone back into the breast pocket of his dark overcoat. As he grabbed the door of his dark Mazda, he glanced back down the street. There were no signs of the drunkard. Clicking his tongue, he got in, started the car, and pulled up the GPS to ferret out the fastest route.

At least Samantha Englund was safely in the air. The girl knew something more than she was saying. With what happened to her friend, hopefully she'd be more open.

As he shifted into gear, his cell phone rang a second time. "Agent Montgomery," he said again.

"I'm sorry for another interruption, but I thought you'd want to hear this."

The line fell quiet for a moment.

"I'm listening."

"We just received a potential lead," said the analyst.

Jason put the car back into park and licked his lips. *Finally, some good news.*

"We reached out to the precincts along all major highways stretching back to Los Angeles. Salt Lake City police reported receiving a call from a nun who picked up a hitchhiker in Vegas. She said that he felt *off*."

"Heh." Agent Montgomery mumbled, giving the analyst pause. He wasn't sure why the image of a gambling nun picking up hitchhikers surprised him. This damn case was anything but ordinary. "Sorry, go on."

"The nun, uh... Sister Mary Elizabeth, found an individual snooping around the bus lot of the Cashman Center and gave him a ride back to Salt Lake City. During the trip, she noticed the man had several stolen wallets in his pack. One of those was a woman's California driver's license."

Jason sat up in the seat. "Where the killings started," interrupted Jason.

"I got them to follow up with her and they just sent back a computer-generated composite. I'm sending it to your phone now. She said his name was Skylos."

Jason pulled the phone away from his ear at the same time a soft beep indicated an incoming text. The image of a young man in his twenties filled the screen.

"Sonovabitch..." The agent jumped from the car. A blue van honked as he sprinted across the street and down to the corner. The man who'd stumbled in front of him was long gone. He breathed deeply and raised the phone to his ear while turning in circles.

"He walked past on the street not five minutes ago. Circulate his photo among Chicago P.D. immediately." Jason stopped. The lead he'd been dreaming of finally dropped into his lap. However, something nagged at him. The suspect had murdered nearly a dozen people, including ones he'd traveled with.

"Why on earth did he spare the nun?" he mumbled.

"What's that?"

Jason stood on the street corner, staring down Blackhawk Street. "Nothing. I'm just thinking aloud, but I should know better than to try and get inside the head of a psychopath... Thanks for the information. Let me know if anything else comes up."

Chapter 42

Samantha and Christopher – Somewhere over Ohio – Wednesday Evening

Samantha shifted in the middle seat of the last row of the plane watching lightning silhouette the dark clouds outside the window. Christopher sat beside her in the aisle seat. With each clap of thunder, he dug his fingernails deeper into both armrests. Samantha felt awful. He'd given up his seat toward the front to sit with her. To make things worse, he hadn't complained once. At least the woman at the window was engrossed in Korean soap operas on her tablet, completely oblivious to their conversation thanks to an expensive set of noise-canceling headphones.

"A Muse," Christopher said, shaking his head. "If I heard myself saying this a month ago, I would have committed myself. I thought I'd be glad to finally know what we were up against."

"It seems to fit. I cached some web pages before we left the terminal. Muses were the source of inspiration within Greek society. But they had no ties to death. I don't understand why one would motivate someone to kill."

"It's pretty easy to change history when you're the one writing the books."

She nodded.

"Or..." he said, raising an eyebrow. "What if they were always malevolent? Society's portrayal of them may have changed over the years—like Grimm's Fairy Tales. I presume you're aware most of the original versions were laden with sexual undertones and over-the-top violence."

"I'm surprised you knew that."

Christopher crossed his eyes, bit his lip, and looked at her. "I'm not just another pretty face."

Samantha laughed. "You could be right. Muses certainly aren't worshipped now like they were during ancient Greek rule."

He raised an eyebrow. "So, it's revenge?"

"Or a roundabout way to get back into the limelight. But your theory is just as plausible. Perhaps there's a symbiotic relationship and they've always manipulated people to some degree."

"You think they feed off us?" he asked. Samantha nodded. "If that's the case, why are we getting visions from them to stop Skylos?"

"Group dissension? It sounds like Calliope went rogue, and the others are out to stop her."

Christopher rubbed the stubble on his chin. "Maybe we have been trying to stop Calliope this entire time instead of focusing on Skylos. Did these websites have any information on how to destroy a Muse?"

"No. Muses aren't supposed to be the bad guys. And besides, they're goddesses. I've never heard of anyone killing a god before."

"Then we'll have to hope that stopping Skylos will be enough."

Samantha nodded and leaned forward to see out the window. While the lightning had died down, the storm continued to rage on. The plane jostled again with turbulence and Christopher let out a faint whimper.

She turned back to him and tried to keep him distracted.

"There's plenty of other things troubling me."

"Oh, ya think?"

She overlooked his sarcasm. "Not to sound self-centered, but why me?"

"A fair question. You do seem to be the linchpin, aside from Calliope, of course. Everything seems a little too coincidental. Of all the billions of people on the planet I was somehow drawn to you."

"I don't think I believe in destiny," she said.

"You're okay with Muses and vampires, but fate is where you draw the line? I'm not saying that I'm a believer either, but everything feels too... orchestrated." Christopher paused before broaching the next topic. "If you want my honest opinion, your digital footprint is too high. Forget fate, I think website attracted everyone: me, the authorities, Marcie, and probably Skylos. But it was all for the better." He swallowed a lump in his throat as he thought about her neighbor. "No offense, but you can't do this alone."

Samantha nodded. "I know. And it's a long story, but I think I've finally figured out how it all started."

"Well, we're stuck in this metal death trap for a while."

"When I first set up my site, I used my real name out of the desire for notoriety. While I quickly gained a following, things took a dark turn. The site attracted trolls who flooded the chat with vulgarities and requests to see my tits.

"I appointed moderators to police the site, but the damage was already done. A couple of weeks later an overzealous fan somehow tracked me down. After following me for days, he cornered me in a coffee shop. He shoved a printout of one of my stories in my face and demanded an autograph. It freaked me out and I asked him to leave.

"He blew up, going on about how he'd donated hundreds of dollars, and that I *owed* him. I got the police involved. He stopped following me but continued to harass and threaten me online. Apparently, he was on probation for another offense and the protection order cost him a promising new job.

"The whole thing scared the crap out of me. I dealt with depression, took myself offline for several months, and ended up completely re-branding the site and myself. I dyed my hair and adopted a pseudonym. He never resurfaced." Samantha snorted. "But I imagine he's been watching. He was probably the one who alerted the authorities and posted that arrest video. Hell, maybe Skylos got in touch with him via my forums."

"I'm sorry you had to go through all that," Christopher said. "But I never would have found you without that video." He sat quietly for a while and then said, "This reminds me of a high school game of dodgeball."

"I don't think they allow kids to play dodgeball anymore, but please elaborate."

"Don't get me started on that. Anyway, when teams are picked, you go for the heavy hitters first. You, me, and Elliot. We're from different backgrounds: law enforcement, writing, the occult. If I were forming a task force to stop this psycho, those are qualities I'd be looking for in my top picks."

"Perhaps Agent Montgomery is part of this destiny too. I'm looking forward to getting some rest and passing along everything we can to the FBI in the morning."

The corners of Christopher's mouth turned down. "With what happened earlier, I imagine they'll be waiting for us as soon as we land."

"Oh, gods. Yvonne..." Tears started to form in Samantha's eyes again. "I can't believe I pushed that out of my mind. I've never met her parents. How do I make sure she's taken care of? If I hadn't flown to New York..."

"Then your parents and I would have been mourning you," Christopher said, lifting Samantha's chin. "This isn't your fault. And the police have probably already notified her next of kin. What's important is that you take care of yourself and remember you're not alone. You'll be staying with Martha and me tonight."

Samantha shook her head. "I can't ask you to..."

"You didn't have to, and I'm not giving you a choice. I'm sure Agent Montgomery can escort us to pick up anything you need from your apartment. Until this is over, you're not leaving my sight."

"Thank you. I don't know what I'd do without you." Samantha yawned and allowed her eyes to close for a moment. With a gasp, she snapped them back open and spoke in a shaky voice. "Do you have any pills at home that would knock me out? I can't handle watching him kill Von."

Christopher fought to maintain his composure. He'd lost people throughout his life, but none to a situation anything like this. Turning his face toward the aisle, he feigned a cough and wiped away a tear. "I occasionally take muscle relaxers for my back. They'll probably do the trick. I know they knock me out." The plane dipped and both their stomachs lurched into their throats. "I could use some right about now."

The corners of Samantha's mouth turned up slightly. "I didn't know you hated flying. I meant it when I said I could have come by myself."

"What kind of friend would I have been if I'd let you? You needed me here... especially with what happened."

Samantha stared at the headrest in front of her. "We haven't talked much about Elliot."

Christopher snorted. "He was a piece of work, huh?"

"Well, yeah, but that's not what I was referring to. He looked like shit. I keep thinking about what Deb said. That whatever is affecting Skylos is taking a toll on his mind. Do you think the same thing is happening to all of us?"

"That hasn't been far from my mind either. But I don't feel any different."

"Ladies and gentlemen, as we begin our descent into Chicago Midway, we ask that you raise your tray tables and seatbacks to their full, upright positions..."

Samantha reached over and grabbed Christopher's hand as he closed his eyes and took deep breaths.

Chapter 43

Samantha and Christopher – Chicago, IL – Wednesday Night

Agent Montgomery was at the gate when they disembarked. The tailored suit coat Samantha had seen him in last time was replaced with a black Kevlar vest and a large pistol resting on his left hip. He stepped forward as soon as he caught sight of her.

"Yvonne?" Samantha asked before he reached them. She already knew the answer but had to be sure.

Agent Montgomery lowered his head. "I'm sorry." She closed her eyes and bit her lip to stave off more tears. He waited patiently for her to open them. "I'll take you to the station. Do either of you have a car here or any checked bags?" They both shook their heads.

"Can I use the bathroom first," said Samantha.

"I need a coffee," said Christopher, setting down both of their carry-on bags. "Anyone else?" The FBI agent gave his head a single shake.

"Black and iced, please," Samantha said before ducking into the restroom.

Samantha cringed when she saw the girl staring back in the mirror. Her eyes were bloodshot and her hair a mess of split ends. She ran the water ice cold and splashed her face a dozen times.

"I'm sorry, Von," she whispered. She stood there for a long time as if waiting for the mirror image to go on without her.

"You okay in there?" Agent Montgomery's voice echoed off the tile walls.

"Yes," she yelled, patting her face dry with a paper towel. When she came out, Christopher handed her a large coffee. "Thanks," she said with a sniffle.

With both men flanking Samantha, the trio wound their way out of the airport to a dark sedan waiting in the no-parking zone. He took them to the precinct where they were interviewed together, at the agent's behest.

After two hours of discussions, Agent Montgomery led them out of the room. "I think that's enough for tonight. I'll take both of you home."

"She's staying with me tonight, but she needs to stop for some things."

"Of course. Whatever you need."

"Give me a few minutes," said Christopher, disappearing into the bowels of the police department. He returned a few minutes later with a large evidence bag in his hands.

"My laptop!"

Christopher smiled and handed it over.

...

Samantha walked up to her apartment door. Even though Christopher kept his pace half a step ahead of hers to block her line of sight to Yvonne's apartment. She turned her head and brought the key up to her own doorknob before noticing the faint red smudge in the center of her door. Before she could turn the handle, Agent Montgomery pulled her back. He pressed his finger to his lips, pulled his backup weapon from an ankle holster, and handed it to Christopher.

Agent Montgomery pulled his sidearm and counted down from three with his other hand. On the signal,

Christopher shoved the door open. The agent leaned to the left and slowly pivoted into the room, clearing the blind corner. Christopher sheltered Samantha with his body, his sausage-like fingers tight on the small pistol. After a few tense moments, the agent gave the all-clear. Samantha stepped into the kitchen where he stood processing the jumble of notes scrawled on the kitchen wall.

"About that..." she said, joining his side.

"I'm Impressed. It looks like the one in my office. Looking for a new job?"

"Not if it'll be like this."

"Fair enough," Agent Montgomery said with a nod. He excused himself and chatted with Christopher in the hall.

Samantha rushed around the apartment, throwing clothing, toiletries, and charging cords into a duffel bag. As she returned to the hall a tear came to her eye along with a smirk. There was evidence tape surrounding Yvonne's door. *They do have money in the budget for tape after all.* Christopher wrapped his arm around her and guided her back to the elevator.

The drive to Christopher's was silent aside from Christopher providing directions. Samantha leaned against the car door and stared out the window. The white noise the car tires on wet pavement was soothing. Samantha slapped herself gently as she fought to keep her eyes open. She noticed Agent Montgomery watching her in the rearview mirror. He maintained eye contact.

"I know this is a stupid question, but are you okay?" he asked, alternating focus between her and the road. She managed a faint smile and then nodded.

"We're only a few blocks away." When the car finally pulled into the driveway, the porch light came on. "This will be fun," Christopher said.

Samantha grabbed the door handle but didn't move. Noticing her hesitation, Christopher walked around the car and opened it for her. In the meantime, Agent Montgomery carried their luggage to the porch.

"Don't make me drag you out," Christopher threatened.

Samantha got out and passed the FBI agent on his way back to the car.

"You have my number. Call me if... If you need anything. I'm a light sleeper."

"Thanks," she said, leaning forward and planting a kiss on his cheek. Her face turned red and she put her hand over her eyes. *What possessed me to do that?*

Christopher unlocked his front door, grabbed all three bags, and stepped into the house. Samantha followed. A woman significantly shorter than him rose from the recliner. Her hair was in a neat bun and she was dressed in a dark blue paramedic uniform.

"You're back already? I thought you..." Martha's voice raised an octave. "Hang on. Is this the person you flew off to New York with on a moment's notice? Jessica said you were acting odd, but I didn't expect this."

Christopher dropped the bags and approached her. He slipped his left arm around his wife's waist and tried to guide her out of the room. Crossing her arms over her chest, she held her ground.

"You can say whatever it is in front of her. Is this what you've been up to these last few weeks?"

Christopher let out a deep sigh and leaned forward. She leaned back at first, then drew closer when he started whispering. Christopher recounted Yvonne's death in hushed tones.

"Oh," Martha said. "Oh, God."

Martha wrapped her arms around Samantha and squeezed.

"I'm sorry, honey. He doesn't tell me anything." She looked back long enough to give her husband a death glare. "You are welcome in our home as long as you need. Is there anything I can do?"

"Pizza and muscle relaxers," said Christopher.

The woman nodded without question and went to the kitchen while Christopher grabbed Samantha's bags and motioned her into the hall. The first room off the family room held several plastic bins and cardboard boxes, an old dresser, and a full-sized bed made up with a blue comforter decorated with a field of stars.

"This was Jessica's room," he said, placing her belongings on the bed. "Shove her crap aside and make yourself at home. Our room is across the hall if you need anything. Allow me to apologize in advance for my snoring. The Wi-Fi password is 'cops house'—one word."

"Here you go," Martha said, coming to the doorway and tossing an amber pill bottle to her husband. He caught it and handed it to Samantha. "I've got to head to the hospital now. Can you let Jessica know she can bring the twins around at the usual time?"

"Sure. I'll walk you out. Be right back, Samantha."

Samantha opened the closet and hung up the few shirts she'd brought before ducking into the bathroom to change into a pair of shorts and a tee. She opened the medicine bottle and swallowed one of the small round pills and returned to the bed. The power button failed to bring her laptop to life.

As she plugged the cable into the wall Christopher knocked on the doorframe. He stepped inside, cradling a small black safe in his hands. He brought it to the closet where he gingerly lifted it onto the top shelf.

"The safe's combination is one-five-nine-eight, the first four of my badge number. The back door is set to the same code."

She stood up and interlaced her fingers. "Do you think he'll come here?"

"I doubt it, but we shouldn't underestimate him. Well, go ahead," he said, gesturing to the safe.

Samantha stepped forward and pressed the buttons on the electronic panel. The lock disengaged with a thunk. Inside was a small pistol, just like the agent's backup weapon. She looked back at him and then removed it, taking care not to finger the trigger.

"The magazine is full, but the chamber's empty. Have you ever fired a gun before?"

"It's been a while," she said with a nod. My dad took me to the range a few times before I moved into the city. I told him he was being an overprotective father." She paused. "I'm guessing I can't carry this without a license?"

"No, and the penalties are steep, but you won't need to leave the house with it. I'm a heavy sleeper and I want to make sure you feel safe."

"Okay."

"You're going to need to pull the slide back to load a round." Christopher stepped behind her. "Hold the pistol in your dominant hand. No, closer to your body so you have more leverage." He held her right arm and extended it. "If you hold it out here, your muscles have to work harder to overcome the resistance of the recoil spring. Grab the slide with your left and push your right hand forward. It's easier to push the frame forward, rather than to pull the slide back."

She followed his instructions.

"Good. That fed a round into the chamber, but it's not ready to fire yet. Here's the safety," he said pointing to a small lever on the side of the weapon. "Once you disengage this, it's good to go."

Samantha moved her arm up and down, getting familiar with the gun's weight. She made a move to put it back into the safe, but he stopped her.

"A few more things. Here's the magazine release," he said pointing to another place on the gun. "Pressing that ejects the magazine. Pulling the slide back while it's out will clear the round from the chamber. It's best not to keep it loaded when the kids will be around. Even if they can't reach up there." He took the magazine from her when she removed it.

When she pulled the slide back, the bullet flew out. Christopher grabbed it out of the air and placed it back into the magazine. He took the gun from her, replaced the magazine, and lay it back down in the safe.

"It feels like only yesterday that I was walking Jessica through the same thing." The oven buzzer sounded from the kitchen. "Good timing."

Samantha followed Christopher into the kitchen where he pulled two cheap, frozen pizzas sparsely dotted with nuggets of sausage from the oven. Plates and glasses of water already sat waiting on the table. They both sat down and ate in silence. After nearly finishing an entire pizza, Samantha let out a roaring yawn.

"I think the muscle relaxers are kicking in."

"I'll clean up everything. Go get some sleep."

"Thank you for everything."

He smiled and Samantha, escorted by a legion of yawns, slumped into the bed and pulled the sheets up to her neck. Her vision and head were fuzzy. Before her eyes winked shut, Samantha remembered the image of Yvonne holding the metal bat the night she met Christopher. Samantha knew she gave Skylos one hell of a fight.

Chapter 44

Samantha – Chicago, IL – Thursday

The door to Jessica's old bedroom burst open, fanning the smell of freshly cooked bacon into the room. She peeled her eyes open, still groggy from the muscle relaxers and half expected Christopher sent his grandkids to bring her breakfast in bed. Instead, Jessica, in full uniform, stood in the doorway with the glint of fire in her eyes. Samantha sat up and froze.

"What the fuck are you doing here?" Jake and Luke giggled in the front room. "Quiet!" Jessica yelled. The twins immediately fell silent.

Christopher came up behind his daughter clicking a pair of kitchen tongs near her head. "It's none of your business, but she's my guest."

Jessica swatted the greasy tongs away. "It's my business when *my* kids are under the same roof as a murder suspect." She turned her wrist to check the time on a military-style watch and pushed past her father. "I'll be sending a patrol car by to make sure she's gone." Jessica stormed out of the room and a moment later the wall rattled as the front door slammed.

"Don't mind her," Christopher said, clacking the tongs again. "Breakfast?"

"She's right, I don't belong here."

"Bullshit. This is my house and you're my guest. Besides, the kids are old enough to make their own decisions."

One of the twins ran into the room. "I'm sorry Mommy woke you up."

"That's okay."

Christopher knelt down beside him and pointed to the bed. "What do you think, buddy? Should Samantha stay for breakfast?"

"Yes. She's pretty and I like her hair." The boy turned to her. "Do you like pancakes?"

She smiled. "Yes. I'm hungry."

"Hi Hungry, I'm Luke." Christopher laughed and stood back up as Luke darted back out.

Samantha failed to stifle her laughter. "You did not teach him that..."

Christopher smiled and the other twin ran into the room.

"This was Mommy's room. Do you like it?"

Jake ran back out of the room before Samantha could answer. In no time both children returned as a pair.

"Do you want to go play?"

"Go wash up and sit down for breakfast. Samantha will be along when she's fully awake," Christopher said, ushering the kids out and closing the door.

Samantha put on a bra, used the bathroom, and then joined them in the kitchen. The table held a large bowl of eggs, a platter of silver dollar pancakes, and a tray of crispy bacon. The kids were already enjoying pancakes drowned in syrup. Samantha took a seat opposite Christopher and started filling her plate.

"Orange juice?" he offered.

"Sure."

"Thanks again for everything. This almost makes me forget what's going on."

"Pssh, you're family now." Christopher looked between the twins. "Do you guys want to spend the day with Auntie Samantha?"

"Yeah!" they cheered in unison, syrup dribbling down their chins.

Christopher crunched a piece of bacon and met Samantha's eyes. "How'd you sleep?" he asked, resuming a serious tone.

"Like a baby..." she said, knowing what he was really asking. "No dreams."

"Good. Me neither."

She pushed the eggs around her plate. Would he lie to protect her feelings? *Probably not.*

After the table was cleaned up, Samantha tagged along as Christopher took the kids through their daily paces. It was a whirlwind of a day between spending time at a playground in the morning, the play area of McDonald's, and the Shedd Aquarium in the afternoon. They were a welcome distraction, but it didn't lessen her paranoia. Everywhere they went she looked over her shoulder. She saw commonalities from the face rendering Agent Montgomery provided on everyone man that crossed her path.

It was a relief when they returned home that afternoon. Samantha retreated to the bedroom with her laptop hoping to avoid another run-in with Jessica. Fortunately, she came and went without incident. But with the kids gone, the house felt empty. Samantha offered to help with dinner, but Christopher insisted on doing it himself. Martha woke in time for dinner and they discussed the kid's doings. Christopher retired in front of the television after Martha agreed to let Samantha help with the dishes.

"Do you want to watch something with us?" asked Martha after they'd cleaned up.

"Thanks, but the kids wore me out." It wasn't a lie, but the kids were a great excuse.

Samantha lay in bed, scouring news sites for any additional deaths since the night before. There was nothing reported so far. She imagined he was lying low, waiting for the right time to strike. Her fingers moved to her cell phone and brought up Agent Montgomery's contact information. *He did say I could call anytime.*

He answered before the first ring ended.

"Everything okay, Samantha?"

"I'm fine, Agent..."

"Please, call me Jason. What can I do for you?"

"Have there been any breaks in the case? Anything you can share?" She took a deep breath, realizing how neurotic she sounded. "Sorry. I'm guessing you can't discuss an open case."

"That's a misconception. There are no laws preventing officers from revealing details on cases."

"Oh," remarked Samantha, shifting on the bed.

"Nothing more from when we spoke last. But we will find him," he reassured. "Even if we don't have an I.D., we know who we're looking for. Just stay close to Christopher. I'll contact you as soon as I know more."

"Thanks," she said with a frown. "Goodnight."

Jason sounded determined but it did little to put her at ease. Even the combined resources of the Federal Bureau of Investigation and the Chicago Police Department couldn't stop him.

The more she avoided thinking about the situation, the more her brain entertained the worst-case scenarios. Christopher, Elliot, Skylos, and the Muse— or Muses—were all linked to her. Therefore, it was plausible that Calliope could have been leading Skylos to her all along and her old stalker was inconsequential.

If Yvonne died simply by being close to her, how would Christopher's grandchildren fare? Samantha never thought about having any kids. And she'd never thought about losing any either. Christopher's words on the plane stood out. Fate pulled them all together.

Their shared visions were the only thing that could stop Skylos. More accurately, she was the only one that could. As much as she hated to admit it, Elliot was right. They wouldn't find Skylos unless she drew him out. It was up to her alone to finish it.

Her eyes drifted to the safe in the closet. Christopher wouldn't have put the pistol there if she weren't destined to fire it. She broke into a goofy grin thinking about Chekhov's gun—a literary concept pertaining to the usage of dramatic elements. If a story details a gun hanging on the wall in one act, it better go off in the next.

Samantha drafted an email to Elliot detailing her plan. She could trust that he'd forward the information along without trying to talk her out of it. Tears welled up in her eyes as she wrote a letter explaining everything to her parents and then a thank you note for Christopher. It felt like a suicide note.

She wiped her eyes and then logged into her website for the first time since being detained weeks ago. Dozens of private messages awaited her attention. She ignored them and dug into the most popular thread on the forums. *Where is Samantha Blackblood?*

It was hard not to laugh at the ridiculous theories. One surmised her recent absence was because she was the killer and had gotten caught. Another suggested the police department had sequestered her away, taking advantage of her psychic talents. Her favorite by far explained that the killings were faked as an elaborate publicity stunt. Bless the fools on the internet.

Samantha read through other posts, some amusing, some offensive. After an hour of catching up, Christopher came by to say goodnight. She waited for a good thirty minutes after Christopher's snoring stretched through the walls. She called a cab and gave them the address at the end of the block.

While she waited, she pulled the computer back onto her lap and fired off the email to Elliot. On both Twitter and her site, she posted details for a private meet and greet at a bar by the Sedgwick Brown Line stop. It was a small dive bar Yvonne liked to hit up. And it would be an ideal setting to keep tabs on anyone coming and going. She took a deep breath and slammed the laptop shut.

The buttons on the safe chirped as she entered the code. She withdrew the pistol and chambered a round like Christopher had shown her. She slipped it into her purse, grabbed her jacket, and crept into the hallway. The wooden floorboards groaning beneath her feet gave her pause. Christopher's continued snoring signaled the all-clear and she slipped out the back door and down the block.

...

Samantha entered the bar and headed for an empty table near the back. Aside from the two men at the billiards table, she was the youngest person in the place by a dozen years. She took a seat and placed her purse in her lap.

A waitress came by. She ordered a cranberry juice. Her knee bounced nervously as she fixed her gaze on the door. People came and went. There weren't many new faces, mostly individuals stepping out for a smoke. Nobody matched the picture of Skylos ingrained within her mind. And nobody showed any interest in the girl sitting by herself in the corner.

Half an hour passed. Forty-five minutes. An hour. Samantha checked all her accounts on her phone. The posts had numerous likes and retweets. Either Skylos hadn't seen it or was wary of falling into a trap. If he wouldn't take the bait, she'd have to hunt him down somehow. The Muses only communicated via dreams and napping on a wobbly bar table was ill-advised.

Think, Samantha, think. Deb had offered some suggestions but jetting to New York hadn't left her time to attempt anything.

She lifted her phone again and typed 'Binaural Alpha Waves' into YouTube. The same boastful videos she'd seen the other night flooded the search results. After looking through several pages she settled on an hour-long video promising to rebalance misaligned chakras. She clicked on the video as the waitress returned and sat another drink on a napkin in front of her.

"Thanks."

Samantha pulled a pen from her purse and yanked a pair of tangled earbuds free from beneath the heavy pistol. Absent any paper, she pulled the drink napkin in front of her. Taking one last look around the bar she popped the tiny speakers into her ears and pressed play.

She lowered the media volume to a point where it barely drowned out the bar. A multitude of sounds filtered into her ears: chimes, ocean waves, and heartbeats along with tones reminiscent of middle school hearing tests. The various sounds rose and fell in both pitch and volume, giving the illusion of a dozen items in motion around her head. Samantha closed her eyes.

If Skylos comes to kill me, someone better intervene.

Samantha flinched as someone touched the back of her hand. She reached for the gun and opened her eyes. A couple who scarcely looked old enough to drink sat across from her holding hands. Samantha took her hand out of her purse and tapped her phone to stop the audio. The ringing continued to orbit her right ear for a moment.

The player showed twenty minutes remaining. *I've been sitting here for forty minutes? Did I fall asleep?*

"Samantha?" the girl said. "Kathy and Steve. We're big fans."

"Nice to meet you," mumbled Samantha.

There were black ink marks on the napkin in front of her. Two indecipherable words had been written enough times to partially tear through the cloth: 'lnadts' and 'sllem'. Though she had no recollection of writing anything, the recognized her own writing. She typed them into her phone. Nothing. An attempt to translate the words from Greek was equally fruitless. Samantha's face scrunched up as she tried to make meaning of the strange syllables.

Steve pulled on his girlfriend's sleeve and got up. "She's kind of rude, let's go."

"What's at St Paul and Wells?" Kathy asked, tapping the napkin.

"Huh?" Samantha said, looking up.

Kathy turned the napkin a hundred and eighty degrees. "St Paul and Wells. Are you supposed to meet someone there? Is it part of a riddle from your new story?"

"Maybe," Samantha responded, still staring at the napkin. "Sorry. I'm scatterbrained today." The man sat back down, and the couple re-introduced themselves.

After another quick scan of the bar to confirm that Skylos wasn't lurking around she chatted with the couple for a few minutes. Kathy was a literature major looking for recommendations on pursuing a career in editing. Samantha passed along a few tips and resources, promising to put her in contact with her old employer.

Around midnight, when Kathy and Steve left, Samantha paid her bar tab. Taking one last look around the bar she headed for the door. A few men followed her with her eyes but didn't follow her out. They weren't killers, only nervous fans, or pervy old men.

She felt stupid coming here, but the intersection of St. Paul and Wells was only a few blocks from the bar. After checking it out, she'd call for a car back to Christopher's.

The small shops backing up to the condo developments along Wells were shuttered and dark. Except for the occasional car, the street was equally quiet and devoid of people. She kept her hand in her purse and resting on the pistol as she walked. The cold, metal grip gave her reassurance.

When she turned onto St Paul something palpable hung in the air. An intense static charge that can sometimes be felt before a thunderstorm. The small hairs on her arms and neck stood at attention as a loud pop came from the street behind her. Samantha gripped the gun tighter and spun around. The street grew darker as the bulb in the streetlight failed.

She flipped the pistol's safety off and moved to the small, metal gate in front of an alley. It blocked access to a private parking area for the condominiums. She placed a hand on the top and swung one leg over. Ahead something heavy clanged to the pavement.

Samantha dropped down as a lanky man in a gray T-shirt and shorts limped around the corner of the U-shaped building. She raised the gun at his chest.

"Not another step!"

The man froze and threw his hands up. "Don't shoot. I just came out for a jog. My wallet is at home."

His face didn't have the right proportions. His lips were larger and nose skinnier—it wasn't him. She lowered the gun. "Get out of here."

The jogger retreated around the corner and slammed his apartment door.

Great. He's definitely calling the cops.

Samantha took a deep breath and slipped the gun back into her purse. Hopefully, Jason had the power to get her out of a weapons charge. She hopped back over the fence and bumped into a man with a royal blue hoodie pulled over their head.

"Excuse me," she said instinctively.

An arm slipped around her waist and then another around her neck. A trickle of blood dripped down her neck from a knife in his left hand. As she reached for the gun a second blade pressed into the flesh at her side.

"Drop it, Samantha," Skylos said, sinking the curved Karambit into her side.

Samantha cried out in pain and dropped her purse. Skylos turned his head as a car drove past on Wells Street no more than fifty feet away. Seizing the distraction, she grabbed his wrists and fought for control of the knives. It was easy to secure the knife at her throat, but simple movements of his wrist plunged the curved blade into her side several more times. She groaned and struggled as blood soaked her shirt and jeans.

"Stop fighting fate."

She didn't have the leverage to overpower him. Her best bet was to stall until the police responded to the jogger's call. "Calliope isn't what you think. She's using you."

"No!" he yelled. "She's my angel." She held his wrists tight, keeping the blades away from her skin. Skylos squeezed her stomach with his forearm, quickening the flow of blood from her side. She grunted.

"Would an angel force you to kill innocent people? She messed with your head." Samantha moaned in pain as the tip of the knife bit into her side again. "Skylos means dog in Greek. You're nothing to her."

A chill ran through the air. Skylos' muscles went rigid momentarily as Calliope made her presence known. Samantha gasped. A shiver ran down her spine and she shook in the same manner.

Liar! Calliope hissed.

She fought harder upon hearing the voice. Remembering how he was always limping, she kicked backward at his knees. Unfortunately, he was pressing too hard against her, and she didn't have the leverage to do any meaningful damage. She'd have to try something else. Samantha moved her head forward, feeling the knife jab into her neck, and then slammed it back.

Skylos' nose broke with a sickening crack. His arm loosened around her neck enough for Samantha to push the knife away from her throat. But the blood dripping down his lip and into his mouth seemed to renew his vigor. Samantha's head jerked forward as he head-butted her back, the knife slashing her above the eyebrow.

Dazed from the strike, Samantha lost hold of his wrist. Skylos pressed the tip of the knife to her throat, sending a drop of blood rolling down her blouse. The surrounding buildings took on a red haze as blood from the gash on her forehead obscured her vision. She let out a hoarse cry for help. Her head swam and she realized she'd bleed to death unless someone stumbled by.

She had to do something drastic. Her side was already ripped to shreds. If she concentrated on the knife at her throat, she might be able to get away. There were numerous apartment doors no farther than fifty feet away and her assailant had a bad leg.

Samantha swallowed the lump in her throat. With a deep breath, she released his right hand. Skylos wasted no time before burying the Karambit deep into her side. She felt pressure more so than pain. With both arms, she pried the knife from his other hand. The blade clanged against the bloody sidewalk. Samantha pushed away from him, tearing a five-inch gash in her side.

Skylos lashed out with his foot and caught her sneaker. She went down hard and something in her knee popped against the pavement. Samantha army crawled forward, blood trailing behind her like a nightmarish snail. She no longer had the strength to get to her feet, but she refused to give up. A scrape came from behind her—Skylos picking up the blade she'd knocked free only moments earlier.

"I've been dreaming of this moment, Sammy," Skylos said with a smile.

Samantha reached out with one hand over the other and inched toward the gate blocking the alley. Her palm connected with something bulky. Through vision clouded with tacky blood, she saw her purse. Fate had placed the butt of Christopher's pistol just within her grasp. With all her remaining strength, Samantha grunted and rolled onto her back. Skylos stood above her, both weapons high and prepared to deliver a final blow. She raised the gun a few inches and squeezed the trigger twice. The pistol let loose two deafening retorts just before she passed out.

Searing pain in her side jolted Samantha awake again. Thick hands pressed into her wounds. Her eyes fluttered open. Christopher cradled her head in his lap.

"Hang in there Samantha. The ambulance is close," Christopher said competing with the screeching of both sirens and Skylos.

Skylos writhed on the ground only a few feet away, both knives still in hand. Blood oozed from his shattered right kneecap. Agent Montgomery stood out of his reach, yelling at him to drop the weapons.

Samantha turned her head toward the commotion. At the same time, a shock wave rolled out from Skylos with a dull thud. His screams ceased as the air was driven from his lungs. Samantha blinked as a gust of wind rushed into her face. A secondary blast wave of negative pressure blew her hair in the opposite direction.

"What the hell was that?" the agent asked, keeping his gaze locked on the killer.

Skylos' eyes went wide and the knives clattered to the ground. "Calliope! Calliope, come back!"

Jason lunged forward and slapped handcuffs on the young man as an ambulance and three squad cars arrived. Two officers lifted Skylos from the ground and placed him in the back of a patrol car. He didn't struggle at all, instead bawling and screaming for his Muse to return. Paramedics rushed forward and loaded Samantha onto a wheeled stretcher. She looked up at the medics, half expecting one of them to be Martha.

"How did..." she asked in a weak voice.

"Shh..." Christopher said. "Save your strength. Elliot forwarded your email to Marcie and she called me. On the way here I called Agent..."

"Just Jason," he interrupted, as he joined them at the back of the ambulance.

"Agent Just Jason. He got to the bar just behind me. And just in time to stop the waitress from tossing the napkin you left behind." Christopher wiped away a tear running down his cheek. "This is why I refused to use you as bait."

"I put my trust in Fate," she said.

The paramedics pushed the gurney to the back of the ambulance. "She needs to get to the hospital and into surgery."

Jason took a step back. Christopher stopped the ambulance door from closing and climbed into the back.

"Are you family?"

"Yes," blurted out Samantha.

…

Christopher and Jason sat silently in the emergency waiting room. Christopher flipped mindlessly through a magazine.

Jason worked at a scuff mark on the floor with the edge of his boot. Military training had taught him to disassociate and compartmentalize, but there was something about this case. Something about this girl. He shook his head and looked up.

"I should have stopped him…"

Christopher tossed the magazine on the table beside him. "What?"

"I ran into him in front of Samantha's apartment yesterday…" He looked at his watch. Samantha had gone into surgery several hours ago. Christopher sat up and waited for him to continue. "I stuck around her building after Samantha called from New York yesterday. I had a feeling he wouldn't be able to stay away. A car alarm went off and…"

"Come on… You know better than to second guess yourself."

"He was no further than you and I are right now. He looked like any other drunk and nothing seemed off about him. Not five minutes later, I received a sketch of his face. He was already gone."

"He didn't elude the authorities all this time because he's stupid or careless." Christopher went silent for a moment. "Not to mention his accomplice is a supernatural force we can't fully comprehend." The truth did nothing to ease the morose look from Jason's face.

Before either man could say anything else, the restricted door at the end of the waiting room opened.

They both shot to their feet and met a tall, red-headed female doctor a few steps from the door. She lowered her clipboard and smiled as they approached. Christopher let out a sigh of relief.

"Samantha's out of surgery. We successfully repaired the perforations in her small intestine. We'll need to keep an eye on her for a few days, but she'll fully recover. She's still hazy from the anesthesia but has been asking for both of you."

They thanked the doctor and Christopher led the way through the maze-like corridors to Samantha's room. He pushed his way in without knocking and found Samantha lying still in bed.

"Go home to your wife. I'll call you when she wakes," Jason said.

"Not a chance." Christopher opened the closet door and carried a folding chair to her bedside.

The heart rate monitor let out a long beep as Samantha flat-lined. A dull thud reverberated through the room muting the high pitched of the machine. Christopher dropped the chair as the wind was knocked out of him.

The machine returned to a barely audible hum as Samantha's eyes fluttered open. She smiled upon seeing the men.

"I'm fine," she said to the nurse that hurried into the room and squeezed past Jason to check the leads of the monitor. Her voice was hoarse and came out softly.

"Make sure you let her rest," the nurse said, glaring at Christopher as he picked up the chair and unfolded it.

Christopher nodded. He waited patiently for the nurse to leave and then sat down beside Samantha. "I'm going to skip the obligatory 'What the hell were you thinking' speech. I'm glad you're okay."

She pressed the button to raise the head of her bed a little and licked her lips. Jason grabbed a plastic cup, filled it from the pitcher in the room, and handed it to her.

"Thanks," she said after taking a swig. "I couldn't let something happen to the kids..."

Christopher held his hand up, stopping her. "It's exactly what I would have done if I were in your shoes. I still don't have to like it."

"Stupid question, but how are you feeling?" Jason asked.

"Groggy and a little nauseous, but thanks to the morphine, not much else. I'm just glad it's over." She looked between Jason and Chris. "It's over, right?"

"Skylos is in custody, if that's what you're asking," responded Jason.

"Good." Samantha winced in pain and lowered the bed again. "Thanks for staying but I'd like to get some sleep now."

Christopher kissed her on the forehead and then rose. "Of course. I'll bring the boys by in a few days when you're feeling up to it."

Samantha smiled. "I'd like that."

"I'm going to stay if you don't mind," Jason said pointing at the poorly padded chair.

"You don't have to do that. I'll be fine."

"I know, but I'd like to stay all the same. The paperwork can wait a day or two. There's no way I'll be forgetting any of this."

Chapter 45

Calliope

Shortly after Skylos' worthless body hit the cement Calliope passed through the veil, reuniting with her sisters. Although they'd been interfering since the murder in the train station, none of her eight siblings challenged her upon returning. This was nothing new. Every time Calliope went on sabbatical, they followed the tethers binding her to her plaything and peeked in on her. In turn, they requisitioned their own puppets to stop her. Hypocrites.

Within the physical plane, Calliope's influence was difficult to deny. However, it came with a cost. While away from her sisters, she lost connection to their shared consciousness and memories. For whatever reason, her kin did not have the same limitation. They followed their charges as they saw fit, delivering whatever details they gleaned through Calliope's experiences. One day Calliope would find a way to overcome this and strip away their advantage but at the end of the day it didn't matter. They were too slow to keep her from having fun.

Now in proximity to her sisters, Calliope saw everything. The full narratives of Samantha, Christopher, Elliot, and the five failures lay at her fingertips. Calliope ached to dissect every aspect of the excursion. How else would she learn and improve?

She found it particularly interesting the way that her sisters managed to bring three individuals together.

But that could wait. First, she wanted to celebrate her success and experience everything Skylos had wrought again.

As the prostitute led Skylos into the stall Erato interrupted her rapture. The train station faded into the aether.

No more killing!

Calliope let out a high-pitched cackle. *Foolish little sister. This is what makes you so weak.*

Calliope had proven countless times that the energy released via destruction was exponentially greater than from creation. The others refused to adapt, leaving Calliope much stronger. She drifted away and continued to relive her experiences.

Calliope laughed as Skylos fumbled about in the ridiculous outfit she'd forced upon him. Why did the others not find this humorous?

She critiqued his mistakes as his exploits played on. Skylos had proved to be abnormally receptive and surprisingly adept for such a crippled little thing. He managed ten kills. She figured he would have burned out before achieving half that. The young man wasn't as charismatic as Charlie or as efficient as the doctor but was able to attain a certain ruthlessness. And he reminded her of another plaything from long ago...

The memories of Skylos grew dim and his came into focus. Her pride dipped a little. She'd forgotten being likened to a talking demonic dog. At least Skylos elevated her to the status of an angel. The irony wasn't lost on her; Skylos was her dog. Calliope dismissed this impression as well and started following Samantha.

Calliope viewed this woman with fear, jealousy, and awe all rolled into one. Albeit not directly, Samantha heard Clio with striking clarity. She stepped forward and took decisive action all along the way. If only Calliope had come across her instead of Skylos...

The other Muses sought her out again. Melpomene spoke up this time.

We know what you're doing. Stop.

The humans once served us. Do none of you remember what it was like to be a God? Look. Samantha's black hair flowed in front of them as she sat at her desk, typing away. *See how receptive she is? We can force her to do our bidding. Force her to bow as they did in the old times. The good times.*

No! No more killing! That is not our way, the eight of them said in unison.

Calliope laughed again.

Hypocrites. You destroy almost as many lives trying to stop me as I do.

In an instant, she forced them to relive their failures from this go around: the four-year-old boy in Spain with constant night terrors, the teen in China who took her own life, the war veteran in Australia driven to addiction...

Erato prevented the mockery from continuing. *All your fault. No more killing!*

No more killing, Calliope promised.

At least for a while... She would be busy for quite some time anyway. There was much to review from this story: every plot point, every character, and every detail no matter how insignificant.

Calliope snuck more peeks at Samantha's timeline. She was a natural leader and others flocked to her. There were minor players too who were equally intriguing: the witch and the tall, dark man she showed interest in. Calliope wondered how malleable he was...

Chapter 46

Chicago, IL – A Saturday Three Weeks Later

Jason sneaked up behind Samantha, wrapped an arm around her, and pulled her close. She giggled and closed her eyes. His warm breath danced on her cheek. He was such a tease. She licked her lips in anticipation and then the shot rang out. A fiery pain spread through her chest and she struggled to draw a breath. She tried to scream but he covered her mouth with his, kissing her deeply.

"Calliope sends her regards," he whispered, before letting go.

She fell for what seemed like forever. Something restrained her as she gasped for air and attempted to sit up. A seat belt. Jason reached over and squeezed her hand.

"Another nightmare?" Jason asked. Samantha nodded. "I can call Christopher and tell him we can't make it if you're not up for this."

"No," she said, wiping the corners of her eyes. "I'm tired of being cooped up in the apartment. Besides, we're only a couple blocks out."

"Good," Jason said with a smile. "He's been waiting to see you. And he's got a surprise."

"He does? What is it?"

"If I told you, it wouldn't be one. You'll see in a minute."

He brought the car to rest in front of Christopher's house and then walked around the car and opened the door for her. Hand in hand, they walked up the driveway and behind the house where the twins ran in circles shooting foam darts at one another.

Members of Christopher's extended family sat around drinking beer at tables set up around the yard. Samantha's eyes lit when she saw Marcie sitting across from Christopher at a picnic table.

"Marcie! What are you doing here?"

Marcie smiled and rose from the table, meeting Samantha halfway. She wrapped her in a bear hug before pulling back abruptly. "I didn't hurt you, did I?"

"Not at all. It's good to see you again."

"Chris and I have kept in touch. He wanted to have a sort of reunion once you recovered."

Samantha introduced Jason, and they filled in the empty spots Christopher had apparently been reserving for them. She looked around the yard but didn't see any other familiar faces. "Elliot didn't come along?"

"No," Marcie said with a sigh. "After you left New York he deleted his entire manuscript—including backups and all offline copies. He's been plagued with constant writer's block and has become a shut-in."

"Oh... I'm sorry to hear that."

Marcie shrugged. "It is what it is, I guess."

"Can I grab you guys a beer?" Christopher asked.

"Sammy's still weaning herself from the painkillers," Jason said. When Christopher held one out to him, he added, "And I'm five years sober."

"Well, I'll gladly pick up their slack," said Marcie setting aside her empty bottle. Christopher stood, handed her another, and walked over to check the grill. "I like your hair blonde. Did you do that when you shut down your site?"

She nodded. "Samantha Blackblood is officially retired."

Marcie hesitated a moment and shifted her attention to the FBI agent. "So, what do you know about Skylos?"

Samantha stared at Jason as well. It was a topic she'd brought up numerous times but one he'd never given a satisfactory answer to.

Jason looked at Christopher who smiled and gave a faint nod. "Alright... Full disclosure. Skylos is currently in a psychiatric hospital as a John Doe. He's either a screaming or a weeping mess, depending on the day. Attempts to interrogate him haven't yielded much. The doctors say he displays textbook signs of Post-Traumatic Stress Disorder, early-onset dementia, and half a dozen different neurological and psychological disorders."

Marcie lowered the beer from her lips and muttered something under her breath.

"During the rare lucid periods, he's taken credit for each of the ten murders attributed to him. He's also confessed to others—some of which I've been able to tie to cold cases. Though he wouldn't have been born before they'd occurred. He blames them all on the angel of death. So, there's that..." Jason lowered his head.

Samantha put her hand on his. "If there's more, I need to hear it."

Jason looked up, but not enough to meet her gaze. "Skylos still expresses a desire to kill you. He says doing so will draw Calliope back. Barring that, he's also attempted suicide a few times. The bottom line is that he'll never be fit to stand trial."

"You haven't figured out who he is yet?" Samantha asked.

"FNUK LNUK," said Jason. The girl's eyebrows furrowed.

"What nationality is that?" asked Marcie.

Christopher chuckled as he threw another set of thick hamburger patties on the grill. "It's an abbreviation. First name unknown, last name unknown. It's less commonly used than John Doe, but much more fun to say."

Jason smiled and continued. "Every lead I found was a dead end. The only ID on his person was an L.A. library card registered to a Vincent Jones. The address on file pointed to a volunteer at the Friends of Hope shelter. That was the same logo silk screened on the blue hoodie he was wearing when we caught him.

"I flew out and did a round of interviews. All the staff knew him by first name only. And they refused to believe that he could be responsible for the murders."

"What about the other places we dreamt of?" Samantha said, shifting to the edge of the bench.

"He was a regular at the theater too. They spouted the same rhetoric—he was a polite, but quiet, young man incapable of these atrocities. The local police discovered a storage room in the basement where he'd been squatting. The Altadena neighborhood was a bust. Nobody recognized his picture. I doubt we'll ever know his identity unless he tells us."

Samantha relaxed her posture again and shrugged. "I guess it doesn't matter. He's incapable of doing Calliope's bidding now."

Marcie looked relieved. "So, no more dreams?" Christopher shook his head.

"Just the occasional nightmare," said Samantha.

"Did you feel it? When the Muse... let go?" Marcie asked. Everyone nodded. "So did Elliot. Right after he passed along your email the phone went dead. He told me later that was when it started; when his creativity was siphoned away." She took a long pull from her beer. "You guys haven't noticed any after-effects?"

"No, we're fine," Christopher and Samantha said in unison.

"I think it's his punishment for not listening," said Marcie. "I've done more digging into the lore. There are a total of nine Muses, all the daughters of Zeus and Mnemosyne, the goddess of memory. There are plenty of stories in which they punished mortals who either questioned their ability or challenged them and lost. These consequences ranged anywhere from removing their talent to blinding them. Whatever it took to make sure their supremacy went unquestioned."

Samantha swallowed the lump in her throat.

Christopher rejoined the table. "Better off than crossing Calliope, though." He opened a fresh beer for himself. "You mentioned nine Muses. Do you think..." Samantha giggled as he counted on his fingers. "There were five others who also received visions?"

"I wondered that myself," said Marcie. "Even though Elliot was in denial, something drew the three of you together. Wouldn't the others have sought us out?"

"You're talking about nine people out of a population in the billions," said Jason. "It's a statistical anomaly that even two of you found each other. The others could be on another continent, incarcerated, or even..."

"Children," said Christopher ducking a stray foam dart from his grandsons.

Jason frowned. "I was going to say, victims."

"It doesn't matter. It's over," said Christopher.

A chill ran up Samantha's spine as a breeze swept through the backyard. "At least until Calliope finds herself another dog."

About the Author

Michael grew up avidly playing Dungeons & Dragons with other, like-minded nerds. These activities fostered a vivid imagination that he still remembers fondly.

Since becoming an "adult" with "responsibilities", the days of 10-hour binge sessions are long gone. Writing has now become the official outlet to keep his mind entertained. He loves urban fantasy and is excited to share his reinterpretation of old myths with a broader audience that a few individuals huddled around a table.

Michael lives with his wife and two children in the suburbs of Chicago. During the day he works full-time in IT. Once the screaming of children has subsided in the evening, he retreats to read, write, and/or absorb himself in video games.

You can follow Michael via these outlets:
    Facebook: @DerelictBooks
    Twitter: @MJAAuthor
    Instagram: @MJAAuthor

Stay up to date by joining his newsletter: